Tangled

CHARM CITY THREADS BOOK TWO

Tangled

STEPHANIA THOMPSON

ORANGE BLOSSOM PUBLISHING

Maitland, Florida

Orange Blossom Publishing
Maitland, Florida
www.orangeblossombooks.com
info@orangeblossombooks.com

First Edition: April 2025

Library of Congress Control Number: 2025902896

Edited by: Arielle Haughee
Formatted by: Autumn Skye
Cover design: Sanja Mosic

Print ISBN: 978-1-949935-91-2
eBook ISBN: 978-1-949935-92-9

Printed in the U.S.A.

Dedication

For my family, whose unwavering support and everyday chaos inspires my writing and fills my soul. And to God, the Author of truth, and the Redeemer of all things woven, tangled, and torn.

Table of Contents

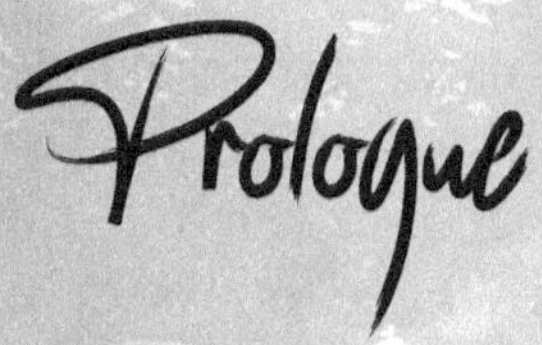

The Grave

Carol Brennan
Tuesday, June 13th 4:26 am
Great Falls Estates Potomac, Maryland

Rain pooled at Carol Brennan's feet.

A collection of mud and leaves clung to his worn boots. He cursed beneath his breath, wiping at a cool trickle of water as it slid down his neck. The leaves and dense overgrowth he had expected, the rain he had not.

And he should have, familiar as he was with the erratic weather in Maryland. He'd lived here half his life, after all. Spring storms were common. But Carol hadn't been thinking about the weather when he left his hotel an hour ago. He hadn't been thinking at all.

A bitter laugh caught in his throat as he scanned the dark woods. Several hundred yards in the distance loomed a sprawling, cottage-style home, blurred slightly by the rain and overgrowth.

Its dimly lit windows, a reminder he was not alone. Even fifty feet into the dense forest, his actions might be observed.

He hadn't considered an explanation, should someone catch him digging up Angela's remains. How would he account for his knowledge of the young woman's whereabouts behind this seemingly innocuous home once owned by Nick and Vivian Janney?

Not that the current owners would take kindly to Carol's trespassing at 4:30 am on this bleak, June morning. He looked every bit a criminal: gloved, dressed in black, and toting trash bags and a shovel.

No. Carol had not thought this through.

Guilt gnawed at his belly. He shouldn't even be here. He should be in Baltimore at the hospital with his nephew, David. In a few hours, the young man would be undergoing a risky, complex surgery to remove a brain tumor. That's what Josh said in his message. He left several last week, but Carol couldn't bring himself to respond.

It was Josh, after all. Joshua Janney, his nephew's best friend and son of the murdering shitbag, Nicholas Janney. The same Josh who grew up on this property. Whose birthmother, Angela, was buried, even now, somewhere beneath Carol's feet. The same Josh he had been trailing for months along with Kate, Josh's sister, and of course, David.

Carol hadn't planned to reveal himself or the secrets he carried. His intention had been to use the three of them, or rather, photographs of them, to taunt Nick. But everything changed last month when the boys turned up in front of Carol's North Carolina home.

And now they were in possession of evidence that could destroy Nick and prove him a murderer, two times over. Evidence that would prove Elena, David's mother, had been an accomplice. Evidence that showed he, Carol, knew of both murders, making him party to the cover up. Details he shared with the boys for David's sake in a moment of incredible stupidity and weakness.

But now?

Carol swallowed hard and dug harder, desperate to push aside thoughts of his nephew. The beautiful, blue-eyed boy bore a striking resemblance to his mother on the day she sat across from Carol twenty-five years ago and shared the horrifying news.

He remembered gaping at her, disbelieving.

"Ian insisted we bury Angela in the woods behind Nick and Vivian's house," Elena had explained, her voice a trembling whisper. "There's a trail, but no one goes back there." Shaking, she'd pushed an envelope at him with all the details. "It was an accident, Carol, I swear. Nick didn't mean to kill her." Tears streamed down her cheeks. "You can't tell anyone. Promise me!"

He'd taken the envelope, unblinking in his shock, hoping, pitifully, that he had misunderstood. That his gentle, cerulean-eyed sister, and her piece of shit husband had not been involved in a murder and cover up, accident or not. That she was not asking him to protect their secret and, by doing so, to protect not only her, but her husband,

Tangled

Ian, and Nicholas Janney—the two men Carol hated most.

Only that was exactly what she'd been asking, and what he'd done. Until two weeks ago when he'd come face to face with Josh and David. And now?

Carol had been sickened to hear of his nephew's tumor. To learn tragedy struck yet another member of his sister's family. After listening to Josh's message, he immediately dialed David but hung up before the call went through.

What if David didn't survive the surgery? And even if he did, who knew what he would remember? What he'd be like? But Josh would remember. He knew. Carol had given them enough ammunition to destroy Nick and drag Elena's name through the mud, should they choose. And without David, why wouldn't Josh do just that? He might even point a finger at Carol.

Carol had hidden the truth about Josh's birthmother, after all. And not only that, for seven years he concealed evidence that proved Ian, David's father, didn't die in an accidental house fire, but rather at Nick Janney's hand. Evidence that could absolve Josh from the burden of guilt he carried because of his actions that night.

Hell, it was Josh who should hate him.

White-hot panic had gripped Carol at the thought. If David died, Elena's memory was all he had, and Josh would certainly destroy that. But not without a body. He might have Elena's envelope—a confession of sorts—but it was all circumstantial if Angela's body was gone.

Carol dug faster, comforted by this knowledge, certain the boys hadn't come looking yet. Only two weeks had passed. Two weeks since he betrayed Elena and desecrated her memory. Two weeks of sleeplessness, shame, and regret so crushing that he'd resorted to grave digging.

Cold sweat mingled with rain as Carol hefted the shovel over and over, lamenting his actions. Following his nephew and the Janney kids, stirring up trouble . . . the photographs. He should've gone straight for Nick without involving them. Should've revealed what he knew rather than protect Elena. But had that ever been an option?

No.

What Carol should've done was keep his mouth shut. He shuddered, remembering the boys' stunned expressions in the back of his truck two weeks ago. Telling them had seemed the right thing to do. The rational thing. But now?

Fuck rational. And fuck Ian Shaw and Nicholas Janney.

Their callous actions led to Elena's death, separated Carol from his family, and drove him to madness. But it all ended here. He would dig until he found Angela's body. He would cover his tracks and burn her remains before anyone came looking. Because regardless the outcome of today's surgery, no matter what happened to David, it was Elena's memory Carol vowed to protect.

Besides, he had a much better plan to destroy Nick Janney.

One Month Later

Soggy Remains

:: The aftermath of a rupture

Joshua Janney (Josh)
Thursday, July 13th 4:43 pm
Foster Avenue Baltimore, Maryland

We should have abandoned this house and moved to Portland when we had the chance.

Kate squeezes past me and shuts off the industrial-sized drying fan currently straddling our upstairs hallway. "Seriously, Josh. How are you living here?"

I've been asking myself that same question.

Aside from the chaos, it's deafening. Extraction and drying equipment from the mitigation company running twenty-four hours a day. Not to mention the smell. Imagine rotten wood got together with wet socks for a drunken night of poor decision making. And then forgot to wash the sheets. A sulfur spring might be less putrid is what I'm saying.

Less contaminated, too. Who knows what nineteenth-century bacteria is lurking around the city water. Or more accurately, our row house.

Kate gawks at the tiny space that was once our bathroom. All the drywall and tile has been ripped out, only a toilet and pedestal sink remain. It's hard to reconcile this wasteland with the once cozy, checkered tile, sky-blue room we spent months renovating.

"One pipe," she says, as if repeating the words somehow makes this less of a nightmare.

One pipe is right.

One rusty-ass-copper pipe burst left unattended can wreak havoc on eleven hundred square feet. Couple that with all the rain we've had this summer? Kind of feels like drowning.

I glance at my phone. "Better get busy packing if you want anything else. He'll be here soon."

Here, being the soggy remains of our Baltimore row house. The fixer upper Kate so prophetically nicknamed *Canton Catastrophe* when she, David, and I moved in. Hard to believe that was less than a year ago.

She's leaning on the doorframe, concern etched in her lovely hazel eyes. "Are you sure you want to meet with him today? Maybe we should wait."

I shake my head. "We need to make a decision." And keeping busy will take my focus off today, our twenty-fifth birthday.

A milestone weighing heavy on both our minds, given the events of last month. It's David's birthday, too. Fifteen years we've known each other. Kate is wise enough not to mention him, though. Ironic, given he's the only one actually born on this day.

Whatever.

Don't think about David. Fly the plane.

That's what the counselor told me last week after we returned from work to discover our home was the new Baltimore Aquarium. I lost my shit in front of Kate—guess she figured I'd need help finding it. Help in the form of her massage client, Judy, who happens to be a grief counselor.

One minute Kate and I are grabbing lunch in Canton Square, the next we're being joined by this woman with gray braids and an empathetic smile. And then Kate's up and gone, and I'm pouring my heart out to a stranger.

"Visualization," she'd said. "Use mental imagery to achieve a relaxed state of mind."

She suggested I picture myself at the beach, but all I could think about was flying. I might as well envision sleeping on the couch for all it's working, though. At least then I'd get some rest.

"Josh." Kate's hand is on my arm, but I yank it away.

I don't need her lamenting my choice to stay. Who else is going to deal with this shit? Kate? I wouldn't do that to her. Besides, I've picked up some hours at the station. I'm rarely home.

Home.

It's a bitter word. I turn before she can read my expression and plod off to the room David and I share. Shared.

How about this for irony? Our room is closest to the bathroom yet suffered the least harm. Mostly the floor and drywall. It was still a mess, though. I boxed everything salvageable and hauled it off to a storage place last week. Besides, I only care about David's stuff at this point anyway. And most of it was fine. It had all been above the water, stacked neatly on shelves.

Because he hasn't been here to use it.

Flying, Josh. Focus on flying.

I focus on the mattress instead. The bare mattress. All our bedding reeks of stagnant water and decay. I borrowed an old sleeping bag from one of the guys at work. Not that I'm sleeping. Most nights I'm staring at the ceiling, waiting for dawn to come. Because, who are we kidding? I'm not piloting any planes. If I'm flying, it's in economy hunched over a barf bag. And that's on a good day.

"Hello?" a voice calls from downstairs. "Josh? Kate? You guys up there?"

Zach. The contractor.

Oh, thank God. Distraction.

5:20 pm

"Two months," he says.

Kate and I glance at each other. Two months is longer than we had hoped, but better than the other estimates.

Zach removes his ball cap and runs a hand through his spiky, blond hair. His shirt stretches tight in the chest when he moves. The guy is massive. Tall and solid, hands like a freaking giant. I force my eyes away. Kate is so small beside him. He could crush her with those hands. My pulse quickens at the thought.

I fight the urge to wrap my arms around her, protect her sweet body and soft, spiraling curls. Not that Zach poses any danger. But everything feels like a threat since David's tumor was discovered. And if something happens to Kate?

Easy, Josh. Zach is here to help.

Nonetheless, my anxiety builds. I grab the waist of her skirt and tug. She stumbles backward, then leans against me, steadying herself.

"Didn't want you stepping on that nail over there," I mumble, covering.

Doesn't matter. Zach isn't paying attention. He's taking in the kitchen with an appraising look. This floor and the basement sustained the most damage, water traveling the path of least resistance and all. The kitchen's directly beneath our bathroom—it's a disaster. When I think of all the work David, Kate, and I put into this place? I can't. It makes me ill.

"Might take less time if I get a bigger crew in here," Zach says in a non-committal tone. "I'll have a better idea once the guys get started."

Zach's the third contractor we've met with. He and his buddy just started this home improvement business. They're offering a break on the labor cost if I help, spread the word, etc. Even with insurance, I doubt we're getting back all the money we've put in. A half a year's worth of work gone in a matter of hours.

Whatever.

I just want the house fixed, and Zach's willing, available, and a friend. Kind of. Kate met him back in May at the wedding of our high school friend, Isabelle. Zach was there with Anna, who has since become her new BFF.

According to Kate, they're on-again-off-again high school sweethearts which sounds like drama to me. She's been staying with Anna and her roommates a mile from here in Brewers Hill since the pipe burst. Or water-gate, as she's calling it.

Kate has this habit of coin phrasing everything. I used to find it amusing, but I'm struggling with humor in general these days. And really, water-gate? As if we're not drowning in our own real-life scandal? Clandestine, illegal activities, conspiracy, large-scale coverups? Basically, our lives in a nutshell . . .

Kate elbows my stomach, and I focus long enough to follow her and Zach to the door. "I'll email the quote tomorrow," he says.

Right. The quote. Probably need that.

He extends a massive hand in my direction. "Looking forward to working with you, Josh." He flashes Kate an easy smile. "See you at Anna's, Sunshine."

Then he's sauntering off without a backward glance at Kate, whose expression immediately punctures. And the tears are falling before Zach rounds the corner, completely unaware of the avalanche his careless nickname triggered.

6:35 pm

She cries for an hour.

This might be an exaggeration but trust me, it feels like an hour. Somehow during this time, I manage to hold it together, lock up the house, and load Kate plus a dozen bags of storage-bound crap into the Jeep. In the rain. Because, why fucking not?

At the hospital, one of Julie's friends kept saying raindrops are heaven's tears. As if that's comforting? It rained the entire time David was in surgery. We don't need tears, I wanted to scream. We need God to kick the shit out of David's tumor.

I hate rain.

Nights like this? It's busy as hell at the fire station. I pull onto Charles Street wishing I could head there rather than Michael and Julie Bennett's house. For our birthday party, no less. Like that's what we need.

Literally, the last thing I want is to celebrate. Besides, I don't even know my real birthday. Neither does Kate. But Bennett has been like a dad to David ever since they met his freshman year at Towson. Bennett and Julie have done a lot for the three of us. Especially this past month.

So, thanks to their persistence and a shit ton of guilt, Kate and I will uphold the dutiful role of twins tonight and pretend our family's not a fucked-up pack of murderous liars. We'll sit across from them and their kids and eat cake, ignoring the fact that our current home is drowning right alongside everything else.

We'll look Bennett in the eye and pretend he's not wondering about Kate and I and how she miscarried the child I fathered, or David and I and the bed we share. Shared. Because that is what you do when the foundation is crumbling—you pretend.

I should know, I do it every day.

It's what I like about my job. When you're a paramedic, there's no space for panic attacks, freak-outs, fucking meditative visualizations. Not with lives at stake. You hold that shit together, even if every fiber of your being wants to lose it. Walk the fine line between compassionate human and machine: get in, get it done, and get out. Wait until it's over to let it go. Or better yet, bury it and move on.

If only my personal life played out so neatly...

It's pouring as we merge onto Falls Road, and Kate is hiccupping, the tears having finally dissolved. I've got to hand it to her, she may cry, but this is the first epic meltdown in weeks. Her first; I've lost count of mine. I reach for her hand.

"Zach didn't mean to upset you," I say for like the hundredth time.

"No, I know." She dabs her eyes with a tissue. "I don't know why it hit me so hard. It's just . . . him saying that? I can't handle it. Not today."

I understand why she's upset. What is the chance Zach would randomly use David's pet name for her?

Sunshine.

Here's a fun fact about Kate, until David came into the picture, she hated anything yellow. The night we met him, she had worn a bright yellow sundress, mostly to spite our parents who insisted on conservative attire for the party they were hosting. That dress was the least conservative thing she owned, plus Vivian detested the color.

Double win.

But then, in rolled David with his ivory skin and satin curls and those ridiculous eyes. And he liked yellow. He told Kate she looked like sunshine because, let's face it, David's an idiot. I overheard him say it, then teased her for days after. Jealousy, I'm sure. Not that I would have recognized the emotion back then.

I squeeze Kate's hand. "I never told him I overheard."

"Might be the only thing you didn't tell him," she says, then smiles sadly. She stares into the rain. "Funny how we both love the color now."

"It's true. His fondness wore on us. We even painted our little Canton shit box yellow." Not the brick part, but the window and trim are this color Kate found called Sunnyside. Only, she's not just talking about yellow, she's talking about him. And that is not a conversation I'm having right now. I turn onto Bennett's street.

"We need an exit strategy," I say.

She rolls her eyes, but I'm not kidding. As comfortable as we've become with them, some nonconforming part of my brain wants to flee.

"It'll be fine," she says and pats my arm.

I pull the key from the ignition and turn, but she's already out the door, beckoning me to follow. "Come on," she shouts over the rain. "We're late!" And she's sprinting up the driveway toward their cozy, rambling colonial before I can say another word.

I trudge behind, not caring if I get soaked. My chest tightens with every waterlogged step. I try to conjure an image of the beach, a plane, something. Anything. Doesn't work; I see nothing but water and despair. And then the front door opens.

Light spills onto the porch, and the sidewalk, and the yard, and the whole damn world. This dizzying warmth envelopes me and everything stops. Even the rain.

Because holy shit.

Faulty Floodgates

:: When a minor leak creates an
indoor waterpark

Katherine Janney (Kate)
Thursday, July 13th 6:47 pm
Boyce Avenue Towson, Maryland

Josh is unraveling.

Piece by heart-shattering piece. I've been watching it happen for a month now. No. Scratch that, months now. Since David's first blackout. But the pipe burst last week was the final straw. Something snapped and he can't mend it. Defeat on top of despair. That is Josh these days.

And that is the look he's wearing before David opens the front door.

David.

Calm, unshakeable David, who breezed through nine hours of brain surgery. Yes, hours. It went well, but the tumor was bigger than expected; too difficult to remove fully. He woke to that unsettling news. And to find they'd clipped a tendon in his jaw, making it difficult to talk. That, plus an angry, jagged scar from the tip of his left ear to his forehead, all the hair around and in between shaved and gone. To find half his face numb, and his left eye bruised and swollen to the point of closing.

A side effect, the doctors said. Fluid drainage. They assured us it would all go away in a few weeks. And as for his headaches? Worse, not better.

But despite all this, he'd been hopeful. Optimistic, even. Soldiered on, came home days later loaded with prescriptions and painkillers. But he was too restless to settle. Agitated and uncomfortable. Nothing we tried seemed to work and he digressed. Wouldn't eat, couldn't sleep. It was awful. And then came the fever.

We rushed him back to the hospital where it took a week to treat the infection. And then Bennett and Julie insisted on caring for him. We didn't argue. It was clear Josh and I couldn't handle things.

And the recovery since? Slow. An achy, painful, watching-paint-dry kind of slow. He sleeps. A lot. And won't answer his phone or text or communicate in any way. Every time we visit, he's sleeping, won't get out of bed, huddled on the couch. You can barely reach him. It is the worst kind of hell imaginable. He's right there, but like, miles away.

So, Josh and I reason he needs to recover at home. Our home. We throw ourselves into getting the house ready. Design work schedules so one of us will always be with him. Plan meals, stock the pantry, prepare for every scenario possible. Exhaust ourselves with details. Finally decide on a day.

And then the fucking pipe bursts.

The one scenario we had not considered. Defeat on top of despair. It's understandable.

So, when David opens the door on our birthday, bathed, dressed, grinning, and seemingly alive for the first time in a month? Well, there is no describing the feeling. Words can't do it justice. It is the best present ever. And me, being me, hurdles the front porch step and launches myself at him.

I hang like a koala from his leaner-than-before but deliciously warm body that smells of all things David. And tears come again because when am I not crying lately? And he's saying something that doesn't register but might be in the realm of Kate, you're crushing me.

And then I remember Josh.

Soggy, stunned, slightly unraveled Josh who's hanging back on the driveway looking lost and elated and close to tears himself.

Painful as it is, I detach from David because we both know who needs him most. And I have no idea where Julie and Bennett are, but I sequester myself in their foyer bathroom for a good five minutes until the ugly crying stops and my curls are properly beaten to submission.

I emerge to find the hall and foyer empty, but voices trickle out from the kitchen. Julie wanted this celebration. Twenty-five is the last birthday you'll appreciate, she teased. It's all downhill from there.

That, and the fact David made it. That he's here. She left that part unsaid. How could we not celebrate, after what he's been through? What we've all been through.

The front door is ajar, and I move to close it before realizing Josh and David are still outside. I back into the shadows and watch, heart caught in all kinds of places. They're on the porch swing, side by side. Josh's head rests on David's shoulder, and his eyes are closed. He's drenched: shirt, shorts, shoes, everything. David too, by sheer proximity. Neither care.

They're talking. David's saying something I can't make out, and Josh is sporting a lopsided grin, biting at his lip with a shy, childlike expression. He looks so content, I feel the tears well up. Again.

And David. Our sweet, David. Gaunt and wiry, paler than before yet so beautiful in the shadowed light. He's wearing a skull cap, but those dark, irresistible curls peek out from beneath. You'd never guess the angry scar he's covering, or the hair that's yet to grow.

And his eyes. Slightly swollen, but alert, finally, and animated. The two of them sitting there reminds me of that picture he texted from Isabelle's wedding before Isaac drove them home. On a bench, so happy together.

Seems a lifetime ago, that night. Hard to believe it's been less than two months. And I'm just over ten feet from the boys, but even at this distance I feel it. Like a warm blanket cloaking us.

Hope.

Faint, but monumental. And timely. With so much uncertainty, we needed this. Josh needed this. Reason to hang in there. I let out a long breath and slowly shut the door. And, for the first time in a month, I'm sensing light at the end of the tunnel.

7:39 pm

But then it fades.

As does our party. If you want to call it that. Basically, it's Bennett, Julie, their kids Jack and Grace, and a handful of neighboring families gathered around the kitchen table to sing and to eat a Costco-size sheet cake Julie must have spent days constructing.

One family, to my intense mortification, I recognize. It's the eavesdropping couple next door who overheard David and I at the fro-yo shop a few months ago. The dad straight up gawks during our birthday song and then has the nerve to ask, in a stage whisper, if I've solved my bathroom problem. I mean, good grief. You make one joke about poop and it's like the world is ending. Does the man not know about our pipe burst?

But I just grit my teeth and laugh. Bennett's already questioning my integrity, given the whole miscarriage-twin-cest situation between Josh and me that he thinks he's privy to. And I don't want to embarrass myself or their family further, which obviously includes telling off creepy fro-yo stalker-neighbor guy.

Stalker.

That is not a term I ever imagined in connection with myself. Though, technically I guess you wouldn't call Carol Brennan a stalker. He's David's uncle, after all. Is it considered stalking if the person is related to you? Maybe.

He's a creep, either way. I don't care how nice David's mother was, her brother is bat-shit crazy for following us. And hiding the evidence about Josh's real mom and the fire all these years? Deplorable. Besides, he's clearly not concerned about David. Josh tried contacting him before the surgery, but apparently David's long-lost uncle wants to stay lost—he never called back.

We've heard from Nick, though. Poor Josh. Between the pipe burst and David's setbacks, his anxiety is through the roof. Add all the past crap we haven't dealt with and Nick's near-constant harassment? He's a mess. We are a mess—all three of us.

Ugh.

I promised myself I wouldn't describe us that way. So, I'll say we're...tangled. That's a better word. The earth shifted when David's tumor was discovered, and nothing's been right since. Only, shifting implies permanent change. Tangling merely requires a little course correction. So, maybe that's what I should go with. Tangled, but course correcting. That's us.

Clinging, too. To each other. To that sliver of hope I felt on the porch. And to the ginormous sliver of cake Julie hands me...

"It was almost impossible coming up with a birthday cake you'd all like." She laughs. "David hates chocolate, vanilla is boring, and he told me Josh has an aversion to strawberries."

All true. We don't generally celebrate birthdays. Not since the year we turned eighteen and learned the truth. It was shocking enough to discover Josh and I weren't twins, let alone not related. And with the fire and all its aftermath?

We had been too stunned to question Nick and Vivian about dates and silly things like, oh, I don't know, birth parent names. Neither Josh nor I know the exact day we were born. Not that they would have been forthcoming.

I mention none of this to Julie, though. She's so happy; I don't want to rain on her parade. "No, this is perfect," I say and take a grinning bite of something moist and gingery with layers of decadent sweet cream—carrot cake.

Holy deliciousness.

I don't need a glance in David's direction to know he's watching. Clearly, he told Julie of my recent obsession. Since the pipe burst, I've been living with my friend Anna and her roommates Rosa and Demetri. They just opened the most adorable café in Brewers Hill. It's called Joe Mama's and it's amazing. They serve Greek and

American coffee and pastries, but their carrot cake is to die for.

That David remembered this little detail with everything else going on sort of wrecks my appetite. I swallow hard and turn. Sure enough, his eyes are on me. Josh too. Both their plates, untouched.

It's so familiar, them sitting together in this kitchen, I could almost pretend nothing has changed. That we're here celebrating Jack or Grace's birthday instead. That we will pack up and drive home together. Back to a house and world intact.

I have a sudden, desperate urge to run. To the boys, away from them, I don't know...just run. My hope drains like bath water, and I stifle a sob. The cake lodges in my throat, and I cough to free it. The sound is mangled and loud and grossly unattractive. Josh hurries over with some water.

"Eat much?" he whispers, pounding at my back. "You're making a spectacle."

I glare over the cup's rim at his soggy clothing and damp hair. "Said the kettle . . ."

David struggles over. "No bickering on our birthday," he chides. And though his tone is light, his eyes are tired. Seeing him fade this fast knocks the wind from my sails. Josh, too.

"You should lie down," he says, then turns to me, frowning. "And what the hell are you doing glaring at that guy?" He nods toward fro-yo stalker who's taken up residence on the couch. David and I exchange a glance.

"Kate shits a lot," David says, and I dissolve into giggles. This infuriates Josh, who is clearly on edge and has no patience for inside jokes.

"Real fucking funny," he growls, but instantly softens as David sways, clutching a chair to right himself. Josh takes his arm. "Come on," he says gently, "let's get you upstairs."

David doesn't argue.

We file out of the kitchen, and I give a little thumbs up to Julie, who's watching with concern. My hope further deflates as David climbs the stairs. I pretend not to notice how pale he looks. How baggy his clothing, an outfit I bought only months ago, has become.

I swallow hard, battling another siege of tears, bracing for the emotional storm front. But once inside his room, he seems better. Surrounded by the comfort of books and blankets and cozy oak furnishings, he's more himself. This room is familiar. Quiet and safe, like David. He lived here during college, after all; it's basically his.

The three of us collapse on the tall, four-poster bed, staring wordless at the ceiling, just breathing in the silence. It is the next best moment to him opening the front door. After a while he takes each of our hands.

"I'm so glad you guys came," he says, yawning, eyes drifting shut. "Don't leave, okay? Stay here with me."

And so, we do.

Friday, July 14ᵗʰ 5:42 am

I wake in a puddle.

It's thick and warm and distinctly urine-like.

Did I pee myself? Did David? Josh?

I open one eye and discover a white fishnet canopy dangling inches above my face. There's a tiny blond snoring beside me who can only be Gracie Bennett. With equal revulsion and relief I realize it is her urine I'm lying in, and I bolt out of the bed.

I stumble to her door and into the silent hallway. Julie and Bennett have a first-floor master, but Jack and Grace have rooms upstairs. David, too.

Once he drifted off last night, I snuck out and bunked with Grace, something I've done often when staying here. And a monumental mistake, clearly. But it didn't feel right, sleeping with the boys. Not given what Bennett thinks he knows about me and Josh. Although, based on a few comments he made this summer, I'm not sure he's buying our twin story.

Whatever about it.

Josh needed time with David anyway.

I push open his door and slip into the cool, dark room. They're still asleep, wrapped tight in each other beneath the thin covers. My heart immediately floods. Here I am, alone and wanting, yet I've never loved them more.

If the last few months taught me anything, it's that life is too fleeting, too sacred to waste on avoidance and denial. The boys love each other...

need each other in ways I can't begin to understand. How can I stand between them? And anyway, if David and I are meant to be, it will happen. I have to believe that.

Waiting might hurt like hell, but he's worth it. *We* are worth it.

Resigned to this, I tip toe past them into David's bathroom. His shower is gigantic and scalding and so decadent I forget to care I'm soaked in pee. It's a million times better than our shower in Canton.

And yet, I can't help missing it. The clanging pipes, the boys bustling in and out, vying for sink space; David's daily rant about water pressure. It'll never be the same. In a few weeks, we'll have a brand-new bathroom. Brand new house, practically. Brand new life if we come forward with what we know.

But where does that leave us? Where does that leave me? Once we're free from Nick's clutches, anything could happen. David could choose Josh, and maybe he should. What would I do then? Could I move on apart from them?

I don't want to even think about it.

I stand trance-like beneath the hypnotic spray until the water cools. My skin is puckered and flushed when I finally emerge wrapped in David's towel. He's awake and blinking through the dim morning light.

Those beautiful eyes. I can't even.

"Where'd you go last night?" he asks, beckoning me over.

I sit beside him and recount my Gracie bed-wetting tale, to which he laughingly wonders how I know it's her urine and not mine. Honestly, it feels so good to be teased by him, I don't give a damn who wet the bed.

"Either way, I need to wake her. Change the sheets and get her in a shower. Or at least tell Julie what happened."

"Do that in a minute," he murmurs, nuzzling me with his cheek. He slides a finger along my thigh. "You're like, all warm and naked and stuff."

I suck in a breath at his touch, at the sight of his bare chest and torso peeking from beneath the blanket. Heat pools in the most pleasant of places as I take in the achingly familiar landscape of his body. Those beautifully sculpted arms, his narrow waist and firm stomach...that seductive happy trail separating the V-lines. And good Lord, his skin. Soft and smooth as ivory in contrast to...

Josh.

His arm rests possessively on David's hip. Tan by comparison. Taut with muscle and a light dusting of golden, sun-streaked hair. Beneath the covers I can make out their legs, all entwined.

It's not an unfamiliar sight, and I wonder, for the millionth time, how I managed to blind myself for so long. "Um...the bed looks a little bit crowded," I say.

He frowns, gently shrugging away from Josh as he motions for me to lie beside him. I want nothing more than to curl into his arms and let him have his way with me. But not here. If Julie or

Bennett walked in on the three of us? Holy Mother of embarrassment.

"Not happening," I tell him, turning before my body betrays me. I feel his eyes slide over me as I dig through a drawer.

"You're so pretty," he says, watching as I slip into boxers and a faded Vans tee. And though I no doubt look a mess, his appraisal makes me feel pretty. And, pathetically, wilts my resolve.

Seconds later I'm in the bed, basking in a cozy cocoon of breath and skin and comfy bed sheets. He strokes my neck and shoulders while I ramble on about the house and meeting with Zach yesterday. About living with Anna and Demetri and Rosa in Brewers Hill. I tell him about my job and the recent drama at the spa. I go on about a host of things he could probably care less about. Yet, he listens.

He always listens.

What I don't mention is him coming home, or his recovery, or the sordid Nick situation we haven't dealt with, or anything Josh related—he tends to sleep with one ear open. Not that there's anything hidden between the three of us anymore.

Anything worth mentioning, that is.

I don't tell him about the date I went on last weekend. It wasn't by choice—Rosa forced me, and it was a disaster. We doubled with two of Demetri's friends. The guy was nice enough, I guess. A little handsy. Horrible breath. I kept offering him gum, but he didn't take the hint.

All I thought about was David and Josh. They've ruined me for other men, I need to accept that. Regardless of who ends up with whom, I'm never moving past them. And speaking of other men. Anna's boyfriend, Zach! What a jerk that guy is. I'm not telling David about him either, or Josh who's bent on hiring his crew to fix our place.

From what I've witnessed this summer, Zach doesn't treat Anna very well. I'm not sure exactly what happened, but she had to leave her job back in June and, while he appears supportive, he doesn't miss an opportunity to take a dig.

They're high school sweethearts with a long history, which I obviously relate to. According to Rosa, he's never been overly kind to Anna. This begs the question, why does she stay with him? Why does anyone stay?

I push back thoughts of my own high school years. Of Josh and David and how we suffered. What we did. What they did—together. As if sensing these thoughts, David's arm tightens.

Behind him, Josh stirs. He makes a grunting sound and sits up. "Damn, it's quiet. What did you fall asleep, Kate?" He leans over David and tugs at one of my curls, sniffing. "Is that coffee? You think Julie's making breakfast? I'm starving."

Of course, he is.

"Seriously, Josh," I grumble. "When aren't you starving?"

But before he can respond, we're interrupted by a blood curdling scream followed by Gracie Bennett's plaintive cry from across the hall.

"Mommy! Come quick! Kate peed in my bed!"

Three

Reclaiming Spaces

:: Turning chaos into comfort,
one step at a time

David Brennan
Sunday, August 13th 9:02 pm
Foster Avenue Baltimore, Maryland

Josh is singing.

He's loud and off-key and I've never loved him more. I'm tempted to stand on our front step while he butchers an entire playlist, but it's late, and I'm tired, and I just want to see him.

I give a nod to Bennett, who pulls away looking every bit the anxious parent. He was against me coming home this soon. Julie, too. They wanted me to stay until the house is finished and I return to teaching full-time. But it's been two months since surgery and, while I'm grateful for their help, I'm ready to get on with my life.

Besides, they're feeling guilty. Like, maybe the tumor would've been detected had I stayed with them longer last spring. Only I don't buy that. Things happen for a reason, even the pipe burst. Josh is all gloom and doom about it, but I believe there's purpose in the chaos.

Just wish I knew what purpose.

Regardless, I'm home and that's all that matters. I push open the front door and, speaking of chaos, our living room is a disaster—spotlights, drop cloths, buckets, a half-empty rolling pan, and Josh. He's crouched in the corner painting trim, singing his ever-loving tone-deaf heart out.

It's the best sound I've heard in days.

Also, the only sound. He's using AirPods, so there is no background noise. He doesn't hear my bags drop or notice when I cross the room to where he's left his phone charging. I pick it up, fighting a tearful grin as I glimpse his screensaver. It's a picture of Kate and I playing in the snow outside last winter. Taken before Nick's interview, before the blackouts. Before my uncle's meddling lit a fuse we've yet to extinguish. It feels like a lifetime ago.

I want to run to Josh, but I take another moment, pausing the song he's listening to instead. He stops painting, taps his ear, and the music resumes. We do this several times as his irritation builds. Finally, I shut the music app completely, and he curses, rising to his feet. And that's when he sees me.

I give a little wave. "Hi."

He blinks.

"I'm back." I point to my stuff by the door. "Bennett just dropped me off."

He glances at the bags, then me, then the bags again. More blinking. It's nine o'clock Sunday night and I'm the last person he's expecting. We haven't discussed my return, but I'm sure he assumed it'd be after the repairs are done, weeks from now.

I take a step toward him. "Josh, say something."

He shakes his head looking stunned and irresistibly wrecked in a worn T-shirt. You Fall, We Haul, it says, and it's so tight; I see the contour of every hard, shredded muscle. I'm not the only one who's lost weight this summer, but it looks good on him.

A warm ache floods my stomach, and I can't hold back. I'm across the room in seconds, tackling him with a crushing hug.

He stumbles. "The wall, David! I just painted—"

"Forget the wall," I say, grinning as we slam into it.

He fists my shirt, pulling me close as we slide to the floor, laughing. I cling to him, overcome and overwhelmed, and so grateful to be home, there aren't words. They say facing death makes life taste sweeter, and it's true.

I cradle his face in my hands and kiss him. Graceless and open-mouthed and so long he's gasping into it, blushing furiously as I pull back to get a better look at him.

"I love you so much," I say, not even caring that we don't say this. These last few weeks of recovery, it's like waking from a coma. Bennett claims they removed my filter along with the tumor. Maybe so. Whatever they did, it feels wonderful and terrifying, and I want to share every part of it with Josh and Kate.

Only, he's so thrown by my arrival he can hardly string words together. "If you had told me you were coming . . ." he sputters.

"You would have worked yourself to death."

Which is why I didn't.

"That's not true." He pauses. "Okay. Maybe it is, but fuck, David." He yanks his AirPods out and sits up. "You can't just show up with no warning when I'm like," he looks down at himself, "I'm a mess! And this place . . ." He gestures helplessly.

We both glance around the living room. It is a mess, but farther along than I expected. Mostly touch up and finishing work left. Not that I care. Josh, though . . . much as he wants me home, the loose ends are no doubt plaguing him. And not just the house stuff—it's all the other crap we haven't dealt with. Which is exactly why he needs me here.

"I'm better now," I tell him. "Stronger and ready to come back and help. Paint, pack up, move forward. Whatever you and Kate need. Doesn't matter what the house looks like, I just want us back together."

"Together?" His tone has a bitter edge. "Might just be me and you for a while. Kate's busy slumming it in Brewers Hill with her new bestie. She might never come back."

I think this is more his perception than the truth. Kate's as anxious as I am to return. Besides, what could she have done here? At least Anna and her friends have been a good distraction.

"We should call and tell her I'm home," I say.

"Yeah," he agrees somewhat distractedly. His smile is hesitant. Hopeful. "You're really back to stay?"

I nod and the remaining tension seems to drain from his face. Something akin to relief brightens his soft, puppy-like eyes, and it's a wonderful sight. He stands, offering me a hand.

"Well, it's about fucking time," he says, fingers tightening around mine. "Come on, you're not going to believe what they've done with the kitchen." He tugs me along, talking all at once about a countertop mishap, and cabinets on back-order. I'm reminded of the brazen ten-year-old who rescued me from my father's clutches and then wouldn't let go.

Still hasn't let go.

I give his hand a squeeze and swallow the lump threatening to form. "Show me everything."

10:47 pm

An hour later the paint is put away, I've toured the entire house, and he and I are in the doorway of our room.

The walls are now a soothing, earthy sage with fresh white trim that meets sleek laminate. Gone are the dingy oak floors we never refinished. It's a far cry from the bedroom I remember.

The dresser and desk are gone, too. Zach's guys built a custom hutch and bookcase around the window seat. They also finished the closet shelf project Josh started. With two beds and no furniture, the room looks huge.

"Wow," I say stepping inside, "it's so different." And empty. "What happened to all the balls?" We've been collecting souvenir balls for years, most of which ended up on our bedroom floor. I bet a lot of them were ruined.

"Storage," he says, watching me, worried, wondering what I think of all the changes.

I notice neither bed is made, but mine is partially covered by a worn, army-green sleeping bag and some flat looking pillows. Something fractures at the thought of him sleeping there. Alone. I run my hand along the dingy fabric.

"Been sleeping at the station, mostly," he says, then clears his throat. Whether that's true or not, the bags under his eyes tell a different story—he's hardly slept.

I stifle a yawn, aware, suddenly, of my own fatigue. Pain twinges behind my eye even though I'm still numb there. I press at it, unfeeling. It's a bizarre sensation. As is the sleep thing which overtakes me with little warning. I sag against the wall.

"You should lie down," he says, and I don't argue.

In fact, I don't change or brush my teeth or do anything. I just crawl inside his sleeping bag, hug a pillow tight, and close my eyes.

He chuckles. "Make yourself at home, why don't you."

But I'm already drifting, vaguely aware of him moving around. Of water running in the distance and lights flickering off. It seems only moments pass before the bed moves and he's beside me smelling of paint thinner and toothpaste, and clean cotton body wash—scents so achingly familiar I could cry.

It's not the big things I've missed, but the mundane. The small, everyday minutia that make a life. My life.

He settles in closer and wraps his arms around me. "Is this all right?" he whispers, breath warm against my neck. I shiver, wanting to tell him it's more than all right. It's perfect. But I just nod as he relaxes, his chest and stomach comfortably molding into my back. I feel his heartbeat, strong and steady, slowing as he stills, its rhythm matching mine.

And for the first time in a long time, we're drifting together, fading into a blissful, dreamless sleep.

Monday, August 14th 10:12 am

The distant sound of Josh's laughter rouses me.

A low, throaty rumble that warms my...everything. I peel a lid open and check my phone, dismayed, but not shocked to see it's after ten. It takes a few moments for my eyes to focus and the grogginess to abate. Waking has become something of a challenge since surgery, but another rumbly outburst has me sitting up.

Josh only talks to a handful of people, and he's not prone to laughter. At least, not the man Josh. As a boy, he was always laughing.

Stumbling out of bed, I make my way down the stairs and into our kitchen where I find him leaning against the counter, AirPods in, grinning at his phone. He's on a Facetime call.

"Hey!" He startles. "You're up! I didn't think..." He looks back at his phone. "Yeah, it's him. Listen, I gotta go." His smile broadens. "No, I won't forget." He rolls his eyes at the screen, still grinning. "You're a pain in the ass, you know that? Yeah, yeah . . . all right . . . you too. I will. Talk to you soon. Okay, bye." He ends the call chuckling, a telltale crimson dusting his cheeks which can only mean one thing.

"So, Tessa," I say, and he nearly drops the phone.

"How did you—?"

"Lucky guess."

It's not. I may not be on my A-game, but I'm attentive enough to know they've been talking since my collapse at the art gala. Besides, he never blushes like that with Kate.

"Well, she was checking on you, asshole. I wouldn't even answer, except she'll keep calling." He frowns, as if talking to my college ex-girlfriend is some kind of hardship. But I'm glad they've connected. I always thought the two of them would get on well.

"So, you guys are bonding over me, huh? I told you there would be an upside to my tumor."

"Yeah, we're bonding, David. Talking to Tess is totally worth your brain surgery, months of sleeplessness, and . . ." He gestures around. "All this shit."

I survey the kitchen which is as much chaos as repair. All that time and hard work we put in, erased in a matter of hours. It is still hard to believe.

"When will Zach and his crew be here?" I ask.

"They don't do Mondays. And I'm off until tomorrow, which means we have all day to get you settled." He catches my wrists suddenly and pulls me into a fierce hug. "I still can't believe you're here. Did you sleep all right? How are you feeling?"

I feel a bit overwhelmed, but I'm not telling him that. Since surgery, my moods and emotions are all over the place. It's given me a new appreciation for Josh and his struggles with panic and anxiety. How he's thrived despite the crippling attacks.

A surge of love has me hugging him tighter, pressing my cheek to his skin, grateful for his ever-steady presence. For the comfort of our sunny little kitchen. I forgot how cozy it is here. How right I feel with him. With Kate.

Kate.

"We forgot to call Kate last night!" I groan at the same time his phone vibrates. He shows me the screen. It's Tessa.

"Reminding me to text her with an update after I talk to you. Because she's concerned. About *you.*" This last part is said rather pointedly.

I don't doubt Tessa's concern, but it doesn't mean she's not interested. "You know I don't care if you guys talk, right? I'm glad you've connected. She could be good for you."

This, of course, is the wrong thing to say. "What is that supposed to mean, 'good for me'?"

"Nothing. It's just—"

"You and Kate," he mutters. "Always trying to pawn me off."

"That's not true, J. I just want you to be—"

"Happy? Is that what you're going to say? You think I'll be happy with Tessa because, why? You dated her? She feels sorry for me?" He steps back, bristling. "Do you even realize what I've been dealing with this summer? I'm not thinking about relationships, David. And even if I was, you think she's who I want?"

No, I don't.

He wants me, or at least he thinks he does. But what does that even look like for us? And what about Kate? We haven't told her I'm home, let alone discussed how the three of us move forward. Not to mention the Nick situation or my uncle's disturbing news.

A dull ache spreads across my forehead. Yesterday's optimism seems like a distant memory. "Look, I'm sorry." I take a step, narrowing the distance between us. "I'm just saying, she's nice is all. She could be a good friend."

"Yeah. I know she's nice. That doesn't mean I'm into her." He gets all blustery when he's fired up. It's kind of adorable. I've missed that so much. Missed *him.*

"No, of course you're right. I'm not thinking straight." I take a sweeping glance around our first floor. "Give me a few days to adjust before we start . . . dealing with stuff." Ripping open old wounds is more like it, but that doesn't sound nearly as appealing. "Let's get Kate back home, sort everything out with Carol and your father. Put the house in order. We finally have our chance at starting over. I want to do things right."

It's what we agreed, moving in here—deal with the past so we can focus on the future. Only, standing with him now in this new reality? Things seem less . . . clear. Especially where the three of us are concerned.

I love him, but I need her. I love her, but I want him. It was an impossible choice before my surgery, but now? I don't want to be apart from either of them. Ever.

His brow furrows, as if reading these thoughts. And while it's a conversation we need to have, now isn't the time. "We can worry about all that later," I say, stepping backward. Formulating a plan. "Right now, I could use a hot shower, black coffee, and some really greasy food."

In truth, I need none of these, except maybe the shower. But Josh is task oriented, and I've just outlined his ideal morning, as evidenced by the dopey grin that immediately lights up his face.

"Come on." I laugh, tugging him with me toward the stairs. "Let's shower and get out of here."

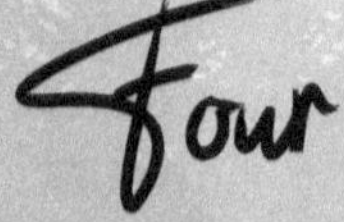

Shower Shenanigans

:: When a bathroom remodel exposes more than plumbing secrets

Josh
Monday, August 14th 11:05 am
Foster Avenue Baltimore, Maryland

When David says let's shower, he doesn't mean together.

I, however, take it as an invitation, and join him—platonically speaking, of course.

Thanks to Zach's crew, our new shower is double its previous width. Which is to say, a few inches shy of standard. Not exactly equipped to handle two guys our size. Or, my size, David is a bit...shrunken. An observation I, unfortunately, share out loud.

His nose wrinkles. "Really, J? Shrunken?" He lathers soap into his hair, squinting at me. "Could you use a less flattering term?"

I let my eyes trace the contours of his slender yet ridiculously beautiful body, still awed that he's here. These last two months felt like a decade, but looking at him now, I'd hardly know what he's been through.

The scar from surgery is there, obviously. And his hair hasn't fully grown in. But the weight loss? If anything, it sharpened his appeal. All that smooth skin and lean, taut muscle? His body is the perfect symmetry of softness and strength and so stunning; it should be a crime.

It *is* a crime, because all I want is to touch him. But I don't. I watch instead, breathless, as he turns into the water, tilts his head back, eyes closed, lips parted. Streams of soapy bubbles cascade down his neck and shoulders, dripping invitingly on the swell of his ass, which is anything but shrunk.

I swallow. "Nope. Shrunk is about right." I'm literally dying here. And like, what the fuck? Is he auditioning for porn or something? How is this fair?

I shouldn't touch him, right?

We are definitely not doing that. Not after the whole starting over conversation. But what the hell does that mean at this point? What, I'm supposed to pretend I don't want him? Not likely.

"David . . ."

I can't take it. He's too close. My fingers graze the perfect curve of his back, and I pull him too me, thumbs pressing into the sexy little dimples above his ass. And holy hell, I could go all day on these things.

I wrap my arms around his waist and we both shiver at the sudden, electrifying heat of skin on skin. We haven't been this naked this close in months, and it's everything. For me, at least.

But not for him. He immediately stiffens, and not in a good way.

"Josh . . ." he says. A warning.

I sag against the wall at his tone, still holding him, hating myself for pushing. For the tension that settles between us. But I don't want to let him go.

He exhales, shoulders slumping. "I'm sorry. I'm not . . . I just can't—"

"Don't apologize." I'm still holding him. Still stroking his skin. "It's my fault."

He shrugs away, the loss of him . . . like a slap of cold. "No, it's not. I just . . . I don't know. I don't feel like myself, yet. And I'm a wreck. No one's seen me like this, and I haven't even—"

"Like what? Naked?" *Is he kidding?* I know his body better than my own. We've never hidden from each other. "Don't be ridiculous. You know I don't care what you look like. Besides, you're perfect."

He's more than perfect. I can barely stand because of him, as is painfully obvious to both of us. But there's clearly something else bothering him.

He shuts off the water. "I'm not perfect. Don't say that." His hand lifts to the incision, as if shielding it from me. He's been keeping his head covered, even when he sleeps.

"What? You're worried about the scar? Come on, D. It's hardly noticeable."

He's already out of the shower, towel cinched tight around his hips. "It's not that. I mean, it is. But . . ." He's blushing. Actual, splotchy, neck reddening heat. A jarring sight. David is rarely embarrassed, and like, never with me. "Quit staring," he chides. "You're making it worse."

I don't know what to do with this troubled version of him. "Sorry. I'm not used to you being so . . . awkward?"

His blush deepens. "Yeah? Well, me either, okay?"

The worry in his tone gets me out of the shower in a hot second. I join him by the sink and grab my own towel. "Something else is bothering you. Spill it."

He shifts, avoiding my gaze. "It's stupid, really. Not even worth mentioning, but . . ."

"But what?"

"I don't know. Since surgery, I haven't, you know . . ." He gestures vaguely toward his groin area. "It's not like I wanted to. Not in the beginning. But now? I'm pretty sure everything's working. Like, all the necessary functions are happening. I just haven't technically . . ." he leaves the sentence hanging, and it takes my brain a moment to catch up.

"What are we talking about here? Jerking off?"

He nods, looking about as mortified as I've seen him. "I read a few recovery articles. There was this one about brain rupture, and it kind of freaked me out, so I just . . . stop laughing, Josh!"

"I'm not!"

I am, but not *at* him. "Come on, a brain rupture? From an orgasm? You know better than that. I mean, yes, an aneurysm can rupture, but you had a tumor. It's not the same."

I resist the urge to lecture him about the dangers of internet diagnosis, which is a legit problem. The number of calls we get at the station from people with cyberchondria would fill an ER five times over. But David? He's not one to fall for that kind of stuff. Only, he looks genuinely concerned.

"All right. Let me get this straight. You're saying, since surgery, you haven't—"

"Nope. Not even once."

He glances, reflexively, at the still evident bulge beneath my towel. "I know it's ridiculous, but I can't get past it." He scrubs a hand over his face. "And this anxiety thing is new for me. It's so frustrating, like a mental block. I don't know how you've dealt with it for so long."

Yeah. That makes two of us.

But we're talking about him. And that is a lot of frustration he's carrying around. *How is he functioning?*

I try to keep my voice even so as not to reveal, one, how humorous I'm beginning to find this whole situation, and two, how inappropriately turned on I am by it. "Well, I can give you a few tips for anxiety, but your other problem?" I intentionally lower my gaze. "Sounds like we're dealing with some built up tension, am I right?"

He barks out a laugh. "You could put it that way."

I'm about to suggest exactly where he can put it when we hear the very distinct, very squeaky sound of our front door opening. Both our heads snap up.

"Zach?" he whispers.

"No. It can't be." The crew isn't coming out today. And there's only one other person with a key. Which means . . .

"Josh?" Kate's voice echoes through our construction zone. "Where are you? I've got breakfast!"

11:32 am

She bounds up the stairs before I can respond.

The bathroom door swings open, and . . .

"David!" Her shriek bounces off the freshly tiled walls and ricochets inside my eardrum. She hurls herself at him. "What are you doing here? Are you home for good? I can't believe it! Why didn't you call, I would have . . ." She trails off, noticing me. "Oh, Josh. Did I . . . ? Are you guys . . . ?" Her arms fall from around him and she straightens, taking in our wet bodies and skimpy towel coverings. "Oh," she repeats. The bag slips from her hand and her cheeks turn the same shade as her onesie.

Yes. That's right. I said onesie.

"What the hell are you wearing?" Probably not the right time, but I can't stop myself. Kate doesn't look like Kate at all. She's sporting a skin-tight purple leopard print condom looking unitard thing, complete with socks and a matching headband. It's a statement.

My gaze shifts to the bag she dropped. Joe Mama's Café it says in bold print. My stomach, much like the rest of my body, has inappropriate timing. It picks that moment to rumble happily. Kate's eyes narrow, and David cuts me a withering look.

"I'm sorry, Sunshine. We were going to call last night, but I fell asleep, and then Tessa called this morning, and . . ." he tapers off lamely as tears flood her hazel eyes. Guilt tugs at my chest. We should've called.

She uses the condom sleeve to wipe her face. "Whatever. It's fine. I should go. Leave you guys to . . ." She gestures at our . . . towels. And before we can protest, she scoops up the bag and all but flees downstairs.

David's behind her, yanking on underwear as he goes. I grab shorts and a T-shirt and join them in the kitchen moments later.

". . . Bennett dropped me off last night," he's saying. "It was a last-minute thing, I swear. We were going to call—"

"After you spent the night and showered together?" she offers. "How thoughtful."

I muss her curls as I slink past. "Don't give David a hard time, it's my fault." I lean against the counter between them and pick through the Joe Mama's bag. "Besides, there's a more pressing issue to discuss." I nod at Kate's outfit. "What are you, an eighties poster child for contraception? Explain yourself."

She snatches the bag from my hand. "You're not funny, Josh. And quit acting like this isn't a big deal. It's my house too, you know. You guys can't just be doing . . . showers all the time."

Doing showers? Did she really say that?

I mean, I get why she's upset. But the reality is, we weren't just doing much of anything. *Yet.* And even if we were, it's all on the table now, isn't it? Only, they're looking at me like I hold some kind of answer, which I don't. The only thing I have to offer is honesty.

"All right, Kate. I'm gonna tell you how it is. David came home late last night. It wasn't planned and I had no idea. He slept like the dead for twelve hours, got up thirty minutes ago, then took a shower to clear his head. And yes, we were in there together, talking, because, among other things, he's afraid his brain might explode if anyone touches his junk. Now, can you please explain why you're dressed like an overripe moon grape? And for god's sake, hand me a muffin. I'm starving."

12:20 pm

"Aerial yoga? Is that even a thing?"

Kate's explanation makes less sense than her outfit. She rolls her eyes at me in the rearview mirror. "It's all about anti-gravity, Josh. You wouldn't understand."

"What's not to understand? You paid for-ty-five dollars to dress in a grape-colored condom, hang upside down, and swing from the ceiling? Am I right?"

She shrugs. "I mean, kind of. But there's way more to it . . ."

"Do you at least get your money back when you return the uniform?"

"What uniform? This is mine," she says. "I bought it."

"You mean, like, on purpose?"

"Yes, Josh. Anna and I picked it out at Towson Town Center, in that new athletic store. It wasn't cheap, either."

"What athletic store?" I suddenly feel incredibly old. When was the last time I even stepped foot in a clothing store?

"Oh yeah, I know what you're talking about," David says, because of course he would know. "Julie bought me shorts from there this summer." He buckles his seat belt. "You'd like them, Josh. Kind of fitted, but comfortable, too."

I almost make a comment about liking him in anything fitted, but something tells me that won't go over well. It already took a half hour to talk Kate down. David and I polished off the Joe Mama's pastries while alternately apologizing and bringing her up to speed on the house.

Besides, I want to savor this moment. The three of us, together again. In the Jeep, doing something simple and ordinary like grabbing lunch. As if the last few months never happened.

"Let's go to Matthew's," I say, heading toward Eastern before either of them responds. Matthew's

Pizzeria is a Baltimore treasure and hands down, the best pie in the state. It's also like a block away.

Kate grabs a table while David and I park. "We should've called her," he repeats for the hundredth time.

Like I don't know this?

"She'll get over it," I say as we make our way to Kate, who starts talking before we reach the table.

"So, what's the plan? Am I coming home? How's that going to work? My room isn't even painted yet." This is because she hasn't picked out paint, but I keep that criticism to myself.

"Come home whenever you want. You can stay in our room until yours is done." Her eyes narrow. "Or the couch. I don't care. I'll sleep there if you two want the room, or . . ."

They glance at each other, then me.

"What? You guys make a suggestion, then. It's not like the three of us have never shared a room before. Or a bed." I give them both a pointed look. "Besides, it's temporary. We'll tell Zach to make Kate's room a priority."

She sits back in her chair. "What is it, like mid-August? I already paid Demi, Roe, and Anna my share for the full month. Why don't I come back on September first? That will give Zach time to finish my room, and you two can . . ." She makes a suggestive gesture with her hands.

"Can what? Flap around like butterflies? What the hell is that?" I mimic her motions, and she shrugs.

"I don't know what you do."

"We don't do anything," I mutter, quieting as the server sets drinks on the table. "And if we did, it wouldn't look like that."

David thanks him, then turns to me, the picture of innocence. "What would it look like, Josh?"

"Yeah, Josh," Kate snarks. "Show us."

Well, he's got a lot of fucking nerve. I'm gonna clobber them both, I swear. "Us. What us? Isn't David a participant in your twisted butterfly scenario? I don't even know what the hell we're talking about. I've been alone in a moldy house all summer, in case you two haven't noticed."

Her arms cross. "You weren't alone last night."

David sighs and leans back, stretching. "Can we move past this?" His arm falls easy around Kate's thin shoulders. He rubs her neck with his thumb. "We should've called, okay? I'm sorry. Please don't be mad."

Kate, much like me, literally melts beneath his touch, and I find myself warmed by their interaction. Soothed by the familiar site of them, together. The ease we three have always shared. It feels good.

It feels right.

It feels . . . too good to be true.

A pensive shiver ripples down my spine. Good things never last—that's my experience. There's usually a downside. David's tumor, the pipe burst, my father's bullshit, Carol Brennan's lies? What if those were just tremors? Little preludes to something worse. What if David coming back isn't a new beginning at all, but a final step toward the end?

I watch them talk, desperate to squash these thoughts. I want to be happy. Start fresh, do things right, like David said, whatever that looks like. I want to forget about my father and the trail of wreckage he's left. I want to pretend Carol Brennan and his envelope don't exist. That there's no tape of Ian dying, no shallow grave in my old backyard, awaiting discovery.

Kate smiles, unaware of my darkening thoughts. She rests her head on David's shoulder and reaches for my hand. "I've missed you guys," she says. "It's not the same when we're apart."

No, it isn't.

I clutch her slender fingers, nodding, not looking at David. I want, for his sake, to keep the promises we made before moving in here. To put our friendship first. Love him from a distance, so he and Kate can be together as they should be.

I want these things. I do. And then, I don't.

I really fucking don't.

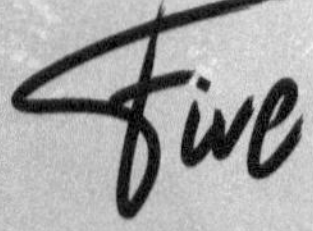

Rubble and Wreckage

:: When dreams crumble like a bad brownie

Kate
Saturday, August 19th 5:49 pm
Dillon Street Baltimore, Maryland

I don't tell the boys about my date.

Not the one from a month ago with bad breath guy, but the date I'm going on now. It's not even a date, really. Just dinner. He's one of Demetri's friends—I don't even know him. Which makes it a blind date, I guess.

A blind . . . dinner?

"It'll be fun," Anna says, her voice barely audible above the traffic. I'm meeting the guy, Chad, at Of Love & Regret. A short walk, and clear mistake. Humidity levels are at swamp hot, and I'm literally wilting.

"What kind of name is Chad West, anyway? It sounds fake." I cradle the phone between my shoulder and ear so both hands can fan my face. Heat this oppressive should be illegal. "How did Demi meet him, again?"

"At the gym, a few months ago. He's friends with one of the trainers." She chuckles. "Maybe it's an alias. Who knows with a name like that; he could be a porn star."

I'm momentarily tempted to search him online. We exchanged numbers and pics, but I know almost nothing else about the guy, which is probably not that smart on my part. Not that it matters. I'm only doing this to spite Josh and David because while they might prefer each other, they'd hate me dating.

And yes, I am that petty. It's been a week, and I'm still seeing them in that bathroom. *Our* bathroom.

"He could be the next Magic Mike for all I care," I tell Anna. "I'm not interested."

I have no desire to meet someone. I don't even need the boys to know I'm dating. Just going out feels deliciously defiant. Like a victory, and not one I expect Anna to understand. I haven't shared the details of my past or our unorthodox little triangle. She knows I'm in love with David, though. And Josh? I'm not sure what she thinks.

She sighs into the phone. "It can't hurt to give him a chance, Kate. Comfortable isn't always better. In fact, comfortable totally sucks sometimes."

I sense this comment is more about her and Zach's relationship than my situation. She's had a rough summer, what with losing her job and all. And Zach only makes things worse with his fake smiles and semi-veiled digs.

Like, he came to pick her up for dinner the other night and she wore this new dress she bought on sale at the Town Center. He kissed her nose and was all, it's cute how you try to bargain shop, but I'm not taking you out in that cheap piece of trash. And he wouldn't get in the car until she changed! Worse yet, she listened. We returned her dress the next day.

Meanwhile, he's like that all the time, even on the job with his crew at our house. Honestly, he reminds me of Nick.

Nick.

I shiver despite the stifling heat. Between his interest in David's surgery and the lingering concern for our pseudo stalker/photographer—he still doesn't know it's David's uncle—Nick hounded us the entire first half of summer. These last few weeks, however, he's been eerily quiet. Calm before the storm, maybe?

His stupid new television show, *Exposed*, premiers in a month, and publicity is bound to ramp up. And since we've yet to investigate Carol's bombshell news, we're still trapped beneath Nick's murderous thumb. Pawns at his disposal.

I just want it all to go away.

"Kate?" Anna's voice startles me back into the moment. "Are you okay? Listen, you don't have to go on this date if you don't want to. Demi can be a little pushy, but he means well. He just wanted you to have some fun."

Demitri is a lot pushy, but with good intentions. If he likes Chad, I'm sure I will too. "It's fine," I tell Anna, lowering my voice. "I'm walking up to the restaurant now. I gotta go, okay? Have fun tonight. Say hi to everyone for me."

My current roomies are in New York with college friends who had last minute tickets to some new Broadway show. The boys are busy, too. Josh is working, and David's at a college function with Bennett in Towson. I only agreed to this date because I knew I'd be alone.

A tall, trim blond with too-bright teeth and impossibly broad shoulders waves at me from a small table. I pocket my phone and make my way toward him.

And I'm alone with Chad West.

6:40 pm

We're not alone long.

Ten minutes into the date, Chad's friends Carlos and Sabrina "just happen" to show up and join us. It's a little awkward because Chad no doubt coordinated it. But they're easy to talk to, and Chad is funny and attentive, and definitely used mouthwash before coming, so that's in his favor.

I hadn't planned on staying long or drinking, but after an hour of appetizers and small talk I'm somehow brushing legs with him beneath the table, laughing at Sabrina's jokes, and sipping a Moscow Mule.

Chad's arm rests on the back of my chair in a slightly possessive way I don't hate, but don't like either. He's a bit of an over-sharer but seems like a decent guy. A hygienist—hence, the teeth. If David and Josh hadn't ruined me for other men, he might even be a contender.

I take a long sip and close my eyes as fizzy, gingery vodka infused warmth floods my veins. The truth is, even nestled beside a handsome man, my thoughts aren't far from the boys. I turn away and discreetly check my phone, warmed farther to see both have sent texts in the last hour. Four from Josh, and one from David.

Josh: KATH – ER – INE?

Josh: Bring me food

Josh: Busy night

Josh: Starving

I roll my eyes and fire off a response.

Me: Seriously Josh, when aren't you starving?

He must be on his phone because text bubbles pop up immediately.

Josh: Pleeeeeaaassseee?

Me: Sorry, can't. Uber Eats?

Josh: ☹

Josh: 🖕

So, he and I are status quo. I check David's message.

David: Sunny, did you know today is National Potato Day? There are more than 4,000 varieties of potatoes in the world. How do I know this?

Tonight's speaker is a potato farmer. Bennett and I are eating baked potatoes, listening to a lecture about potatoes, from a guy who looks like a potato. Send help. Also, I miss you. Are you coming over tomorrow?

I get that squeezy, painful-pleasant swooping feeling that accompanies all things David. I want to respond with a million verses and beg him to rescue me, but I settle for a GIF of a dancing Mr. Potato Head, a heart emoji and a pathetic, *I miss you, too . . . see you tomorrow*, instead.

Chad rubs my shoulder. "Who are you texting, pretty girl? Got another date after this?"

He and his friends laugh like it's the funniest comment in the world, but something sharp flashes in his eyes. He's all smiles through dinner, though. We hit the bar for a drink after, and he's the perfect gentleman, pulling out my stool, ordering for me. So, maybe I imagine it.

A plush sun is setting over the city as we wrap up at the bar. Sabrina and I head to the bathroom while the guys settle the tab and stroll outside for a smoke.

"Chad's like, so sweet," she chirps about fifty times, hugging me. She's had four drinks to my two and it's starting to show. "You guys are a-dor-a-ble!"

She's still hanging on me minutes later when we find them outside leaning against a sleek BMW. Carlos pats the top lovingly. "My baby," he purrs, flicking his cigarette to the ground, smashing it. "You girls ready? Let's go."

"Oh." I glance at Chad. We hadn't discussed plans, but it's close to nine and I'm done with this evening. I thought I'd head home, only he's opening the car door, ushering me inside.

"Friends of ours are having a party," he explains, sliding in next to me. "They've got a sweet place. Super chill. You'll like it."

I'm about to tell him he has no idea what I like, but Sabrina is closing her door, and Carlos is backing up, and my protest gets lost inside the deafening thump of techno pop. Chad squeezes my shoulder and leans close, his lips on my ear.

"It's not too far. If you don't want to stay, I'll get you an Uber, all right? No pressure."

I nod, only mildly comforted. This feels . . . off. I hardly know Chad and his friends. And they didn't mention going to a party when we were at the bar, did they? I don't know, maybe this is what people do. I'm usually with Josh and David—parties aren't really our thing.

A dull ache closes around my heart. I wish we could go back. To our house when we first moved in. To David before the tumor and his uncle's crazy medaling. To Josh, before he and I were battling for the same heart. I want the three of us, full of hope and fresh beginnings.

Whoever said ignorance is bliss is a genius.

I love ignorance.

Serve it with a side of naivety, and I'm good to go.

My melancholy must be evident because Sabrina turns with a glossy, wide-lipped grin. "I'm so glad you're coming, Kate. It'll be fun, really!

Relax." She rummages through a bag, then hands me something wrapped in tissue. "Here, this will help," she exclaims, winking.

I unwrap a large, thick brownie oozing with chocolate chunks. It looks divine. She hands one to Chad, who has magically produced a cooler. He offers beer to us girls, and water to Carlos.

"To relaxation," he says, clinking his bottle against mine. "Eat up. Sabrina's brownies won't last long."

Carlos leans over and snags one from her bag. He plants a kiss on her nose. "These are fucking dope, babe," he says, and they all laugh.

I get that flushy, hot feeling, like I'm on the outside of their joke. I sense I'm missing something obvious, so I cram half the brownie in my mouth and laugh along to cover.

Carlos cranks up the music, and before I know what's happening, I've polished off my beer, am devouring a second scrumptious brownie, and we're on the Interstate heading north, singing cheesy '80s tunes. I no longer feel outside of them, but I don't feel like myself, either. Time seems oddly still, yet somehow, skipping, and everything is wonderfully bright, if not a touch dizzying. I roll my head from side to side, testing out this new reality, marveling at the sensation.

I squint at the approaching headlights which seem blurrier than normal. Vibrant and colorful, like dancing fairies. Maybe they're fairies. How cool would that be? And wasn't the party supposed to be close? *Why did we leave the city? How long have I been in this car, anyway?*

I want to ask these questions. But it's cozy in the back seat, and Chad's arm is closing around my shoulders. I lean into him, drowsy-warm and lightheaded, my eyes growing heavy. A twinge of concern hangs in my periphery, nagging at me, reminding me something isn't right. I'm too tired to focus on it, though. So, I snuggle into the crook of Chad's arm.

"That a girl," he says, cradling me. "We'll be there soon."

Be where soon?

I want to tell him to take me home, but the fairy cars whiz by, and my eyes won't stay open. Chad strokes my hair, and I imagine David's gentle hands. He leans in for a kiss and I melt, pretending his acrid lips and foreign tongue are soft swirling pools of buttery sweetness, familiar as sunshine and blue skies, and safe as the boy waiting for me at home.

Sunday, August 20th 3:12 am

And it seems only moments later I am home.

Not my home, but someone's. A loud, crowded home. And I'm. . . dancing?

What happened to the car?

"More shooters coming through!"

A shrill, female voice cuts the air, decibels above the grunting thump of music. Something sweaty and cold is pressed into my palm. As if acting on its own accord, my hand then lifts to my mouth and sends a glob of slippery, sweet, boozy gelatin down my throat.

I immediately gag, stumbling backward into the small crowd.

"What the hell?" someone hollers. Peals of laughter erupt all around me.

"That girl Chad brought is on the floor again," another shouts.

Before I can right myself, rough hands haul me up and out of the crowd. ". . . taking her upstairs . . ." I hear Chad say, his voice thick and slurred with annoyance. "Damn it, Sabrina. I told you those brownies were too strong."

The brownies!

Of course, those damn brownies! I'm carried, bumped, and jostled through a crowded living room as snatches of the night return with nauseating clarity. The long car ride. The music. Their laughter. The inside joke. *Those brownies are dope,* Carlos said.

How many did I eat?

Chad tows me through a kitchen littered with empty takeout cartons, crushed beer cans, and plates piled high. A group is gathered around the table playing cards. One girl waves, and I have a vague sense I, too, played cards at that table.

What else have I done?

Uncertainty rockets through my poor, addled brain. I'm not sure where I am or what's happened, exactly, but I want off this brownie train.

I'm suddenly quite done with Chad West and his friends and their . . . brownies.

We're lumbering up the stairs, away from the kitchen and the crowd when my better sense finally takes over. I squirm and writhe in his arms, upsetting our balance and he curses, nearly dropping me. "Fucking chill," he mutters. "I'm just taking you to lie down, okay? Relax. You gotta sleep this shit off."

Like hell I do.

I may not be strong, but after years of massage, I know the body. I wait until we're off the stairs, then, with a precision I shouldn't possess, I drive my middle and index fingers into the hollow dip where his collar bones meet. Chad crumples like a wounded animal, releasing me with a girlish shriek.

And I'm on the floor.

It takes a moment for my head to stop spinning as Chad unleashes every curse word in the book. He lunges for me, clawing at my leg.

"You bitch!" he seethes. "Get in the fucking bedroom."

There's that glint in his eyes again, and a barrage of warning bells clamor inside my head. I might be high as a kite, but wild horses couldn't drag me into that bedroom. So, I snap my leg back, wrench it free from his grasp, and I run.

Down the stairs and past the crowd of sweaty strangers. I find a door and stagger through it, my ankle twisting painfully. I don't care. I kick off my heels and run. Off the porch, through the yard, down a road, and into a forest.

I run until the trees swallow me whole, and I collapse, dizzy and gasping for breath, and so grateful to be away from him and out of that house, I could weep. I take a brief inventory, relieved to find my clothing and purse intact, and my cell phone still miraculously charged.

But holy mother of bad brownies, it's almost morning. I've lost hours, freaking hours of my life. The gravity nearly levels me, and I fall back hard, my head thumping on the moss-covered ground. I've been alone and incoherent with complete strangers and a guy who is unbalanced, at best; any number of horrid things could've happened.

Would I remember? I'm sure I would remember.

Think Kate. Breathe.

There's a sharp crack beside me and I nearly jump out of my skin. Okay. Forget thinking. There'll be time for that later. I need out of here, like now. Hugging myself, I roll to a sitting position, squinting through the trees. Lights twinkle in the distance.

I don't even know what city this is. If I had an address, I could call for an Uber, but I'm not going back to that house. I don't think I could even find it. I could walk to a main road, I guess, but that seems daunting. And dangerous. Painful, too. I'm barefoot. My stomach churns a hopeless little song as the world begins to spin. I lie back and close my eyes.

I could call the boys.

Just the thought lifts my spirits. I mean, it's mortifying. I don't want them to see me like this or know what I've done. But deep down, I know they would never turn their backs on me. Their love will never change. Of this, I am certain.

They would come for me without question. They would find me. They will *always* find me.

Heart thrumming and spurred on by these thoughts, I lift my phone and dial a number I memorized years ago. A number that, like the man it belongs to, hasn't changed since childhood.

He answers on the second ring; his voice a mixture of fatigue and concern. "Kate? What's wrong? Are you all right?"

"Josh!" I go limp at the sound of him, suddenly sobbing so hard I can barely get the words out. "Josh, I'm in trouble, and I want to come home."

Six

Mending Walls

:: Healing rifts one room at a time

David
Sunday, August 20th 9:40 pm
Foster Avenue Baltimore, Maryland

I sleep through Kate's entire devastating date ordeal.

After an impassioned evening of potato propaganda at Towson with Bennett, I was ready for a long, uninterrupted night of sleep. So long, in fact, I didn't wake Sunday until noon when I discovered a wildly disheveled Kate asleep on the couch with an exhausted looking Josh slumped beside her. Still shaken, he followed me into the kitchen where the sketchy details of Kate's night unfolded over coffee.

He'd been at work when she called, resting in the bunk room, thankfully, and not on a call. It had taken an hour for him to reach her in a dense, wooded area north of Baltimore. She was scratched up and barefoot and half a mile from the nearest home with little memory of where she'd been or how she got there.

He used her phone's location service to find her, something I wouldn't have thought to do. But Josh is clever like that, and in an emergency, there's no one more capable. I can only imagine how devastating it was for him, receiving the call, driving all that way, not knowing how he'd find her.

"It was like high school and her fucking overdose," he whispered, face drawn in misery. "I kept thinking, what if I can't find her? What if something happens before I get there?"

He'd been inconsolable. No matter Kate's overdose in high school was an accident. Or that she, despite our mistakes and failed intentions, knows how much we care. The truth is, he's right. Only, it's not just his fault—he and I share the blame.

We spent the remainder of the afternoon hovering while she slept, keeping watch. Something we did often as boys. Chad, to his credit, did call and check on her. Josh talked with him, or rather, threatened certain death if he fucked with his sister again.

The asshole claimed a misunderstanding. Kate didn't speak up, he didn't realize her ignorance to the whole brownie situation, he figured she was down to party, whatever.

Don't get me wrong, he should've insisted on taking her home. But his claim she was a fall-down vomiting mess half the night jives with the scant details she relayed to Josh. And is further supported by her camera roll, which includes a dozen blurry selfies of her antics.

When she ran off, Chad said he assumed she called an Uber and left. A cop out, let's be honest. And I have no doubt he was planning to take advantage of her. Bad brownies, evidently, are a godsend. And a smack in the face.

Josh and I hardly spoke while she slept. Not that we needed to; I sensed his resolve. Could taste his guilt, razor sharp and bitter, like my own. If only we had insisted she come home last week. If we had paid more attention to her needs, if we hadn't been so focused on each other . . . this wouldn't have happened.

By evening, he could no longer hold it in. He pulled me aside in the kitchen, pale and vibrating with determination.

"It ends with this," he whispered. "All of it. You and I, Nick, his fucking show . . . your uncle? All the bullshit ends right here, right now." He gripped my shoulders. "All day, I can't stop thinking this whole thing could've been avoided. If I wasn't around, if she'd been with you, if I had just walked away years ago and let you be, none of this would've happened. Not even the fire."

I shook my head. "That isn't true. And you don't have to—"

"Yes, I do. I owe it to her. *We* owe it to her. What if something worse happened last night? What if she'd been lost without her phone? If she overdosed again or, God forbid, that asshole tried to . . ." He choked, unable to voice this, our greatest fear.

Protect Kate.

That was our number one goal as boys; to keep Nick and Ian from getting to her. From using Kate like they used us. It's ironic, really, that our vow to keep her safe is what ultimately drove us together. That it should drive us apart now seems so wrong. And yet, what option is there?

She'd woken after that, hungry and hungover, and our conversation dropped. But I wasn't so focused on her that I missed the shift in Josh. The deliberate way he sat apart from us as she recalled the night, in fragments. The foyer trim he suddenly had to paint while she and I ate dinner. The call he made to Tessa, minutes after Kate suggested a movie.

By bedtime, even she knew something was off . . .

"What is he doing?" she whispers. We're on the couch together when he comes lumbering down the stairs with a pillow and blanket from our bed.

"You two take the bedroom. I'm sleeping down here."

Kate and I are on our feet in seconds. "You're not doing that," she protests. "I'll just take the other bed. Or I can drag the mattress into my room. It's fine, Josh."

Except, it's not.

Despite our efforts to finish her room, Zach and company hit a few snags. There's still patches in the drywall, only half the ceiling is painted, and we're waiting on the floor to come in. No way she's sleeping there.

Josh is right, she should be with me. He's doing what we should've done all along—put Kate first. Make good on the promises we made, moving in here. And I want nothing more than to take her upstairs and comfort her. To lay beside her and make her feel safe and loved.

Only, the emptiness I feel watching Josh set up a make-shift bed on our couch?

It nearly guts me.

Monday, August 21st 12:49 am

It's the middle of the night and Kate is awake.

My eyes are closed, and we should both be sleeping, but I feel her gaze. There's a science behind gaze-perception, the mind's ability to detect what or who someone is looking at. But I don't need that—I know Kate.

"You're staring," I say, eyes still closed.

She sniffs, and I turn in time to see a tear slide down her cheek. I lift a hand to catch it, my thumb smoothing across her delicate skin. I hold her face so she's looking at me.

"Don't cry, Sunshine. It'll be all right."

She nods, resting her hand atop mine. Our fingers lace together. "I really didn't want to go on that date," she says, even though we've already been through this a million times. No matter how much I reassure her, she can't let it go. She makes a distressed guttural sound. "It was just so stupid.

And now look what's happened. I've ruined every-thing. And for what?"

I pull her into me. "You haven't ruined any-thing. None of this is your fault, Kate. It's all on Josh and I. We've been selfish and insensitive. You had every reason to be upset."

"That's just it, though. After all my stupid reve-lations about the three of us before your surgery? All the misery he went through this summer? The way he missed you?" She shakes her head. "I put him through hell today. He shouldn't have to be alone."

I don't want Josh alone on the couch any more than I want Kate dating strangers, eating spiked brownies, and passing out in the woods. But he'll be okay for the night, and she needs sleep. I run my fingers through her hair. "Don't worry about Josh, he can take care of himself. He's probably still painting. Besides, he likes the couch."

She rolls her eyes because the truth is, Josh hates sleeping alone, and we both know it. "If I move back in here, he's staying with you, just like before. I don't want any argument. We'll all sleep together if my room isn't done. Better that than one of us downstairs, alone."

"When you move back, not if." I kiss her fore-head, more relieved by her insistence than I'm willing to let on. "We need you at home, Kate. I need you."

She snuggles closer, nestling her head on my chest. I play with her curls as we hold one another. As wonderful as it is, having Kate in my arms—and it is wonderful—I wish it weren't this way. It feels . . . tainted. Her on the heels of a date that could've had dire consequences. Josh, blaming himself, vowing to keep away.

Especially after last week, guilty as I feel acknowledging that.

It was good for him and I to be alone together. We've been around each other most of our lives, but with others. Parents, Kate, roommates . . . it's rarely just the two of us.

And I wasn't lying to Kate; I do need her. But I need him, too. There's a comfort I can't quite describe when it's just him and me. An undeniable chemistry that's always been there. And after last week? I'm more certain than ever.

More confused, too.

I came home intending to set things right, but I don't know what right is anymore. I only know Kate dating and Josh pulling away is all wrong. I keep a tight lid on these feelings, though, much as my filter-less brain wants to release them. No need to remind her my indecision has kept us in this mess.

"D?" she says after a while, yawning, her voice thick and groggy with sleep. "I didn't tell you this earlier, but remember how I said Chad kissed me in the car?"

Not exactly an image I want to conjure. "Yes, Kate. I remember."

"And remember I told you I didn't tell him to stop?"

Where is she going with this? "Yeah. I remember that, too."

She leans over and presses her lips to my cheek. "I didn't stop him because, in my mind, I pretended he was you."

8:53 am

I don't sleep much after that.

I must drift off eventually, though, because I wake with a jolt to streaming sunlight blocked by a disgruntled looking Josh lurking over the bed, watching me.

What is it with these two?

He holds a finger to his lips and nods at Kate, who is dozing peacefully by my side, her mouth parted, arms bent, arch-like, over her face. She chuffs out a little snore, eliciting a smile from both of us. But his quickly fades.

"We need to talk," he whispers, peeling back my side of the covers. He all but yanks me from the bed. We pile into the hall together, and he shuts our door, then leans against it. He scrubs a hand across his face. "Sorry," he says, exhaling. "You sleep forever these days, and I couldn't wait any longer."

I take in his pale complexion and tousled hair. "Were you up all night?"

He shrugs, and my fingers itch to touch him. To brush the loose, golden strands from his forehead, straighten his shirt, hold him close until the worry lines disappear. I take a step, but he shrinks back.

"Don't." He bites at the corner of his lip. "Did Kate get some rest? Did you guys talk? How's she holding up?"

"She's all right. A bit shaken, but mostly okay. I think she feels bad for upsetting you and," I nod toward the stairs, "this new arrangement."

His lips purse. "Yeah. I did some thinking about that, and other things. I made a few decisions we need to talk about."

Unease settles over me. "Decisions?"

Any decision Josh makes right now is bound to be rash and emotionally charged. But when he sets his mind on something, deterring him is like rerouting elephants. I brace myself.

"Two things," he says, holding up two fingers for emphasis. "First, we're going to deal with your uncle and his bullshit, wherever the fuck he is. The envelope, the dead body? I'm sick of thinking about it, and like, wondering, you know, what we'll find. Even if it is my mother buried out there in the woods behind my house . . ." He swallows. "It's not like I knew her. We can't change what happened, but we can expose Nick and make him pay, like Carol planned. Or at least get him to leave us alone. It's been almost three months, you know? And you're stronger now. I don't want to put it off anymore. I want to go back to the old neighborhood this week. Just you and me. Kate doesn't need that stress, right?"

I nod.

"So, you're in?"

He knows I'm in. "I'll do whatever you want. But are you sure, because—"

"Second," he interrupts, barreling on as if stopping might, in and of itself, be a deterrent. "We're going to make some changes around here. Kate's moving back. Like, today. I told her on the ride home. We're picking up her shit and she's coming back. I don't care how much rent she paid."

Like I'm going to argue? "I think that's for the best. But Josh—"

He holds up a hand, silencing me. "As for the situation here, with us. I think I should take Kate's room when it's finished, and she should move into ours with you." His eyes skirt back and forth between the rooms before finally meeting my gaze. And it's all there. The pain and regret, his fatigue, the hurting. I want so badly to take it from him. But he's squaring his shoulders, lifting his chin, already prepared to battle.

"I don't know what else to do, David, but I know I can never see Kate like that again." He lowers his voice, leaning in. "You two are all I have, and I can't stomach the thought of losing either of you or messing up your lives any longer. If that means digging graves, confronting Nick, and pretending I'm not falling apart without you? So be it."

Unearthing Ruin

:: The uncovering of hidden truths

Josh
Thursday, August 24th 2:20 pm
Great Falls Estates Potomac, Maryland

It's Thursday before David and I make the trip back home to our old neighborhood.

Home.

What a joke.

I pull over, kill the engine, and take a breath as I stare at it. My childhood home. It seemed so lavish back then, now it's just . . . a house. Whitewashed bricks, black shutters, miles of climbing ivy. Eighteen years Kate and I lived there, yet I feel no more tied to it than the burrito I ate for dinner last night.

After much debate, she, David, and I decided it best we make this trip in the afternoon. Some of our friend's parents still live in the neighborhood. Strolling around at night might be questionable, but our presence during the day shouldn't rouse suspicion. Even on the path in the woods behind our house.

"You could say you're digging up a time capsule." Kate suggested. I scoffed until David reminded me, we did in fact bury a time capsule. It contained a pack of my Pokémon cards, his Stretch Armstrong, and Kate's duplicate Beanie Babies, among other things. God only knows why, or where we buried the box, but I guess it isn't a terrible excuse.

Coming back to this neighborhood might prove a terrible idea, though. I clutch the wheel, chest tight as a band about to snap. The seconds crawl by.

"This feels wrong," I tell David. "How are we even here?"

I feel like an actor. My life, it seems, has disintegrated into a made for television drama where the antagonist—Carol—controls the narrative, and the villain—Nick—gets away with murder for decades.

David and I, the unwitting protagonists, armed with the truth and a map, set out on a journey to uncover my mother's remains. You know, because my father strangled her, and David's parents helped cover it up. Oh, and Carol hid the information for twenty-five years.

But the plot deepens. Ian and Elena buried my mother, Angela, in a forest, feet from my childhood home. Within plain sight of my bedroom window, if Elena's directions prove true. A forest Kate and I happily explored as kids, oblivious and

under the deceived notion we were not only siblings, but twins.

So, yeah. Dramatic, psychological thriller
unfolding right here. And entirely fucked up does
not begin to describe it.

I don't need a response from David to know
he feels the same. The three of us spent countless
hours playing in the woods. So much that we wore
a path between his house and ours. Leveled and
rebuilt since the fire, the home he shared with Ian,
is less than a mile through the trees.

"We don't have to go through with this," he says.
"We can bag it, you know. Come back another day."
He's not even trying to mask his apprehension.

Uncertainty tugs at my resolve. I trust David's
internal compass more than my own. But I can't
stop picturing Kate, broken and bruised, crying
as I carried her to the Jeep Sunday morning. And
David, the peaceful way he slept with her tucked
in his arms.

Chad West. What a piece of shit. There are
a million guys out there just like him, and Kate
deserves better. She deserves David, and a future
free from Nick and his disgusting lies. Coming here
is a step toward breaking away from him and getting back our freedom. And maybe, once we have
that, I can finally let the two of them go. So no, we
don't have to do this. We need to do this.

I need this.

I don't respond to David, but instead throw
open the door, grab my rucksack, and hoist the

worn strap over my shoulder. I motion for him to follow.

We walk together down the empty street, the air heavy with rain and the distant scent of pine, past my old house where the ivy nearly covers its windows and around a secluded opening between two neighboring yards. Odd, how familiar yet foreign things can be. How people change, but places don't. How in sync he and I are after all these years. We didn't discuss the route we'd take into the woods, or how to avoid being seen; he just knows—the way he has always known.

"Looks like Jake Patel still has that car," he whispers, nodding at the carousel red sixty-nine Pontiac Firebird parked in front of my old neighbor's garage. "The dent's still there, too." His lips quirk into the faintest of smiles.

It's a harmless comment. A simple gesture. But instantly I feel the dizzying weight of love for him, that irrepressible surge. It's the same way I felt the moment we met, and every moment since. I could not love anyone more.

This last week with Kate home has been wonderful and excruciating as I've discovered the more space and distance I put between David and me, the more I want him. And that does not exactly jive with the current plan.

"Patel was always a cheap bastard," I grumble, willing away the feelings that rush back. The memories. David and I are responsible for that dent. A late-night game of chicken gone wrong. No one ever knew, thankfully, like so many secrets we share from those days.

What if we had lost him this summer?

I don't want to think about how close I came to knowing. I don't want to think about losing him. Ever.

Shivering, and despite my vow to stay away, I grab his arm. We step through the brush and into the woods, not stopping until the trees have us in full cover. I yank the envelope Carol gave us from my bag before I can overanalyze what we're doing. What it means and how it could be leading to secrets nearly a quarter of a century old.

Inside the envelope, alongside David and his twin sister Abigail's birth records are a series of damning emails between Ian and Nick with time and date stamps as well as a distant photograph of Nick embracing a young woman who, according to Elena Brennan, was my mother, Angela.

In addition to the documents is a handwritten note from Elena detailing where she and Ian buried Angela's body. A note I shredded when we first opened this envelope—Kate taped it back together.

And that is what I pull out.

"If we find her . . ." David trails off, glancing at the pieced-together paper in my hand. He gazes down the overgrown path leading toward my old backyard.

"We'll figure it out." This I say with zero confidence. We agreed to wing it once we got here, and I'm still not sure what to do. Involving the police seems premature when we don't even know if there's a body.

Also, we aren't without guilt. True, we had nothing to do with my mother's death and the ensuing cover up, but, coerced by Nick or not, David, Kate and I started the fire that burned his house and Ian's body along with it. Nick has proof. And if we expose his past, he'll no doubt expose ours.

But what if my mother's body really is out here? We're just going to haul her out and tote her remains around in the back of my Jeep? I don't see that happening. And I don't know the legal ramifications, but from a moral standpoint, how could we not tell the police? Maybe she's a missing person. A cold case. A girl whose family has been searching all these years.

My family.

And isn't that a fucking mine field. We walk for several minutes in silence, following Elena's direction as I weigh this. Her description of the place where they buried my mother is spot on, and David and I know the clearing. A small patch between three split trunk oaks in a cluster—they're hard to miss.

And still thriving. Ominously so.

It's David's turn to grab my hand as we approach. "Are you sure about this?"

I nod, despite my growing sense this is a horrible mistake. I can hardly voice that concern now, though. He takes the lead, and I let him, focusing my efforts on keeping upright and the warm assurance of his fingers laced with mine.

We breach the clearing, and I'm about to look up when he stops suddenly and sucks in a breath. I nearly plow into his back as I glance around expecting . . . well, I'm not sure what I'm expecting. But it's not this.

This is . . . chaotic.

The ground is all dug up and disturbed. Unnaturally so. There are several trench-like ditches of varying depth and a large hole, scantily covered by sticks and old leaves. Clearly not the work of an animal, but a human.

A human unbothered with covering his tracks.

And I know, instinctively, we've been played.

"No," David says, his body turning, taking in the scene. "It can't be . . ."

But it is. It so fucking is. And the earth gives way beneath me.

Friday, August 25th 2:58 pm

Here's the thing about timing; it's a bitch.

Hours pass. Days. Months, even, with no significance whatsoever. And then, in the blink of an eye, a careless driver plows through a redlight and slams into your car. Suddenly, you're in the ICU clinging to life, counting every second, wondering how different things would be if only you had left home a minute later.

I've spent enough time in EMS to know—there are no coincidences. Life is all about timing.

So, I'm not shocked when my father calls the day after our grave digging disaster, or Carol-Brennan-is-a-piece-of-shit day, as I'm now calling it.

Because of course it was Carol.

Shame on us for being so stupid. As if he'd hand over keys to all that damning evidence, then walk away? No. Carol is just like my father, a lying piece of shit coward. We tried to call him yesterday, but his number had been disconnected. Carol Brennan is gone.

My father, on the other hand? Very much in my face and in our business. I'm walking into work when he calls.

"Son," he says, "how are you?"

His gravelly tenor makes me want to impale something. I clench the Jeep key so hard it digs a crater into my hand. "Fine," I manage, hoping my icy tone will put him off.

No such luck. "Is this a bad time? I thought I'd check and see how David was doing."

Yeah, right.

I pause mid stride, blood already boiling. "I'm at work, so yeah. It's a bad time. And we both know you aren't calling about David, so drop the bullshit."

There's a beat of silence on his end. "Whatever you want to think, Joshua. Have it your way."

I almost choke. My way would involve shoving his face in a pile of evidence and lies so damning he'd never dig out. But the digging is already done—thank you very little, Carol fucking Brennan.

I close my eyes and try to push out yesterday's nightmare . . .

"Maybe Carol thought he was protecting us," David reasoned after dragging me away from the torn-up clearing. Once the initial shock wore off, he'd been almost relieved. "It's not like we can just go to the police, Josh. Think about the questions they'd ask. We might screw over Nick, but we'd be inviting a world of scrutiny on ourselves."

A valid point. But protecting us or not, Carol is a fucking liar. I hadn't fully considered the fallout from a police investigation, though. Or the ensuing media circus. Only, where does that leave us now? Still in Nick's clutches, that's where . . .

He clears his throat. "I have some news," he says. "But if you're working, I suppose I can call Katherine . . ."

And there's the manipulation.

"Just say it," I bark, bracing myself. Will I ever not be triggered by this man?

"Well, believe it or not, I actually would like an update on David, but I'm calling to let you and your sister know *Exposed* debuts in a month and the network is planning a premiere party. In D.C. An intimate event. You two will need to be there, obviously."

Obviously.

"Kate isn't my sister." I can't resist needling him, and my comment has its intended effect.

"Oh, for fuck's sake. We are a family, and you two better damn well act your parts. It's important to the network, and it's important to my fans. They tune in for more than a show; they want an experience. A kinship. Someone they can really relate to and get behind."

Is he kidding me with this? "Kinship?" I sputter. "Who are you, Mr. Rogers? Fucking kinship. You don't know the meaning of the word."

He exhales heavily, and I swear I can feel venom coursing through the phone line. "Do you really want to cross me, son? You're walking a thin line, here."

I am.

I shouldn't provoke him. It's not like this wasn't expected. We knew there would be a premiere, and that Kate and I would be required to attend. It stings like a bitch, though, having freedom within our grasp, then losing it. But I'm too defeated to put up much of a fight.

"Fine. Whatever. Just tell me the details and we'll make it happen."

He spews out a date and time. "Tell David I'm expecting him there, too. With Katherine. The fans eat that shit up."

Of course, he wants David there, the opportunistic fuck.

David's presence is bound to stir up interest due to Ian's death and his role in the demise of Nick's original series, *Brought to Light*. Even more so if he's there with Kate. Not to mention David's appearance, which is always a draw. Nick has never had a problem exploiting that.

"So, that takes care of them. Now, for you . . ." I hear papers rustling. "My publicist came across an interesting photograph last week. You and some girl at a charity event back in June. Apparently, there's speculation you two are an item. Theresa Fontes? Does that name ring any bells?"

3:04 pm

I nearly drop the phone.

"Tessa?" *Oh, hell no.*

"Is that what you call her?" He chuckles. "I'd call her a sweet piece of ass. Not gonna lie though, she looks like the female version of our boy, don't you think?" His voice takes on a mocking, sinister tone. "But then, that shouldn't surprise either of us, now, should it?"

Of course, he'd notice her resemblance to David. I can't even argue—they do look like each other. And isn't that just twisted on so many levels. I need to end this.

"Look I gotta go. Tell your publicist to check her source. Tessa is a friend, that's all. There's nothing between us."

"Right. A *friend*. Well, you might want to let your friend know there's going to be a half-page spread featuring you two in *What's Up Weekly* coming out Monday."

I halt midway through the station door. "Wait, what? No. No fucking way. You can't—"

"You'd be shocked, how many people read those gossip rags. You can't buy that kind of publicity. And with *Exposed* debuting next month? It's quite a lucky coincidence."

I sag against the wall. This cannot be happening. "No. Nick, come on please. Listen. You can't do this, Tessa, she's not . . . we're not . . . anything. She's going to be blindsided."

"Not if you tell her. Better yet, invite her to the premiere." I can just picture the smug expression on his disgusting face. "You should be thanking me," he continues. "We could be talking about an entirely different spread of photographs, or have you forgotten those are out there? Better you with this Tessa than dry humping your sister in line at Target, am I right, Joshie? You hear what I'm saying?"

Oh, I hear him. Loud and clear. I hang up, fuming. Fuck Carol. This is all his fault. We could be rid of Nick if it weren't for him and his meddling. I dial David, but then remember he has a doctor's appointment and quickly disconnect.

I call Tessa instead, bracing myself. She answers on the first ring. "Josh! I was just getting ready to text you. Have you been online? There are pictures of us all over the internet."

I drop to the ground, eyes closing, acutely aware of my rising heartbeat. Of the sweat beading up on my skin. Part of me had hoped Nick was full of shit. But I know better.

"Yeah, about that." My back sinks into the brick wall as I cradle the phone. "Do you have a few minutes? We need to talk."

Eight

Shifting Foundations

:: A change in plans exposing hidden
cracks and deeper divides

Kate
Friday, August 25th 3:20 pm
Johns Hopkins Medical Center
Baltimore, Maryland

Moving home is a mixed bag.

On the one hand, I'm home. Home. Two months ago, David was on the brink of death, and everything we owned was underwater. Literally. And now, here we are. The three of us, together. Healthy, healing, and relatively intact. Even the house is in good shape.

Zach and his crew aren't finished, but the basics are done. In a bizarre way, it's like starting over. As if the last nine months never happened.

But on the other hand?

It's like everything changed and instead of acknowledging it, David, Josh and I are tiptoeing around, afraid to upset the balance. We seem to have forgotten what it's like to just be together, and no one knows how to fix it, least of all me with my stupid Chad West debacle.

And then, yesterday happened.

"Kate, come on." I feel David's hand on my arm, gently tugging. "They're ready for me."

"This way, Mr. Brennan," a nurse is saying.

My eyes fly open. *Did I fall asleep?*

I stumble out of my seat, tripping after David and the stout nurse who leads him to an exam room. Once inside, she takes his vitals, and I chug what's left of my coffee while digging a package of Pop-Tarts from my purse. Maybe the caffeine-sugar rush will wake me.

"It's gonna take more than that." David smirks, stretching his legs once she's gone. He has phenomenal legs. I take a giant bite and unabashedly gawk at the view. "You were snoring like a chainsaw out there," he says, even as a yawn interrupts my inelegant munching.

"Was not." Meanwhile, I probably was. Sleep has been in short supply lately. And with everything that happened yesterday? I don't think any of us slept.

He pats the exam table, stifling his own yawn. "Come lie down. I have a feeling we'll be waiting here awhile."

Here, being a follow up with his neurologist. Two months have passed since surgery, and despite the infection and initial setbacks, he's doing remarkably well. Back to himself for the most part. A little less focused, maybe. And his eyes bother him. But aside from the scar, there's little evidence of this summer's nightmare.

Looks can be deceiving, though.

I climb onto the exam table and snuggle into his outstretched arms. He smiles, but it doesn't reach the worried blue of his eyes. It doesn't mask the tension, rolling off him in waves, or cover his preoccupation, which has little to do with this appointment.

"Can we please talk about yesterday?" I don't mean to say this out loud.

Or maybe I do. I don't want to add to his stress, but we're obviously both thinking about it. And there's so many elephants in the room . . .

4:15 pm

The boys were home when I got in from work last night, clearly shaken.

Josh wouldn't talk about it, and all I got from David was scant details. Enough to gather his uncle screwed us over, yet again.

Not exactly shocking. I mean, who didn't see that coming? I knew Carol was bad news. But why confide in the boys if he planned to dig Angela up himself? If it even was Carol. He could have told Nick, or someone else altogether.

And what then? We wait? See if anything comes of it? It's like we're sitting ducks . . .

"Your uncle is a piece of work," I mutter once it's clear David isn't going to elaborate. He props an arm behind his head on the exam table and sighs.

"There isn't much to say, Kate. It's all speculation. And we don't know for sure it was Carol. Or if there even was something or someone buried out there."

I cut him a look.

"Okay, fine. It was probably him. But like I told Josh, maybe it's for the best. I mean, do we really want to get into it with Nick? Besides, we still have Carol's tape from the night of the fire, and all the other stuff in my mom's envelope. Damning, but not as concrete as a body, I guess. Maybe he thought it would be enough. I don't know. Maybe he regretted telling us about Angela and tried to undo the damage."

"Or maybe he's crazy and made it all up," I grumble, though we both know this isn't the case. It just sucks, all of it. And there's no point pressing David here in the doctor's office, so I pull out my phone and scroll through the notifications. I'm not that active on social media. Neither are the boys. Rosa and Demetri sure are, though.

Joe Mama's, their café, has a ton of followers. They post daily specials, pictures, run contests, that sort of thing. I try to support them whenever I can. After liking their latest posts, I scroll through some other accounts. A random phrase catches my attention. A familiar name. I do a double take.

Josh Janney is trending with #Exposed?

I blink a few times, certain I've misread. But no, it's still there, clear as day. My skin begins to crawl as I click on the tag. There are hundreds of recent posts and comments.

HOT new couple OMG, who is she???? #Exposed #JoshJanney

Love moment #JoshJanney #Exposed

Serious sparks! #JoshJanneyLoveMoment #Exposed # broughttolight

A sick feeling slides over me. The same photograph is featured in most—a picture of Josh dancing with Tessa. Obviously taken at the art gala, but like, what the heck? *Why is Josh trending with Nick's new show?* I elbow David. "Look at this."

He squints at the screen. "Is that Josh?"

I nod, not really processing what we're seeing here. "He's . . . trending. With Tessa. And . . . *Exposed*?"

David grabs my phone, paling as he pages through screen after screen. "This is a joke, right? It doesn't even make sense. And this photo is from the gala, what does that have to do with *Exposed*?"

I shrug, mind spinning. A fresh wave of panic grips me. Josh!

"We've got to call him, David! He's already unhinged from yesterday, what if he sees this at work?" Then a far worse thought takes root. "What if Nick sees it and thinks we're trying to sabotage his show or something?"

Or worse yet, what if Carol is behind the photograph? What if he plans to publish all the photos he took of us last spring? Before I can voice this or call Josh or do anything, the door swings open. A tall, balding man in a lab coat and glasses saunters in, his face impassive and bland.

"Mr. Brennan," he says, "Sorry to keep you waiting, but we wanted to review the results of your scan before talking to you." He pulls up a chair in front of David and rubs his hands together. "I have good news, and bad news. Which do you want to hear first?"

11:40 pm

David and I wait six grueling hours for Josh to come home.

In that span of time, we manage to find the source of Josh and Tessa's photo, a local magazine that covered the gala and not Carol Brennan, thank God. We scroll through a thousand posts, looking for I don't know what. Something nefarious, maybe?

Nothing stands out but the sheer volume of people invested, not only in *Exposed*, but in Josh and Tessa's budding "relationship." Internet sleuths quickly identify Tessa and tag her social media—a website and Instagram profile with over fifty thousand followers.

Who knew?

It seems our Tessa is a jack of all trades. Event planner, freelance writer, and she used to host a travel blog. I mean, of course she did. I would expect nothing less. Someone even coined a ship name for her and Josh.

Jessa.

Real freaking original.

What David and I do not do is discuss his appointment, or the disturbing news his latest scan revealed. That we table, because you know, avoidance—it's our thing.

I can't even.

We also do not call Josh or Tessa. Well, we try Josh, but it goes straight to voicemail. Which means a busy night at the station. Plus, Josh abhors social media, so we're counting on him staying in the dark until he gets home.

And Tessa? We didn't want to call her without first talking to Josh. So, it goes without saying that David and I are on literal thumbnails by the time Josh walks through the door at 11:00 pm. I see, instantly, that he knows.

His face is pale and drawn, eyes wary. He has the haggard look of a man on the run, but all I see is a boy. Frightened and panicking . . . pretending he's strong. David and I rush to him.

"You guys know then." It's not a question.

He drops his bag and just like that, we're talking at once. It takes nearly an hour for the details to unravel. David and I fill Josh in on his appointment, highlighting the good while delaying the bad. We tell him of our discovery online, and what the subsequent research revealed.

Josh recounts his call from Nick, and his demand for our presence at the premiere, as well as the premature release of the art gala photo. He tells us how Tessa was alerted by a friend and knew of the online buzz long before him. And of the calls he's been receiving from journalists and reporters.

"I finally shut off my phone," he says, groaning as he leans his head back on the couch. He and David are sitting together, legs outstretched. I'm on the ottoman facing them, alternately massaging their feet.

I give Josh's pinky a little tweak. "You might as well leave it off if that magazine is coming out next week."

He covers his face. "What a fucking nightmare."

Ever the pacifist, David pats his leg. "People have short attention spans, J. These things blow over. It'll be—"

But Josh doesn't let him finish.

He pounces like a coil, unleashed, pinning David by his shoulders to the couch. "Don't tell me it'll be all right, asshole. Don't placate me. This sucks and I want to hear you say it."

He hovers, inches above David's face, vibrating with fury. David strains to free himself, but even I can see his struggle is half-hearted.

This is a scenario that's played out between them dozens of times over the years. This faux battle for power in which Josh asserts himself and David pretends to fight him off. It works because, while Josh is physically stronger, David is the one in control.

He holds his ground now, as always, not by escape but with restraint. He just stops moving. Stares up at Josh with empathy in his endless eyes. But there's something else there, too.

"Say it!" Josh repeats, weaker now. Less commanding. I can't see his expression, but I feel the shift. The subtle drop of his shoulders, the way his muscles relax, the current of heat surrounding them.

Not role play, I realize, but foreplay.

David wants this, at least on some level. He likes it. A reality that should have me running or shouting or, I don't know . . . protesting. But it doesn't. I sit, riveted by these boys I love, so in love with each other. Denying what they want for me.

An agonizing truth. I don't want that responsibility on my hands. And I definitely don't deserve that level of sacrifice. Worse yet, and much to my horror, I feel myself growing warm. A pleasant and wholly unwelcome heat settles low in my belly, and try as I might, I can't look away.

The smooth, sculpted contours of David's chest and shoulders, the chiseled plane of Josh's back, his tanned, muscular arms. They always seem to breathe in sync with one another. And when their eyes meet? It's like no one else is around. I'll never have what they have. As if in slow motion, I'm propelled forward. Leaning closer, needing to touch and be touched, to feel part of them, to—*Seriously, Kate? What the hell are you doing?*

"All righty, then," I chirp, hopping up like a jackrabbit. I clap my hands a bunch of times for some unknown reason, and the sound echoes through our construction zone. The boys literally fly apart, and I feel their eyes as I scurry toward the kitchen. "You guys want water?"

I'm practically shouting. I have to grab the counter to steady myself, feeling wholly flush and mildly traumatized. No way that just happened. Nope. I'm tired, that's all. Stressed, undersexed and overheated. Clearly not thinking straight.

I shove my head in the freezer for a moment, breathing, repeating these little mantras until my brain and body cool enough to return to the boys. They are seated on opposite ends of the sofa, looking shamed.

"Water." I shove a bottle at Josh before he can offer some embarrassing apology. I hand a bottle to David, too, and we all chug in silence as elephants dance around the room. "Let's finish this up and go to bed," I say, once it's clear they aren't talking.

It's late and I'm suddenly so tired my brain is bleeding.

Josh nods, still flustered, but David just looks pained. Wondering what I'm thinking, no doubt. And why I'm acting so funny. Also, we haven't elaborated on his scan results, and he likely wants to keep it that way for now.

Thankfully, Josh steps up, clearing his throat.

"So, there is one more thing I need to tell you guys. It's about Tess . . ." His face pinches. "Hear me out before you comment or get all judgmental, okay? I was under duress when I called her. Keep that in mind."

I make a point of not looking at David because with this lead in, my oh-shit detector is up. Also, I'm still sort of picturing him beneath Josh. So, there's that . . .

". . . she's online more than we are," Josh is saying. "The photograph didn't bother her, but she was upset about something." He bites at a nail, regarding us with wide, regretful eyes. "The thing is, her roommate bailed on their lease, and Tessa's contract was up at work, so she left Chicago a few months ago and moved in with her stepbrother and his partner in Nashville." He turns to David. "She said you guys talked about it when we saw her in Ocean City last spring?"

He shrugs. "She may have mentioned something . . ."

I brush off the tiniest twinge of jealousy. I like Tessa. We've gotten to know her pretty well since David's surgery. I think her friendship is good for Josh, and I don't believe there's anything there between her and David. But I feel itchy, all the same, thinking about the three of them chatting it up.

"Well, either way, it's not working," Josh continues. "They've got a small place, and there's not enough room. Anyway, she's waiting on an offer from this cruise company. Events coordinator or something. Starting in November or December. She needs a place to crash until then." He gestures around our nearly finished living room. "I know it's terrible timing with the house in shambles, and Nick, and this Carol bullshit, but . . . we could fit another bed in Kate's room or the basement, or . . ." His eyes sweep back and forth, avoiding us. "I don't know. I'm sure we'll figure it out once she gets here."

David and I look at each other, mouths dropping. "Wait a minute," he says. "Are you asking or telling us?"

Josh's face twists into a pleading sort of grimace, and I'm suddenly wide awake. "Yeah. See, that's the thing." He scratches the back of his head. "I may have already invited her."

There's a beat of silence as we digest this news because *what the actual fuck, Joshua?*

David and I erupt simultaneously as Josh covers his face with a throw pillow.

"I know, okay? I know. I'm sorry! I should have run it by you. But listen." He chucks the pillow and makes a run for the stairs, palms rising. "Just think about it," he calls from a safer distance. "Tessa moving in solves a multitude of problems. She gets a place to stay until her job starts, I get a date for the premiere, Nick is happy, she's happy. You two can do whatever it is you do. Hell . . . maybe Tessa and I can even, I don't know . . ." he slows with each word, his enthusiasm fading.

It feels as if the air has been sucked out of the room. He can't even say it. Of course, he can't. He was on top of David five freaking minutes ago.

Josh doesn't want Tessa. I bite back tears as I watch the color drain from David's face. He moves to the stairs and reaches for Josh's hand as something silent and inexpressible passes between them.

And I know.

I know with sun rising certainty, this won't work. This plan Josh hatched. There's no getting over David. I of all people should know. And we'll never appease Nick. Tessa is just a tool. Does she even know she's being used? Does it matter?

And am I wrong for playing along, because I don't voice these doubts and neither does David. By some well-intentioned agreement, we cave, following Josh up the stairs, chatting, stupidly, about how we can accommodate Tessa, and her arrival date.

Which is in two weeks, for crying out loud!

Once in their room, I slug on a tee shirt and undies and drop into bed beside David, wishing my own room was done. Craving, for the first time in weeks, one of the pills Josh made me get rid of. Oh, the sweet bliss of nothingness. What I wouldn't give for a night of dreamless sleep.

A few minutes later, Josh climbs into his bed, alone and smelling of toothpaste and despair.

Wrong, wrong, wrong, the whole of my being shouts, even as David pulls me close. Isn't this where I want to be? What happens when my room is finished? What happens when Tessa is here, every night? I look over at Josh. What's happening to the three of us?

Silence descends with the darkness, and no one's talking. How can they possibly sleep with this piercing quiet? I'm about to scream or sigh or, I don't know, fart or something . . . anything to break the misery, when Josh's voice cuts the night.

"You guys never told me what the doctor said about David's scan. Did everything look all right? When's the next appointment?"

Of course, he'd ask.

David's arm tightens around my waist, but I don't need the warning. I know Josh better than the lines of my hand. He's hanging from a ledge right now, and I won't be the one to push him over.

And I certainly won't be the one to tell him David may need another surgery.

Nine

Three's Company

:: An unexpected disruption in the balance

David
Friday, September 8th 2:47 pm
Freedom Grove Academy
Baltimore, Maryland

The last student exits my classroom.

Smiling, I close the door and sink into my chair. When I returned home a month ago, part of me wondered if I would ever teach again. Yet here I am, finishing my first week.

Well, technically a half week. The school's administration is allowing a part-time schedule until I get my stamina back. They've been more than accommodating. So have Kate and Josh, who are still driving me back and forth.

My phone vibrates with a text.

I know without looking, it's him—twenty minutes early. The man is nothing if not punctual. I open his message, and sure enough . . .

Josh: D, HURRY TF UP, GOTTA DIP FOR WORK

Gotta dip?

Me: Who is this?

Josh: 🖕

Josh: NO CAP, LET'S BOUNCE. RUNNING LATE

Josh: COME ONNNNNN

He's still spam texting moments later when I climb into the Jeep.

"What are you, channeling middle schoolers? Gimme that thing." I toss his phone into the back as he peels off. "Gotta dip? No cap? You sound like my students."

He grins. "I've been helping at work with the high school volunteers."

"Well, that would explain why you're texting like a preteen."

"You know, we're only twenty-five, David. That's not exactly old." He pauses, eyes narrowing. "Correction. I'm not old. You look like a Yale professor." He fingers the soft, navy sweater vest I'm wearing. "Did you borrow this from Bennett?"

What's wrong with my vest?

"Kate bought it for me." I examine the fine cabling, remembering her words. "She said vests are the new layering essential this fall."

"Bro, what?" Josh laughs so hard his head hits the steering wheel. "Take that shit off. You look ridiculous." He yanks the vest over my head and tosses it in the back. "You know who you remind me of in that thing? Remember that show we used to watch after school, *Three's Company?* The guy, Jack? You look like Jack, only, you know... prettier."

I roll my eyes. "You're just jealous."

"Jealous? I wouldn't be caught dead in a sweater vest." He's laughing, though. A warm, husky sound that makes me ache for those days. For simpler times and the boys we used to be. He rests a hand on my neck, fingers playing at the curls poking beneath my ball cap. "You should take this off, too," he says, tugging at it.

My hand flies up, instinctively. I don't go anywhere without a hat or beanie anymore—a point of contention between him and me. Turns out I'm vainer than we thought.

I pull the cap down farther, and he sighs. "Did you at least make an appointment with the new surgeon?"

Two weeks have passed since our ill-fated return to the old neighborhood and the Tessa-Josh gala photo mess—or Jessa-Jam, as Kate likes to call it. As predicted, Jessa faded into internet oblivion within a few days of the *What's Up Weekly* spread. Several reporters canvassed our street, and one neighbor gave an interview. But overall, little came of it.

Not to downplay the ordeal. We were on pins and needles; certain some rogue media personality would uncover the mountain of scandal we're hiding. But no. At least something fell in our favor.

My scan? Not so favorable.

We knew there was residual tumor—it was too invasive for the surgeon to remove everything. A blow, yes. But not entirely unexpected. I was told there would be regular scans for months, if not years.

I was not, however, prepared for news of growth already, minimal as it was. My surgeon didn't exactly say a second surgery was imminent, but he implied we might be there sooner rather than later. News I'm glad Josh didn't hear firsthand. Kate and I filled him in once everything settled.

Hence, his insistence on a second opinion. His other insistence?

Tessa.

Anticipation ripples through me. Her flight lands in less than twenty-four hours. "Our new roomie will be here soon," I say, shifting the conversation. I tap the digital clock on his dashboard.

"No more *Three's Company*," he deadpans, but it comes off flat. His grip tightens on the wheel, as if bracing for an argument. Because I did argue, initially.

Tessa moving in is awkward for a multitude of reasons, not the least of which is our lengthy history together. We met at Towson, freshman year, both on the heels of a disastrous adolescence, which, if I'm honest, probably drew us together.

We stayed close, though, only drifting apart after graduation. I cared about her. Still care about her. But our relationship was more a friendship of ease, not the deeper connection I share with Josh and Kate.

Not that Tess isn't deep. She's incredibly perceptive, only I was closed off and hiding back then, and so was she. We didn't share much about our respective pasts. A fact that's likely to change when she moves in . . .

"You're sure about this?" I ask Josh.

Opening our home to Tessa means opening our lives. A risk that shouldn't be taken lightly. Things are bound to come out, the question is, how much we want her knowing. Only time will tell, I guess.

He shrugs. "It's a little late for take backs."

"I know, but—"

He waves me off as we turn into the neighborhood. "No buts. She's coming. We already made the decision. Besides, I have good news. Guess what I did today?" An entreating look accompanies this question, and I can't help but relent.

It's Josh, after all. What wouldn't I do for him? If he wants to help Tessa, if he thinks her presence will restore some kind of balance, so be it. It's only a few months. What's the worst that can happen?

He doesn't wait for my prompting. "Zach and I did a walk through, and I gave him the final payment this morning." He beats the air with his fist. "Our house is officially done. No more contractors!"

That is good news. It's been chaotic the last few weeks with work crews in and out. Kate's room, oddly enough, took the longest. They finished painting there a few days ago, and we finally got the furniture and beds put together.

Beds, plural.

We decided on separate rooms upstairs for now and a return to his "plan" after Tessa leaves. For the duration of her stay, it will be Tess and Kate in one room and Josh and I in the other, with the basement as a last resort. It's finished, only Kate swears bugs are colonizing behind the walls. I wouldn't admit this to Josh, but I tend to agree.

He parks in front of our house. "I'm just going to let you off, okay? I gotta get into work."

Kate's outside talking to one of our neighbors—the cat lady. We don't know her name, but she's always pushing her cats around in this little doll stroller. Kate waves at us, then beckons me over. "There's a new kitten!" she calls.

It's all so very familiar. So comfortable. So, us. *Will Tess being here change that?*

Josh must share this thought because a look of concern crosses his face. He grabs my arm. "Tell me this will be all right."

I'm not sure if he means the Tessa situation or our recent chaos in general, but whatever the case, my instinct is to reassure him. "Of course, it will. Go on to work, okay? Everything's going to be fine."

He frowns.

Truth be told, I'm not sure what to expect. Things have been better these last few weeks. And also worse. We've had a lot to deal with on top of the house and my recovery, and it's weighing heavy.

Plus, I'm still feeling off. Unsettled and confused about him and Kate and where we go from here. I guess that's to be expected—it's only been three months since surgery, and already there's a setback. But now isn't the time to delve into it—Josh has a long night ahead of him.

I climb out of the Jeep, shut my door, then lean in the open window. "*Three's Company,* huh? So, if I'm Jack, who does that make you?"

He blanks for a moment, then grins. "Larry, obviously," he says. "Duh."

"You mean the used car guy from upstairs? No way. He's such a player."

"He's Jack's best friend, moron. Who else would I be?"

I pretend to ponder this. "Well, Mr. Roper is the clear choice, but I think I'm going with Janet. You've got reliability written all over you."

I expect a protest, but he just shakes his head. "Janet, huh?" He shrugs. "I can accept that."

We're both laughing as Kate walks over. She hugs me. "What's so funny?" she asks, burying her face in my chest with a world-weary sigh. "You guys won't believe this, but I locked myself out again."

"Shocker," Josh mutters. Zach's guys installed a new front door lock and Kate keeps forgetting the key.

He and I exchange a look. Without missing a beat we both say, "Chrissy."

"What is that supposed to mean?" she demands as Josh drives off. But I don't respond because a disquieting thought suddenly occurs to me.

The saying isn't three's company, it's two's company, three's a crowd. And as the Jeep disappears from sight, all I can think is, what then does that mean for four?

Saturday, September 9ᵗʰ 2:17 pm

Kate practically sprints toward the baggage claim at BWI Airport.

"I see her!" she calls, zeroing in on a tall brunette who's standing off to the side, casually leaning against a large suitcase. Even in black joggers and a gray hoodie with no makeup, Tessa is stunning.

Josh inhales sharply, and I can't help but laugh. "Caught you off guard, didn't she?"

We watch her and Kate hug before walking toward us, arm in arm. I wave, but Josh has yet to move.

"Breathe," I whisper, nudging him as the girls approach.

"Josh!" Tessa runs straight to him. She kisses both cheeks, then takes his face in her hands. "Meu amor! How can I ever thank you?" She plants a soft kiss on his lips.

"Oh . . . um . . ." He casts a helpless look in my direction, instantly reddening. "It's no problem, really. We're glad to—"

But she's already turning, arms outstretched. "Daveed," she murmurs, kissing me. "Louve a Deus! I pray for you every day." She grasps my shoulders, beaming. "You look wonderful! More beautiful than before."

I don't dare glance at Kate because I'm pretty sure I, too, am blushing. This is classic Tessa, though. She's sort of intimate and overwhelming.

We'll get used to her . . .

And we do.

Apart from a few uncomfortable moments on the ride home, the four of us get on like old friends. It helps that she and Josh have been talking regularly since the gala. Kate messages with her, too, though less frequently. And Tess and I have always been able to pick right up.

Thanks to Facetime, she's as familiar with the house as we are. All but Kate's room, which we just finished. After dinner and a walk around Canton, the three of us help her get unpacked and settled.

"It's beautiful!" Tess exclaims, turning around Kate's room several times. I take my own appraising look. The walls are a soothing yellow, and all the trim and fixtures are bright white. The beds take up a decent amount of space, but each is pushed against a wall and covered with plush throw pillows. It's modern, but in a cozy, cheerful way.

It feels like Kate, and I love that.

Josh and I are about to leave them to their organizing when Kate suddenly gasps. She points to the ceiling outside her closet.

"What is that?"

We all look up to see an angry, jagged crack in the drywall.

"You've got to be shitting me!" Josh moves to stand beneath it, neck craning. "That wasn't there yesterday!" After a moment's inspection, he storms from the room. "I'm calling Zach. This is ridiculous! We just did the fucking walk through!"

He's already downstairs with Kate fast behind him. "Wait," she pleads. "I don't think you should bother him tonight. He's with Anna, remember? I told you she fell this morning at the café . . ." Their voices fade as Josh presumably ignores her request.

"Que pena," Tessa murmurs. "Poor Josh. You guys have been through so much."

If she only knew.

We regard each other intently. It's not awkward, but I feel a bit odd, standing alone with Tess in Kate's room. Discussing Josh, no less.

"I'm sure we can get it fixed," I say, for lack of something better.

She nods, moving toward me. She takes both my hands. "Are you really okay with this? Me being here? You guys have so much going on. I don't want to cause any more problems or get between you and Kate, or you and . . . Josh?"

Her eyes are beautiful and piercing. Deeply empathetic. There's no point denying what she's already observed. "I'm not going to lie, Tess. It's complicated. With us, with everything. But I want you here. We want you here. I think it will be good . . . for everyone."

Her brow knits together and she frowns.

After Josh's rash invitation, she and I spoke a few times. She made it clear—without my blessing, she wouldn't come. I did my best to reassure her, but my hesitation must've shown. Must still be showing.

"If it doesn't work, I can stay at Bennett and Julie's," she says. "He offered."

Of course, he did.

He's such a good man. Lord only knows where we'd be without him. He even found Tess a temporary job at the college while she's here. But I don't want her to feel like this is some kind of trial.

"I'm sure that won't be necessary." I nudge her, pointing at the bed where a faded yellow-and-black shirt with the words Study Party lies, unfolded. "You kept that?"

It's mine, or at least, it was. A joke among some of us in the Towson English department. She picks it up, clutching it to her chest with clear exaggeration. "Claro, meu amor! It's my favorite," she swoons.

"So, that's how it's going to be, huh?" Laughing, I pull her into a hug just as Josh's angry voice floats upstairs.

It is both familiar and foreign, holding her. Breathing the delicate vanilla scent that always seemed to linger on her skin. It reminds me of the times she comforted me in college. Brightened my day. Made me laugh.

"Maybe you can work your magic on Josh," I say, only half joking as we exchange a look. Together we empty the rest of her suitcase, alternately bemoaning the last few weeks and reminiscing about college. Josh stalks in at one point and takes a million pictures of the ceiling, muttering something about incompetence. Kate rejoins us for a few minutes, then ducks out to shower.

And Tess and I are alone again. She's quiet, though. Biting at her lip, clearly hesitating. Her eyes dart around the room before she moves to close Kate's door.

"Why didn't you tell me about Josh and Kate's father?" She whispers. "I had no idea he was *the* Nicholas Janney. He's a celebrity. I used to watch *Brought to Light* all the time. You and I watched it together, in college. Don't you remember? Why didn't you tell me?"

"Well, I . . . um . . ." *How do I respond to that?*

But she's not waiting. "And your father! You told me he was an alcoholic, that he died suddenly. But you never mentioned he was part of *Brought to Light*, or that his death was so . . . so . . . tragic."

"Yeah. Well, the thing is—"

"I've done some research," she continues, talking in earnest now. "I don't care if he's famous, I think Nicholas Janney is a shady person, and I don't trust him. The way Josh said he used that picture of us from the gala? How he let your father take all the blame for that man dying? *Brought to Light* was his show!" She shakes her head. "You know, I watched that interview where he talked about your mother, David! Unacceptable! Ele é uma cobra mentirosa desgraçada!"

Tess has never been one to mince words. I have no idea what she just said, but I recognize the word cobra, and Nick is nothing if not a snake. Far be it for me to defend him. Meanwhile, her research is impressive. She would've had to go back nearly a decade to get details on the *Brought to Light* scandal.

Nick's old show still gets coverage from time to time. I think the family of the man who committed suicide started a foundation in his honor.

But the blame for his death always remained with Ian. Nick's actions are rarely called into question.

"Yeah. Nick's kind of an asshole," I agree.

Her lovely features harden, even as she hugs me, murmuring words of sympathy and frustration. Tess knows all about family dysfunction. It's how she ended up living in the states with her stepbrother. Of all people, she can relate to our backstory. Tess would not be shocked by what Josh, Kate, and I have done and what we've been through.

And as we hold each other in Kate's room, I wonder if it's only a matter of time before we tell her the truth.

11:46 pm

The girls are still up when Josh and I go to bed.

We face each other in the dark. "So, what do you think about today?"

He yawns. "I think I'm too tired to know what I'm thinking." A sharp giggle escapes from Kate's room, and he groans. "What can they possibly have left to say?"

"Beats me." I'm yawning, too. "Kate seems happy, right? I think she and Tess will get along."

"Yeah, I guess."

He's distracted. Worried about the ceiling issue and our mounting pile of stress. We can't do much about that, but at least Zach promised to stop by tomorrow and assess the damage.

I scoot closer to the edge of my bed so I can see him better, keenly aware of the distance. This new reality. He seems so far. I stretch out my hand and so does he, our fingers weaving.

"Tess and I had a good talk while you and Kate were downstairs."

"Yeah? About what?"

"Oh, you know, work and college and stuff. The move. Her thoughts on our situation here."

His fingers tighten. "Our situation? What's that supposed to mean?"

"Nothing. She's just observant, is all. And she's done some research on Nick. Let's just say, she's not a fan."

"Is anyone a fan of that piece of shit?"

"Josh . . ."

He sighs. "I just want to go to sleep, David. Tell me tomorrow."

It's rare for him to tap out, so I don't press further. He's still holding my hand, though. The girls have stopped talking, and all is quiet. I rub small circles into his palm, listening to the way his breathing slows, soothed by its familiar rhythm as he falls deeper and deeper into sleep.

My mind blanks, and the air grows thick and heavy. I'm drifting when a loud noise from the hall has me sitting up so fast my head spins.

What was that?

Like a sharp crack. I look to see if Josh heard it, but he hasn't moved. After listening intently for several minutes, I'm convinced I imagined the sound and am about to lie back when I hear it again.

Much louder.

Then, with no warning whatsoever, Kate's shrill scream sears through the wall as an explosion literally rocks the house. It feels like an earthquake, and I fall from the bed, stunned.

Josh is on the floor beside me, disoriented. But he's up in seconds, on his feet, pulling me, pushing me to stand. "The girls!" he shouts, stumbling forward, struggling through the door and into the hall as their cries grow louder.

We burst into Kate's room, nearly falling over each other in our haste. But we're stopped short by the acrid chaos of it all. Startled silent by the horror. Kate's room, unrecognizable. The girls disembodied screams, lost in a cloud of dust and moldy debris.

And the ceiling, in a thousand pieces on the floor.

The Plan

Carol Brennan
Saturday, September 9th 11:46 pm
Sunset Haven Motel Naples, Florida

Carol hunched low in the seat of his rented SUV.

He trained his camera on two shadowy figures approaching the seedy, south Florida motel. As if sensing his presence, the taller figure, a man, glanced in Carol's direction providing a brief, indisputable image of his face.

Nicholas Janney.

Carol almost laughed out loud at the man's stupidity. Could someone as shrewd as Nick be dumb enough to bring a young girl—by all appearances, a minor—to this motel just weeks before the premiere of his nationally televised news series?

The answer, of course, was yes.

But then, Janney had always been a cocky prick, even as a kid when he began coming around for Elena. Carol's attempts to prevent their relationship failed—his younger sister had been smitten with the boy. The two were inseparable.

At least, until Ian Shaw came along.

Carol zoomed in on Nick's face, snapping several remarkably clear shots before Nick turned his attention back to his companion, urging her out of the open hallway and into their room. A moment later, the door closed, and Carol released his breath. That had been far too easy.

But he wasn't done yet.

The idea to follow Janney had come to him on a whim. Carol wanted to kick himself for not thinking of it sooner. He could've avoided the mess in Baltimore with David, Josh, and Kate, and no one would be the wiser.

He swallowed back thoughts of them, ashamed. His nephew's surgery had been a success. Josh left a brief message stating as much—a terse message. Not that Carol blamed him. He didn't return the call, though. There was no point. He destroyed any goodwill with David when he dug up Angela's body.

So, Carol did what he did best—fade into the abyss. He closed the beach place, changed his number, and left the North Carolina shore. Drove south to Florida. To Nick Janney, and the plan he'd finally devised to destroy the man. What he had not imagined was how easy it would be.

How arrogant and careless Janney was with his philandering. Like he almost wanted to be caught. But men like Janney don't change, Carol reminded himself. Nick viewed people as commodities.

Expendable once their value expired. Carol just hadn't expected the women to be so young.

He crept up to the window outside Nick's room, conjuring thoughts of Elena, and the life Nick stole from her. The anger fueled Carol, compelling him to lift his camera and catch one final shot.

The amount of video and photographic evidence Carol had on Nick's sexual deviance was damning and incontestable. On one occasion, the scumbag hadn't even bothered closing the curtains. Carol videoed the entire, depraved affair.

Not only did Nick like his women young, but he liked degrading them. It was disgusting but played right into Carol's hand. He snapped a few more photos, then hurried to his car and took off.

Once back at his rental, Carol surveyed the evidence he'd amassed. It would take time, he reasoned, to put it all together in a meaningful way. And for once, time was on his side. *Exposed* was set to air in three weeks, and the premiere party had just been announced.

He'd seen the photo of Josh and that girl and noted the buzz it created for *Exposed*. A plant, no doubt, if not choreographed by Nick himself. He, of all people knew, a picture was worth a thousand words.

And a video?

Carol chuckled, connecting his camera to the laptop. A video was indisputable. The premiere party would be a night Nick Janney never forgot; Carol was certain of that.

Because Carol planned to expose everything.

Tangled
Part Two

Ten

Framework Failure

:: When strategic changes reveal
unseen structural issues

Josh
Tuesday, September 12th 4:23 pm
VFC Station 30 Lutherville, Maryland

Maybe it's Tessa's presence, but the ceiling collapse does not fully derail me.

"It actually collapsed?" My buddy Greg's eyes grow wide. "Are you serious?"

"Not the whole ceiling. Just a support beam, over the closet. Still a nightmare, though."

He shakes his head. "Damn, J. You guys gotta sell that place. Cut your losses and move." He hops out of the rig we're inspecting and slams the door, yawning. It's been a long shift. "All done. The oxygen's going to expire soon, but everything else checks out."

I make a note in the logbook as we head toward the locker room. He stops me before going inside, clapping a hand on my shoulder. "Hey, I really am sorry about the house. At least no one was hurt, right? The offer from this summer still stands. Shawna and I have a spare room. You're always welcome."

Warmth fills my chest. We've only worked together a few months, but Greg's proved to be a good friend. I give him one of those awkward little single-arm side hugs. "I appreciate that, but I think we're good for now."

And, as crazy as it sounds, we are.

Not that I would've believed this Saturday night. Saturday, I wanted to tear the fucking house down. Discovering that crack, waking up, terrified, stumbling into the horror in Kate's room? Pure misery. It could've been worse, though.

It could've been catastrophic.

One of the rafters gave out, taking with it the surrounding drywall and insulation. The only saving grace? It happened by Kate's closet, away from the beds. Once the dust settled, David and I were able to see both she and Tessa, terrified, but unharmed. Of course, we had no idea of the structural integrity at that point, so we fled.

To Bennett and Julie's house. No matter his thoughts on Kate and me, Bennett loves David. He wouldn't turn us away. Plus, Tessa asked to go there.

She's a tough girl but add a ceiling collapse to a cross-country move and anyone's nerves would be fraying. I'm not even sure how I held it together.

Numbness, maybe? Maturity? Not likely.

But what is a house compared to people? It's nothing. Once I knew David, Kate, and Tess were fine, it was like a huge weight lifted. There we were, covered in dust and debris, driving down the interstate at one o'clock in the morning, frantically dialing Bennett, and all I could feel was relief. Gratitude, even. I've been riding that high ever since.

Kate, on the other hand? Not so high. She calls while I'm in the locker room changing . . .

"I can't believe you're making me do this!" she wails. "I'm exhausted."

"Um, exaggerate much? You've been sitting around the house all day; how are you exhausted?"

"Whatever, Joshua. I haven't sat at all. I've been dealing with contractors and insurance people. I'm not you or David. I don't know what I'm doing!"

This is somewhat true. Kate inherited the task of oversight, which is to say she spent the day at our house dealing with a rotating door of work crews and repairmen. Not her forte. But I'm on days this week, David's teaching, and Tess is working with Bennett out at Towson.

Since Kate dropped her OT job to pursue massage full-time—under my strong objection I might add—she has the most flexibility. Besides, David and I made all the phone calls, and Zach's coordinating the work. We really just need her to be there.

I refrain from this reminder, biting my tongue while she recounts the details, most of which I already know thanks to a call from Zach. Namely that the house has now been deemed structurally sound. Fortunately, the collapse resulted from one failing beam rather than a pervasive problem. Also, it sounds like the repairs will take about three weeks, which totally sucks. But it is what it is.

"At least we can live there while they do the work," Kate muses. "Think Tessa will want to come back with us?"

We've been crashing at Bennett and Julie's since Saturday. They'd let us stay longer, but three days is enough. At least for David, Kate, and me. Tessa is still deciding.

We have limited space as it is. With Kate's room under construction, it makes sense for her to stay with Bennett and Julie. Only Saturday night, before the collapse, it was nice, the four of us. A little awkward maybe, but mostly good. Fun, even.

Like, maybe bringing Tess here wasn't so stupid after all. Like, maybe she's exactly what we need. And maybe, she needs us, too.

8:35 pm

Thankfully, Grace makes Tessa's decision to come back an easy one.

"My friends think you guys are the cutest couple," she swoons as we're finishing up Julie's famous baked ziti. She is a phenomenal cook. "They can't believe you're living in my house!" Grace continues, rocking back and forth in her excitement. She practically falls from the kitchen chair.

Beside me, Tess smiles, but she's got to be annoyed. I'm annoyed. I love Grace and all, but thanks to her fangirling, I'm ready to get the hell out. If only we could take some of Julie's food . . .

"That's enough, Grace," Bennett warns. He gives his daughter an admonishing look.

Jack rolls his eyes. "You should hear her bragging to the neighbors, Dad." He turns to me. "One of the moms offered her money if she could get you and Tessa to sign a copy of *What's Up Weekly*."

"She did not!" Grace glares at her brother. "Okay, she did. But it was a joke, Jackson. And I would never do that. Josh and Tessa are my friends!"

Jack mutters something about her not having friends as Bennett orders him from the table, but Gracie isn't done. "Wait! Oh my gosh, I just thought of something!" She claps her hands together. "When David and Kate get married, Josh and Tessa should get married, too! You guys can have a double wedding! I'll be the flower girl. Tessa and Kate can buy matching dresses . . . Josh and David will be each other's best men . . . and . . ."

Julie stands, clearly irritated. She beckons Grace. "All right, little miss matchmaker, we're going upstairs. Don't you have homework to finish? It's almost bedtime."

Gracie scowls at her mother but rises obediently. "Think about it," she whispers, hugging each of us before making a woeful exit.

Bennett slumps back in his chair. "Sorry about that. Her best friend was in a wedding last weekend. I think Grace has flower-girl fever."

We all laugh, but it's forced.

I watch Kate and David from my seat beside Tess. The brief glance they exchange, her false smile, his distant gaze. They're sitting close, hands beneath the table, out of view. I'd bet anything he's holding hers, squeezing the finger where a ring should be.

Would be, if not for me.

"You know, we could have a double wedding," I blurt, stupidly unable to stop myself. "I mean, crazier things have happened, right?" I sling a reckless arm around Tessa's shoulders, and she jumps, nearly knocking over her glass of water. She takes a giant gulp as I plead, silently, for the universe to erase the last few seconds.

What the fuck was that?

David's eyes widen as Kate's narrow to incredulous little slits. Bennett just stares at us . . . confused. He met Tessa long before he met Kate or me. Bennett knows how close she and David were in college. I'm sure he assumed they'd end up together one day.

But no.

Flash forward to Tessa out of the picture and David living with me and Kate in Canton. Bennett, being the kind man he is, welcomes us with open arms only to learn, quite accidentally, that Kate and I hooked up in secret years ago and that I, her supposed twin, fathered the child she later miscarried, unbeknownst to David or me. And if that weren't bad enough, he finds out David has been lying all along about his past, his family, and his relationships.

And who is at the center of all his deception? Me.

And now, here I sit in his kitchen, eating his food with my audacious arm around David's ex, talking about double weddings. If I were Bennett, I'd hate me. Fuck, I hate me.

But he doesn't. He's not that sort of man.

"Well," he says, leaning forward with a thoughtful expression. "I don't think that sounds crazy at all, Josh. I think you should each follow your heart and go wherever it leads you." He stands, then stretches. "Speaking of which, I'm going to bed. Are you guys still planning to pack up and head home tonight? I'm not rushing you, but it's getting late, and this old man is tired."

And that is all the prompting I need.

Twenty minutes later, I'm in the bathroom gathering the last of our toiletries when Tessa walks in. She shuts the door and leans against it, arms crossing.

"A double wedding? Really?"

My cheeks immediately heat. "Come on. I was joking. That's not even a—"

"—because the more I think about it, the more I like the sound."

Wait. What?

The toiletries fall from my hand as she sidles up beside me. "I know we've only been talking for a few months, but everyone seems to think we make a great couple. What if they're right?" She takes another step, fully in my space now, peering up at me with a sultry gaze. Her hands press against my chest. "I think we should go for it."

She can't be serious. I search her face, swallowing. "Um . . . go for . . . what, exactly?"

She leans in, lips grazing my cheek as she murmurs, "Everything. I want it all. Long engagement, big wedding, cute little suburban home, two kids . . . the American dream. What do you say, Josh? Let's do it."

Let's do it?

"Um . . ."

I'm struggling to speak as she pulls back, and that's when I see it. The glint in her eyes. The trace of a smile. It instantly morphs into this huge grin, and she's straight up laughing.

"Oh, meu Deus! Your face!" She touches my cheek, softly brushing it with her thumb. "Relax, I'm just teasing." Her look turns melancholy. "Don't take this the wrong way, but marriage isn't my thing. I'd be terrible at it."

A tidal wave of relief rushes over me. "Oh, thank God," I mumble, cringing as she bursts into laughter once more. That sounded awful. "Sorry! It's not you. It's just . . . I feel the same, about marriage, I mean." A picture of Claire pops into my head and I wonder how I ever deluded myself into thinking I could marry her, or anyone, for that matter.

Tessa frowns. "But you want David and Kate to marry, no?" It's as much an accusation as a question.

Do I?

The obvious answer is yes, of course I do. Isn't that the point? Bring Tess around, make it seem like we're a couple, so David and Kate are free to be together. I can't bring myself to say it, though. "As long as they're with each other, I'll be happy."

"Happy? That's such an empty word." Her head cocks to the side. "Will you really be happy if they marry, Josh? That's what you want?"

What I want is for this conversation to end, like now. But the bathroom's growing smaller by the second, and there's no dodging her penetrating gaze. "It doesn't matter what I want. As long as Kate's taken care of and David is with the one he loves, I'll be fine."

She blinks. "The one he loves? And you think that's Kate? Your sister?"

Well, fuck.

I'm not entirely sure what she's implying, but it's clear she's seen straight through our little charade. David was wrong, Tessa isn't perceptive, she's fucking supernatural.

"Tess . . ." I begin, but she holds up a hand.

"I'm sorry. I shouldn't have said it like that. And you don't owe me an explanation, Josh. I'm not judging. I care about you and Kate. And I love David—I will always want the best for him." She grabs my arms. "You don't have to hide the truth is all I'm saying. I was at the gala and the hospital with you guys, remember? We've been talking for nearly three months. I know how much you love him. And I don't doubt he loves Kate. But have you asked David what he wants? Who he wants?"

"He wants her." The words fly out before I can contain them, and the break in my voice gives it all away.

"You sure about that?"

I'm not sure about anything. But she keeps pressing, and I'm backed against a wall, literally. My defenses are shit. "I don't know, okay? It's been a wild summer. You have no idea. And I don't know what the hell I'm doing. But I know Kate needs David, and I know he loves her. They've sacrificed everything for me. More than I can explain. So, if I can give them happily ever after?" I shrug. "I at least have to try, right?"

She stares at me for the longest time. "So, that's it, then? I'm here for you. A distraction. Like a game, no? We pretend while they get forever?"

It sounds awful when she puts it that way, but I nod nonetheless, transfixed by her words and the gleam in her mesmerizing blue eyes when she finally says, "If that's what you want, Josh. I'll play games with you."

Before I can move or respond, or gather any semblance of thought, her body presses into mine, fingers curling through my hair. "You're a fool if you think it's going to work," she murmurs, the decadent warmth of her lips sliding over mine.

Her kiss is soft and sultry and so unexpected she's pulling away before I can think to respond.

She cups my cheek, smiling. "It's okay, meu amor. We can have a little fun pretending." And with that, she slips out the door.

Friday, September 15th 11:16 pm

We're home for three sleepless nights before agreeing on the nuclear option.

"All four of us in one room?" Kate looks skeptical. She glances back and forth between David's bed and mine.

"Sounds good to me." Without hesitation, Tessa belly flops onto my bed. "No offense, guys, but anything is better than the basement."

Since returning to Canton, and the temporary closure of Kate's room, we've tried several sleeping arrangements. One thing we all can agree—the new couch makes a terrible bed. Our other discovery? There are no bugs in the basement, but it's creepy as fuck, and no one likes sleeping down there. I'll give Tess credit—she lasted one whole night before surrendering.

"So, who's sleeping with who?" she asks, whipping off her sweatshirt.

Did I mention she also has zero inhibitions and no filter?

David, Kate, and I look at each other.

"How about Kate and David in his bed, and me and you in yours?" Tess grins like a Cheshire cat until I cut her a *could-you-be-a-little-less-fucking-obvious* look, regretting for the hundredth time our bathroom conversation at Bennett's house.

David seems on the verge of objecting when Kate weighs in. "Fine by me. It'll be like a big sleepover."

"Or an orgy," Tessa quips. She dissolves into giggles at Kate's horrified expression. "I'm kidding, Kate, jeez." She tosses a pillow at her. "Like you guys have never thought about it."

And that's my cue to exit . . .

"I don't think I can do this," I tell David five minutes later, feeling mildly panicked despite knowing full well I brought this on myself.

We're in the bathroom brushing our teeth while the girls get settled. Between work and the chaos of moving back and forth, this is our first moment alone since returning from Bennett and Julie's. I have a million things to share with him, but my present angst is taking precedence.

He wipes his mouth. "What can't you do?"

"Sleep with Tessa in my bed, moron. Across from you and Kate!" I lower my voice. "It's weird, right? And here's the other thing. I think she knows, you know? Like, not just about us." I gesture, vaguely between him and me. "About everything. I mean, she doesn't know, know. But she definitely knows something."

"That's a lot of knows," he jokes, side-stepping the towel I flick at him. "What do you want me to say? It's awkward for me, too. This whole situation is weird. And I told you she's clued into what's going on here. She's not an idiot."

No, she's not.

I mentally replay our exchange at Bennett's house. And the kiss. Or the not kiss, because I'm pretty sure I just stood there like a damn gaping fish or something. But, whatever, he doesn't even know about that.

I lean forward, meaning to share the lurid details, but end up catching a whiff of soap and skin and something so indefinably David, my brain short-circuits. I just stand there with my face in his neck, sniffing like a creeper, until Kate hollers that the remote isn't working, and why are we taking so long?

And I say nothing.

We find the girls snuggled into our respective beds, channel surfing because all we have up here is cable. David yawns and all but falls in beside Kate, eyes already closing, the little shit.

Concern momentarily replaces the full-body angst I'm battling. Logically, I know his fatigue is normal, especially given his recent return to work. But I experience a ripple of fear, nonetheless, given what we've learned about the residual tumor and the probability of yet another surgery.

It's funny how medical training flies out the window when it comes to someone you love. *The one you love.* That's what I said to Tess.

She's watching me watch him with a knowing look. I should be thanking her. She's doing what I asked—what I haven't had the courage to do, which is force David and Kate together. Sighing, I plod over to my bed and curl up so near the edge I almost fall.

No one speaks as Kate tries her best to find a show using our ancient remote. She lands, unbelievably, on an old rerun of *Three's Company*. David, of course, isn't awake enough to notice.

Eventually Tessa shifts, leaning close to my ear. "I don't bite," she whispers. "Unless you want me too."

I bark out a laugh, and Kate shoots me a questioning look as David's eyes fly open. He blinks several times, briefly perplexed at the sight of Tessa and me. We lock eyes and it takes every ounce of willpower not to reach for him.

Fuck, how am I going to do this?

Tessa's still by my ear. "I can go downstairs if you want," she says, softer now, so soft only I can hear. She rubs my arm in what can only be described as a motherly way, which is nice, yet fully emasculating.

What must she think?

I turn purposefully, righting myself, resigning to man the fuck up. "No, don't do that, you're fine," I tell her, propping my head on the pillow. I grab the remote from where Kate abandoned it and curse myself for not setting up a streaming service in here. There is literally nothing on cable. "Maybe we can find an old movie or something," I say, irked to discover most of the buttons are sticking.

We end up on some random station where, inevitably, a rerun of *Brought to Light* is playing. Nick's smug-ass face immediately appears, and I hear Kate groan as he touts yet another perv brought to justice. And I can't even turn down the volume.

Fuck my life.

Eleven

Blades of Truth

:: Cutting to the heart of it

Kate
Thursday, September 21ˢᵗ 5:52 pm
Foster Avenue Baltimore, Maryland

It's not like I planned to tell Tessa about the miscarriage.

But plans have a way of changing.

Take today, for example. It started like any other day or any other recent day, post ceiling collapse. Work crews arrived at the crack of dawn while the four of us stumbled around Josh and David's room waiting for a turn in the shower, awkwardly side stepping each other as we guzzled coffee.

It's cozy in a chaotic-ish sort of way.

We've adapted surprisingly well to communal living. Even Josh, who struggled at first. And I do mean *struggled*. But he's so bent on pushing David and me together, he'll do anything, including sleep with Tessa, I guess.

It's heartbreaking knowing I'm the problem. But what am I supposed to do? The boys know where I stand, especially after the Chad West debacle. I don't even want to look at another man.

Only, this is bigger than me. This is between them. And David, true to form, wants to let things play out until Tessa is gone. Don't get me wrong, he's still regaining strength and not in a decision-making state of mind. And I know he likes having Tessa here—it's not about her. It's just the situation in general. Imagine trying to recover from brain surgery with three people you love, and have been intimate with, together under one roof, in one bedroom, inches apart, lusting after you.

While that might be some people's ideal, it's not David's. Especially given the toll it's taking on Josh. But I digress.

This morning, Josh drove David to work since my first appointment wasn't until ten. That left me in charge of getting Tessa to Towson, which would have been fine if not for the sudden onset of pain. Mind-searing, sidesplitting, screaming pain. Like a thousand scalding knives cutting through my body . . .

"Tessa!" I shrieked, shivering as blood trickled into the toilet.

She was in the bathroom in seconds. "Oh meu Deus, coitadinha de você!" She kneeled on the tile, brushing hair from my face. "What's wrong, Kate? What happened?"

"I was in the shower," I gasped, grabbing her arm as another wave rippled through me. "I felt this sudden burning, and pressure, like I had to pee or something. I think it's a UTI. I used to get them in college, but I never had one come on so strong or so fast!"

Her eyes grew wide and she immediately insisted on calling Josh. I almost agreed, desperate for him. But he and David shouldn't have to manage my every mess, and all I really needed was a doctor.

Consequently, Tessa and I spent the morning, not at our respective jobs, but at urgent care, where, after an excruciating wait, we learned I did indeed have a urinary tract infection. Coincidence or not, I started getting them freshman year after the miscarriage, a fact Tessa, unfortunately, overheard me share. She kept her reaction in check, though, and mentioned nothing.

She was quiet as we filled my prescriptions, and quieter still as we drove home and settled me into David's bed, careful to avoid the curious work crew. But the question lingered between us all day . . .

By evening, the pain meds are in full force and I'm no longer peeing daggers. I finally resemble a human again. A human, anxious to clear the air.

"Go ahead," I say, hoisting myself up in bed. "Ask me about the miscarriage."

Tessa looks up from her laptop. She shakes her head. "It's not my business, Kate."

But it is.

She dated David in college. I know he told her about me. That we saw each other from time to time. If I were her, I'd want to know. I want her to know.

"The baby wasn't David's."

"You don't have to tell me."

"Yes, I do. I want to. And it really wasn't. She wasn't." Call it momentary insanity, or fatigue, or just plain stupidity, because I should stop right here. Every ounce of self-preservation tells me to shut the hell up. But I can't. I suddenly have to get this out. "The baby," I say, breathing harder, "I don't know if she was a girl or boy, Tess, but I named her Zoe. And . . . and . . ." *Don't say it, don't say it, Kate!* "And . . . Josh was the father."

I don't know what I expect to happen. A shifting in the clouds, spontaneous combustion, euphoric relief? I don't know. But what I do know is, nowhere on my radar exists the possibility of Josh or David showing up at this exact moment to witness my unraveling.

But they do.

Tessa's shock is loudly overshadowed by Josh's horrified gasp. His face contorts into a mask of shock and rage. "Kate," he sputters from the doorway, "what the hell is wrong with you?"

Behind him David pales, as I try to wrap my mind around the reality of them, here.

What are they teleporting now? How are they home already? Maybe I'm dreaming.

I cling to this notion until I notice the darkened sky and realize David and Josh do not possess superpowers—they're just back from work at the regular time. That, and Tessa's mute look of disbelief at what I've divulged.

Josh sees it too.

He lunges into the room, unleashing a river of expletives as David holds him back. I immediately burst into tears, vomiting apologies and explanations all over myself. It's therapeutically tragic, and there is no stopping me.

"Oh God, Josh. I'm so sorry! I didn't mean to tell her, or maybe I did. I don't know. I'm not thinking straight. I just feel so bad. And I'm peeing blood, and we've been at urgent care all day, and I had to tell the doctor about the miscarriage because, you remember how I used to get those UTI's in college? And I didn't want Tessa to think it was David's baby because she overheard, and . . ." I take an enormous gulp of air. ". . . and I'm so damn tired. Who cares anymore? I need someone else to know, and not just this, but everything. I mean, why shouldn't we tell her?"

I'm shouting, and David looks ill as Josh's mouth drops open, but I can't stop. "We're all sleeping in the same room, for crying out loud. She clearly knows things don't add up. And she's going to meet Nick, Josh! She should know what he's done, what we've done, and what we're dealing with and . . . and . . ."

I'm sobbing too hard to continue. David's on the bed, hugging me, having abandoned a stunned looking Josh in favor of the puddle formerly known as Kate. No one speaks for what feels like eternity, and it's awful. But then Tessa, bless her, reaches for Josh and gives his arm a squeeze. She pulls him onto the bed, so we all sit together.

"Listen, I don't know what you guys think, but I don't care what happened in your past." She looks each of us in the eye, sternly. "Tell me, or don't. It changes nothing as far as I'm concerned. The past doesn't define you anymore than it does me." She cups my chin, forcing me to look at her. "That said, telling me just might free something for Kate, here." She glances at the boys. "And maybe for you, too. And in that case, you should know, I would never betray your trust. Ever."

Her face is stone solemn, and I believe every word. And yes, I know they're just words. Void without action. Yet, somehow, when Tessa speaks, they dance and transform, morphing into something almost . . . magical.

Hopeful.

Even the boys feel it. I see it in their drawn, weary faces—the desire to let go. As if the very act of telling might release our burden. And as unlikely as it seems, we begin talking.

And then we talk.

And talk.

And talk.

We speak in turn and overtop each other as we tell Tessa of our childhood, and how we met. Of the *Brought to Light* years and Nick and Ian's exploitation of the boys, and how they sacrificed to protect me.

I tell her of my overdose and how it prompted Josh to confront our fathers, an act which led to Ian's death, the fire that destroyed David's house, and our discovery that Josh and I are not who we thought we were (cue Tessa's relief at learning we are not, in fact, siblings, though something tells me she never believed this to begin with).

We tell her of college. How hard it was to be away from each other, from David. How Josh and I succumbed to the loneliness, then regretted it. How I kept our baby a secret from both boys, even after I miscarried.

And finally, we tell her about this last year. The news of Nick's new show, David's dwindling health, the threatening photographs, and our run in with his uncle. She is horrified to learn Nick murdered Josh's mother, and further devastated when we tell her all four of our parents played a role in the decades-long cover up.

She weeps as David and Josh describe the dug up clearing and Carol's ultimate betrayal that took freedom from our hands and left us beholden to Nick . . .

It's late into the night when Josh flops back on a pillow, eyes closing. "So, that's it. The story of our lives. We finally learn the truth, only to lose the evidence that proves it. Real fucking fitting." He sighs. "And now, instead of rubbing Nick's face in the mud, we've got to kiss ass at his stupid premiere party next week."

"It's still a step forward, Josh." I'm curled up next to him, inside David's sleep heavy embrace.

We're all back in his bed, having talked through dinner and my second round of medication. I'm exhausted and exhilarated and blissfully numb.

Only, Josh is still fuming. "Yeah? Well, it feels like a step backward to me."

But I don't mean Carol's betrayal or Nick's bullshit. I mean telling Tessa. That's a huge step. A terrifying, yet necessary step toward freedom.

I don't care what Josh says; I'm proud of us, and I'm glad we opened up to her.

She rubs my leg from her perch at the foot of the bed, her sapphire eyes tinged red from crying. "Thank you for trusting me," she says, lifting a solemn hand to her heart. She holds it there.

This, I recognize, is Tessa's way of acknowledging the gravity in what we shared. A silent, yet meaningful sign of solidarity and sisterhood. And as I snuggle closer to David, fiercely tired and fully content, I love her for it.

Tuesday, September 26th 6:22 pm

Telling Tessa does not change everything, but it changes some things.

In the days following my UTI induced share-all, there's a palpable shift. For the first time since moving in together, we're not tiptoeing around the past. We're talking openly and, dare I say, joking, about things that might have incited panic a few months ago.

I'm not sure how, or why, but telling Tessa is kind of like removing a splinter from a lion's paw—the lion is still dangerous, but he's much less agitated. This is how the past begins to feel—it's still a threat, just not as deadly.

Until the week of the premiere, that is, when the lion king himself stalks into town. Nick and his pride of alpha males are swarming...

"Fucking Nick again." Josh glances at the incoming text on his phone, then tosses it to David. Josh is driving and Nick keeps spam-texting party instructions.

"He says the network has a car service lined up to take us into D.C.," David reads. "They'll be at the house Friday afternoon around 4:00."

Josh white knuckles the steering wheel, and I imagine steam coming from his ears. "I told him we'd drive ourselves!"

"We could stay in the city," Tessa offers, glancing at me. "I have a friend who works for Marriott. She can get us a deal."

I love hotels. "That would be awe—"

"Hell no!" Josh glares in the rearview. "We're leaving as soon as possible. No press, no interviews, no pictures. I told Nick. We're in, we're out, we're done. End of discussion."

As confident as Josh sounds, this is far from reality. There are expectations where we're concerned, and he knows it. Which is likely why he agreed to go out this evening on a double date—him and Tess, and me and David.

And it's only a little fake, so that counts, right?

The four of us are heading to an indoor axe throwing place, then dinner at some trendy restaurant in Mount Vernon. Not only did Tessa plan the whole night, but she also convinced Josh it was a good idea. She suggested playing up the Jessa thing before the premiere. Stage a few dates, tip off the press, etc. She's even going to vlog about it.

This way Nick gets the publicity he craves, Josh and Tessa's "relationship" gains validity, and most importantly, we take control of the narrative. It's brilliant, really. If only Josh would be a little less . . . salty.

"Axe throwing," he scoffs once we're set up in side-by-side stalls. The place is large and comfortably rustic, like a chic barnyard. There are reclaimed wood wall dividers, metal accents, soft, ambient lighting, and worn leather couches by each stall. The atmosphere is super cozy, but Josh isn't buying it. "I can't believe people pay for this. I'd rather chop down a fucking tree." He yanks an axe out of the wood stump beside him. "What a dumb idea."

Tessa lowers her camera and rolls her eyes at me. "Is he always like this?"

"Like what?" David grabs the axe from Josh's hand. "This is pleasant for Josh. Sometimes he's downright surly." He flashes the three of us a grin, then, without so much as a glance, hurls his axe toward the target, landing a perfect bullseye.

We just stand there, speechless.

I've grown accustomed, these last few months, to thinking of David as fragile. Not weak, exactly, but delicate. Which clearly, he is not. The three of us engage in a moment of unabashed gawking.

Yowzah.

I don't know if it's the boots I made him wear, or the ass-hugging jeans, or the way his muscles ripple beneath his shirt, but the whole competent lumberjack vibe he's rocking? Totally doing it for me.

"I got that on video!" Tessa cheers. "It's perfect for the vlog."

It's perfect, all right. He is perfect. I'm salivating.

Josh, meanwhile, has shifted into competition mode. "How . . . ?" he sputters, looking from the target to David and back again. His eyes narrow. "Oh, it's on, princess." He yanks another axe out of the stump and makes a grand show of launching it.

Josh might have size on David, but he does not have accuracy. His axe lands with a wood-splitting thud miles from the bullseye, then drops to the ground.

Tessa dissolves into giggles. "Wow, Josh. That was axe-tremely off target." She elbows him. "Get it, axe? Target?"

There is a moment of complete silence in which David and I try desperately not to laugh while Josh fully reddens. His lips twist and I fear the beast.

But—and this comes as a shock to everyone—instead of anger, the corners of his mouth tug up, and he begins to laugh. At himself, at Tessa, at me and David, who knows, and who even cares because the beauty of his laughter overshadows everything.

Tessa gives him a giant bear hug, and he hugs her back, running his fingers through her long, thick curls.

"Don't you dare post that," he warns, but there's affection in his tone, and gentleness in the way he touches her. And for Josh, that is huge.

David's watching, too, of course, beaming like a proud parent. He's far too good an actor to let his feelings show, but I guarantee he's having mixed emotions. After a moment, though, he retrieves both axes and hands them to me and Tessa.

"All right, girls," he says. "Let's see what you got."

7:15 pm

We spend the next hour ass throwing.

Someone (Tessa) posts a pic on her Instagram and tags it #assthrowing by mistake. By the time she notices, the post has over a thousand likes and two hundred comments—most about Josh, whose backside is looking fierce and, much to his dismay, is featured rather predominantly.

But for all his negativity, Josh ends up having a blast. In fact, he is the one we have to drag away when time is up. David walks off the clear winner, but what Josh lacks in accuracy, he makes up for in strength. The target is barely recognizable in Tessa's final photo.

It's fun, but the whole ordeal takes longer than anticipated. We end up bagging our original plan in favor of The Chasseur, which is close by and apparently on Tessa's Baltimore bucket list.

Who knew she had a list?

And, more importantly, why haven't I thought of making one?

She's explaining the restaurant's name and its ties to The Lady Baltimore, when Josh gets a call asking him to cover the night shift, thus drawing our first "double date" to an early close.

He heads into work while David, Tessa, and I watch a movie and eat take out in bed. To clarify, Tessa is in what we've come to consider her and Josh's bed, and David and I are in his. An arrangement that works with Josh here but feels a bit polygamous without him.

Tessa has no qualms addressing this. She rolls onto her belly, cups her chin, and grins at us. "Would we make an adorable throuple, or what?"

David, already half asleep, pulls me close beneath the covers and yawns. "I'm too tired to throuple. But don't let that stop you two . . ."

Oh, good Lord, I can't even with him.

Tessa laughs. "I think you're missing the point of a throuple, David. But if you're talking about Kate and me . . ." Her lips press, and she regards me playfully. "We should at least kiss, don't you think? It's only fair." She begins rattling off pairings. "David and I have been together. Josh and David, you and David, you and Josh, me and Josh . . ."

Wait, what?

Beside me, David twitches. "You and Josh?"

"Oh, so you are awake." She hops out of bed with a Cheshire cat smile, grabbing a blanket and our empty take out containers. "I think I'll let him share those details," she says, winking as she backs out the door. "You two cuties enjoy some alone time. I'm going to work on the vlog."

We listen to her fading footsteps and then the downstairs television comes on.

"She's joking," I say, finally. "We would know, right? Like, literally, they're sleeping next to us. If anything was going on, we'd hear it."

I realize how ridiculous this sounds even before David starts laughing. "Because nothing happens outside the bedroom, right Sunshine?" He tugs teasingly at one of my curls.

I flip over to face him, undeterred. "Of course, how silly of me? Who would ever think of making out in, oh, I don't know . . . a shower. Or a bathroom. Or, God forbid—"

"A mall dressing room?" he supplies.

And I can't help it. A grin spreads across my face as the heat of that memory washes over me. It wasn't so long ago David and I got caught making out in a mall dressing room, and Lord have mercy, what I wouldn't do to go back.

"I can't help if you get off in public places," he jokes, pressing a kiss to the tip of my nose. But his expression quickly turns somber. "As for the shower, though. That day you walked in on Josh and me? It wasn't like that, Kate."

Ah, yes. The shower. We haven't talked about it. Which is not to say I haven't thought about it. Or David's post-surgery concern about his . . . um

. . . junk being touched, as Josh so eloquently put it. A problem I assumed they worked out, together.

In fact, I've spent a good amount of time thinking about how exactly they might have worked it out. Something I never imagined myself doing. But then, I never imagined myself feeling turned on by watching them wrestle, either.

The . . . um, physics of Josh and David's relationship is not something I try to focus on. But lately? I don't know. It doesn't bother me as much. In fact, I think part of me wants them together. Which is just weird on so many levels. But, whatever. I'm learning not to overanalyze.

And I'm not pushing for anything intimate between David and me. One, because he hasn't, and two, because, despite Josh's transparent Tessa plan, I know he wants David, and I can't bear hurting him.

Only, now? Curled against David's willing body, on the heels of watching him ass throw in those snug-fit lumberjack jeans? Hurting Josh seems less an offense. Besides, who knows? Maybe he really is into Tess.

And David?

He's suddenly very awake and very into me, and I for one, am not questioning it. He gets up and shuts the door, then returns, stretching out alongside me. He's so close our breath mingles, and I feel his heartbeat quickening against my chest. It's impossible to misread the longing in his eyes.

"Hi," he says softly, his voice a warm caress. "Remember me?"

As if I could forget?

Every moment with him is burned in my soul, like he's part of me. The best part. But I play along, an impish smile tugging at my lips. "Hmm . . ." I say, pretending. "You remind me of this boy I once knew . . ."

His eyes twinkle as he moves even closer. "Just a boy?" he whispers, lips brushing my ear.

"Maybe more." I'm already trembling with anticipation, damn him. Just one look can turn me into a puddle. But the feel of his lips against my ear? Forget about it. I'm a freaking goner.

"Maybe I should remind you." His tone is tender yet urgent as he traces a finger along my jawline, his touch sending fresh waves of pleasure down my spine.

Our lips meet in a soft, languid kiss as the world beyond our room starts to fade. It's just us, lost in the moment, rediscovering each other with every breath. His hands roam my body, exploring with a familiarity that is both comforting and electrifying.

I melt into his embrace, my hands tangling in his beautiful curls as our kiss deepens. His tongue holds a thousand broken promises, but I don't care. I forget them all at its first caress.

Friends, lovers . . . I don't know what we are anymore, and I don't want to care. I don't want to care about Josh and his feelings, or Tessa, downstairs. I want David, and he wants me, and for now, that's enough.

Foreplay gets tossed to the floor along with our clothing and all rational thought. We cling to each other, breathless and laughing as we roll in a frenzied heap of sheets, and skin, and raw, naked wanting. Screw consequence.

I'm a live wire, trembling at his every touch. Speaking of which, he's clearly worked through his post-surgery concerns, because good Lord, the things he's doing.

"Please," I beg, suddenly desperate for him. I'm wild and alive, and so in love, my skin is bursting. I love him so much, I just want to hear him say it.

"Are you sure?" he murmurs, lips languishing on my belly and the inside of my thighs, finding, at last, the place that has every part of me quaking.

I want to shout, *yes . . . yes, yes!* But I'm so past gone, all I can do is hold on for dear life while he makes utter waste of me. I want to forget myself in the sheer weight and warmth of his spectacular body, his mouth . . . his words. I want to hear him say I love you, over and over as he fills the deepest parts of me. I want this moment, right here, to be our always.

And as we do finally, blissfully come apart together?

I pretend that it is.

Afterward, we lay sleepy and sated in each other's arms, not talking. The silence between us is heavy yet calm as I nuzzle against his chest, memorizing the rise and fall of his breath, and the steady beat of his heart.

He shifts slightly, tightening his hold on me, and I bury my face in his skin, inhaling his clean, musky scent, savoring the closeness. My mind drifts to the future and the uncertainty looming over us, even as I try, desperately to hold on.

"I love you," he whispers, voice barely audible. But it's loud enough to make my heart soar, okay, *skyrocket*, to the stratosphere.

"I love you, too," I murmur, exhaling as he pulls me close, pressing a warm kiss to my forehead. It's not a platitude. I know David loves me. I know he wants us to be together. And for the moment, I let myself believe.

Because I know he wants this as much as I do. But deep down, I know that while for me, he is everything, for him? I might never be enough.

Twelve

Fully Exposed

:: When the carefully guarded
façade finally drops

David
Friday, September 29th 4:23 pm
Foster Avenue Baltimore, Maryland

The car service Nick promised does not come to pick us up for the premiere.

This is an omen or a blessing depending on how you look at it, but either way, we're thrown into a tailspin.

"Nick is fucking with us," Josh seethes, nearly splitting his pants as he hoists himself into the Jeep. It would be comical—his suit being from college and no longer fitting—if he weren't so stressed. Also, I'm pretty sure Nick wouldn't mess with something like getting us to the premiere party on time.

But I keep quiet as Kate and Tessa teeter out of the house on too-high heels and hand me their bags. Their very full, very heavy, bags. I keep quiet about those, too, because what in the world did they pack? The event only lasts a few hours, and Josh is hell bent against staying at a hotel. Seems they might have other plans.

"Ladies," I say, holding the door open while they ease into the backseat. Despite Josh's clear irritation, I pause to admire them and marvel at the unlikelihood of the four of us attending this premiere party. Together. In couples, no less.

It doesn't seem real.

But a lot of things feel that way since surgery. I get this sense, sometimes, like I'm an observer, looking in. Present, but not fully participating. Throw Tessa in the mix, and it's . . . well, it's bizarre, to say the least.

And Kate?

My sweet Sunshine. I don't deserve her, that much is clear. Why she puts up with my nonsense is perhaps the greatest marvel of all.

"You look beautiful," I whisper, leaning in to plant a soft kiss on her cheek.

"David, are you kidding me?" Josh groans. "Could you take any fucking longer?"

Josh, on the other hand? Now, him, I deserve.

"Relax," I say, climbing into the passenger seat. "We have plenty of time. Besides, Nick can hardly blame us for his car service not showing."

This earns me an eat-shit look. He'd probably swat at me if his suit weren't so tight—the fabric clings to his every move. And not in a bad way.

"You clean up nice," I say, watching him drive. He rolls his eyes, but his grip loosens on the steering wheel and some of the tension drains from his handsome face.

It returns as we enter D.C., though, and even the girls are quiet once the venue is in sight. The party is at some trendy, industrial space on 14th street, mere minutes from the White House. It would be impressive if Nick weren't such a detestable fraud of a human.

He and Vivian are outside with a crowd of executive types greeting guests. We park, collect ourselves, and approach the entrance: Josh with Tessa, and I with Kate.

The girls are stunning. Tess, always poised and confident, chose a sequined, billowy mini-dress. The low neckline and thigh skimming hemline leave little to the imagination. Her hair is wild, makeup, dark. Everything about her is meant to draw attention.

Kate, on the other hand, is purposely understated. She has on a beige, fitted calf-length gown, and her curls are locked in a severe bun. The effect is restrained and elegant and unintentionally sexual. I can't stop staring.

Neither can Nick, who notices us long before we reach him. "Katherine," he chokes, clutching the arm she quickly yanks away. "You look so grown up."

Josh steps between them, glowering as he offers Nick and then Vivian the limpest of handshakes. "Your fucking car service never showed," he says through clenched teeth. "We had to drive."

Nick shrugs before faking the appropriate look of apology. Vivian's face, meanwhile, reveals nothing. The entire exchange is uncomfortable and awkward, and the four of them couldn't appear less like family. Still, they pose for the requisite pictures together, smiles plastered.

Nick is a bit flustered by the time he speaks to me yet manages to make a vulgar comment about Tess and I looking like twins. Visions of Abigail flash through my mind just as he seems to remember I am, in fact, a twin, and objectifying my dead sister is probably in poor taste.

Not that he cares, but people are listening.

He mutters something about water under the bridge before turning to Tess, who glides past his outstretched hand without acknowledgement. She's being waved on, so it appears unintentional, but I know better. And so does Nick.

We are then ushered to a sad little red carpet where more photographs are taken. I field the same predictable questions about my father while Josh and Kate are grilled about Nick, their family, the new show, and of course, their personal lives.

But, as we'd hoped, it's Tessa who steals the show.

She dazzles in the spotlight, and the press eats it up. The three of us gladly back into the shadows as she entertains questions about her relationship with Josh, Kate and me, and the now infamous #assthrowing date photo, which went viral days ago and is still gaining momentum.

"She's amazing," Kate whispers.

"I might be in love," Josh says rather worshipfully.

He's joking, but I wonder if there's any truth in his words. I have yet to ask him about what Tess alluded to the other night. Probably because of my own guilt and the fact that I don't want to know. Despite encouraging their relationship, the possibility of Josh actually falling for her is not something I fully considered.

I mean, it would be good, right? That's what he wanted. What we wanted. Kate and I haven't put a label on anything, but after the other night? It's obvious where we're heading.

The crowd grows as Tessa talks, and Kate edges closer, fingers lacing with mine. I can't deny it would make things simpler for us if Tess and Josh got together. If they fell in love.

I should want that.

Kate's hand trembles, and my heart aches to take her away from all of this. To hold her every night as I have this week and give her the love she needs. The love she deserves. I want that, too.

But as we file separately into the venue, Josh catches up with me. It's crowded and loud, and I know he's hating every second. He stands close as we wait behind the girls. So close his breath heats my neck, and his tension becomes part of me.

I'm overwhelmed by the need to touch him, to be with him, to make him feel all right. So much, that I risk a pause, allowing my back to press against his chest, despite the crowd. A momentary connection, but it's enough.

And it's then I realize what I've always known. That no matter what transpires between him and Tess, no matter how much I love Kate or desire a life with her, part of me will always want him more.

And what the hell do I do with that?

7:02 pm

The first hour passes at a snail's pace.

It's excruciating. We mingle with as few people as possible while Nick and his pompous sycophants parade around, celebrating.

"It's not like they found a cure for cancer," Kate gripes. "It's just a stupid television show."

Tessa sets down her empty glass and gives Kate a hug. "Come to the bar," she urges. "Let's get another one of those fun, themed drinks."

Fun is a stretch, but theme is spot on. The network spared no expense this evening. There's even a specialty beverage menu. Predator Punch, Justice Jigger, and Catch and Cointreau, to name a few. They're cringy and awful, and entirely Nick.

The girls leave and I turn to find Josh, several feet away, engaged in conversation with an older woman who looks like Vivian's sister. He casts me a pleading look, and I'm about to rescue him when a member of the security team brushes past.

He grabs my hand, quickly pressing something to my palm before hurrying off. It happens so fast I think I imagine it. But when I uncurl my fingers, there's a tiny piece of crumpled paper.

Meet me in the bathroom, it says. *Come alone.* The note is signed Gillie.

Gillie?

I swing around, but the man is gone.

Gillie . . . why do I know that name? I search my memory, then remember Josh who seems to have untangled himself from the woman. He's heading toward the bar.

Gillie . . . Gillie . . .

It's a dog's name, I think. Carol's dog? Yes! I'm sure of it. But that note couldn't be from Carol, could it? He wouldn't come here. I'm pretty sure he'd rather murder Nick than attend a party honoring him. And why reach out to me? Why use a code name?

I think of the photos and how he stalked us for months, the way he threatened Nick, and the secrets he carried. And Angela's dug up grave.

Yeah, I could see him using a code name. But why now? Why here?

A dull ringing builds in my ears as I stand, debating. Should I go? Tell Josh? Flee? I glance at the exit, then toward the bathroom. If it's Carol, I have to know why he's here. What he wants.

And if it's not Carol?

I don't even want to consider that. I don't consider that, or anything, as I make my way to the men's room. I pace back and forth waiting, breathing deep to keep my heart from racing. I'm about to explore each stall when I hear a lock click into place and the lights cut out.

"I'm sorry, David. I couldn't think of another way to do this."

Carol's voice is close and quiet and holds no threat. Despite the bizarre circumstance, I feel some measure of relief. I don't trust my uncle, but I don't believe he'd harm me, either. At least, not physically.

I have so many questions. "What are you doing, here? Does Nick know?"

He steps forward, and I can barely make out his silhouette. "I doubt Nick remembers I exist," he says, moving closer. "But he's going to know me after tonight."

There's something maniacal in his tone, and I'm reminded of his erratic behavior the day we met at the beach, and in his truck with Josh. How quickly his mood can shift.

"Why—" I begin, but a hand clamps over my mouth. Footsteps pass in front of the door and the handle rattles.

"It's locked," a male voice says, and the footsteps fade.

"We don't have time for questions," Carol whispers. "You just need to listen."

I nod as he withdraws his hand.

"I'll answer the obvious because I know you're wondering. Yes. I dug up Angela's body. She was there, just as your mother said. I burned her remains, and all the other evidence. I'm sorry,

David. I couldn't let Elena's memory be tainted like that." He pauses, breath quickening. "I've made so many mistakes. Not insisting your mom leave Ian, involving you kids, betraying her memory. I should've just kept away."

He grips my shoulders then, turning me so we're face to face. I can barely make out his eyes. My eyes. "But none of that matters now, do you understand? I finally have a chance to set things right." His fingers dig into my skin. "Do you hear what I'm saying? I'm going to get back at Nick and destroy him. And it's all going down tonight."

I swallow as the room begins to spin, every fear from the last two decades morphing into reality. "Tonight? Here?" This can't be happening. He's going to expose everything. The photos of Josh, Kate and me. Ian's voicemail. The fire. My knees begin to buckle, and I pull away from him, stumbling.

I've got to warn them. We have to get out of here.

Carol moves quickly. He blocks the door. "I know what you're thinking, and it's not that. What I have planned for Nick has nothing to do with you, or Josh and Kate. I promise. I know my word means nothing, but I wouldn't betray you kids like that. Your secrets are safe with me."

"Then how . . .?"

I don't even know what questions to ask, and it doesn't matter because Carol's leaving. He's reaching for the handle. "I can't tell you what or how because I need your reaction to be genuine. They'll review the security footage from tonight. I want Nick to know you kids weren't involved. But it's going to happen soon, so you need to go back out there and act normal."

Normal? Is he kidding me?

"Carol . . ." I plead, but he cuts me off.

"I'm sorry it's all gone down like this. That I didn't do more to protect you and Abigail and your mother back then, or Josh and Kate. What I'm about to do will rip their family apart, but it's not much of a family to begin with, is it. And they have you."

The light snaps on, temporarily blinding me. "Last thing," he says, opening the door. "We won't see each other again, David. I don't know what the fallout will look like from all this, but if things go south? If I end up in custody or they find me some-where? I want you to know there's a package for the three of you. In the same place your parents buried Angela. Inside a hollow rock, a few hundred paces north. Go alone once the dust settles. And, David? Be careful."

And before I can gather a thought, before another question has the chance to form, he's gone.

7:53 pm

If the first hour of the party is excruciating, the second hour is unbearable.

I'm on pins and needles all through the hors d'oeuvres service, hyper aware and wholly exhausted from making a show of normalcy. So much, I can hardly choke down the Fugitive Fritter someone hands me. Yes, even the appetizers have ridiculous names. I could laugh if I didn't think I might throw up.

It's Tessa who finally pulls me aside. "Are you all right?" she asks. "You look pale."

I want to ask what else she's noticed, but all I say is, "I just want the night to end."

This, at least, is true. It feels like an eternity since Carol's warning, and I'm beginning to wonder if he's full of crap. Even more so once dinner is over and Nick mounts the gaudy, makeshift stage. A large screen behind him flashes to life as he bows magnanimously.

"Welcome. Thank you all for coming out tonight." Beside me, Josh flinches and Kate reaches for my hand. "It's humbling to see the support our little show has attracted." Nick continues. Tessa leans into Josh and makes a gagging sound. "I say little, but we're doing big things. Important things, like tracking down predators, getting them off your children's screens, and into rehabilitation and correction centers where they'll get the help they need."

This is met with thunderous applause and cheering as Nick invites Vivian, his manager, the show's producer, and some network executives to join him. They engage in a few minutes of self-important musings about the show and its origins. And all the while my anxiety builds.

Carol claimed his plan was going down soon, but it's been well over an hour now. I scan the room looking for him, or anything out of the ordinary. But all I see are swarms of entertainment's elite. Every expression looks plastered. Fake. Does anyone even care about this show. And what's ordinary? What can Carol possibly have planned?

"It's starting," Kate whispers, clutching me tighter. Beneath the table Josh's leg begins to shake. The moment they've been hyping all night—a sneak peek at season one along with clips from the first episode.

The lights dim, and Nick and company take their seats. The intro begins with images set to a catchy, yet ominous, orchestral piece. Nick's talking head appears in the bottom corner, explaining the show's background and format.

After a few minutes I find myself relaxing. Kate's hand loosens. The presentation is pretty vanilla—basically a repackaged *Brought to Light*. Nothing unexpected. It's almost boring.

Did I dream the encounter with Carol?

I'm beginning to question my sanity, when the screen abruptly darkens, and static floods the air. There's a moment of blackness before a grainy image appears.

Horrified gasps ripple through the crowd, wave-like, and Josh's leg stops moving. He leans forward, mouth dropping. "What the fuck . . .?"

On the screen, larger than life, is none other than an image of Nick, bare-chested and bent over what appears to be a young girl. It's hard to tell because her face has been blurred, but her arms are bound behind her and he's pulling at her hair. While their midsections aren't visible, it's clear what he's doing. It's also clear she is not a willing participant. The image is disgusting, and degrading, and I have to blink several times to believe what I'm seeing.

"David!" Kate's fingers dig into my arm. "Oh, my God! What is this?"

The screen dissolves into a series of stills and clips. At the bottom in block lettering is the title, NICHOLAS JANNEY: FULLY EXPOSED. A voice, which I recognize as Carol's, begins to narrate.

"Who is Nicholas Janney?" he asks, as image upon graphic image layer to create a mosaic of depravity. Murmurs of shock and dismay grow louder as, across the venue, guests begin to stand. A woman at our table covers her face.

"Is he a faithful family man or a lying, cheating, predator?" The collage fades and we're treated to a split screen—Nick and Vivian hugging at some fundraiser beside grotesque footage of him assaulting yet another young woman, her face also blurred.

"Or is Nicholas Janney worse than the pedophiles he wants to rehabilitate?" The next clip is atrocious. Kate covers her face as horrified gasps echo across the room. Josh braces the table with both hands, pale as a ghost.

This is what Carol planned? This is . . . there are no words for this. It's appalling.

I glance around at the evolving scene. Technicians rush the stage while dozens of guests with phones in hand record every damning second. The noise level reaches a fever pitch before the entire room goes dark. Emergency lights flicker on, indicating a power loss, and a mass exodus begins.

But we are not in it.

We sit in frozen silence, too stunned to move. At least I don't have to worry how my reaction appears—I'm too shocked to move, let alone speak. If this is Carol's plan, it's beyond anything I could've fathomed.

But how did Carol know? How did he get all those photographs and videos? *Does it matter as long as Nick goes down*, prompts the little voice in my head. It shouldn't.

But it does.

All those women, no . . . girls, in some cases, were obviously not there by choice. And Carol knew? He just watched and recorded and did nothing? That makes him just as bad, doesn't it? I feel sick. I don't know how to respond to any of this. And from their glassy-eyed stares, neither do Josh and Kate.

Thankfully, Tessa keeps her head. The power switches on, and she's standing, beckoning us toward the door. The room, half empty now, is in disarray, Nick and company having exited during the blackout, but the media contingent is swarming.

"We need to go. Now!" Tessa's voice cuts through the shock and fog. We're on our feet in seconds, following her into the chilly night as reporters shout questions at our backs. The girls ditch their heels and we run, none of us speaking until we're safely in the Jeep and blocks away. Josh exhales audibly, but it's me who breaks the silence.

"You guys are not going to believe the story I have to tell."

Thirteen

Damage Control

:: The daunting task of reputation management

Josh
Saturday, September 30th 3:41 pm
Foster Avenue, Baltimore, Maryland

The fallout from Nick's *Exposed* premiere party is swift and epic.

Within minutes of Carol's Fully Exposed video hijacking, clips are posted online, local entertainment outlets begin reporting, and the story makes national news. By Saturday morning, the network has issued a statement, Nick has lawyered up, and the premiere of *Exposed* is delayed indefinitely, pending investigation.

By afternoon we, too, are in the thick of it. Hailstorms of messages, reporters at the door, news agencies casing our street. It's a shit show.

"We can't leave the house," I mutter, peering through a slit in the blinds at yet another nondescript van parked a few doors down.

Who do they think they're kidding?

Kate's phone chimes for the millionth time. Our phones have been blowing up with friends and acquaintances crawling out of the woodwork. Nothing says reach out to me like a scandal, right? And it's not even our scandal.

Meanwhile, most of our current friends and co-workers had no idea Kate and I were siblings, let alone twins. Because we're not. But, whatever. That little deception has been blown wide open along with everything else. Just one more fun fact we've had to address.

Whatever the fuck.

"It's just Mia," Kate exclaims, after reading the message. "She wants me to know I can take as much time off as I need."

"Aww, she's so sweet." Tess joins Kate on the couch. "It must be nice working for a friend."

A friend? I turn from the window, about to spew some venom because I can't stand Mia. She's a bad influence. Not only did Kate quit college because of her, but she left a well-paying job at Hopkins to help with the mobile massage nonsense. Mia doesn't know the first thing about running a business, and she's dragging Kate down with her.

David appears in the doorway, though, beckoning me. Distracting me is more like it, but I let him. We listen from the kitchen as Kate's phone chimes, yet again.

"My friend Hadley, from high school," she tells Tess.

Hadley moved out west for work this summer. We haven't heard much from her since our spring trip to Isabelle's wedding in the Outer Banks. Kate immediately launches into tales from that fateful weekend, and I can only hope she focuses on our run in with Carol rather than my drunken antics. But whatever. I don't care what Tessa thinks.

At least, I don't want to care.

I don't want to care about anything, especially this mess with my father. What a piece of shit. And Carol Brennan is the mastermind behind his undoing? Really? The man has balls the size of Texas, I'll give him that, but he's clearly off his rocker.

Let's ignore the stalking-us-for-months, photo-threatening, grave-digging drama. The fact he collected all that evidence on Nick, infiltrated the premiere party, and fucked with the video feed? Who does that? And all in the name of revenge. I mean, I thought *I* had anger issues. His shit is like, next level.

And he's David's uncle.

David, who doesn't have a revengeful bone in his body, who's never been anything but gentle and kind. David, who almost broke down while telling us about Carol and what he did. So devastated was he for those girls, twice victimized, he could hardly get the words out.

And this is just the beginning. Carol blurred their faces, but identities are bound to come out, assuming the girls were of legal age. Either way, they'll be hunted, hounded, and forever linked to Nick and that disgusting video. Don't get me wrong, I want my father to pay, but not at these women's expense . . .

"What?" David says after a minute. "Why are you staring at me?"

Am I?

I feel a dizzying rush of affection for him. For the boy he was, and the man I know him to be. For the way he loves me, despite my flaws. "I'm just glad you're not like your uncle, is all. There are some seriously fucked up men in our families."

And without him? I might have followed the same destructive path as my father.

He sets down his coffee, seeing through me as usual. "You're nothing like Nick, Josh. You know that, right?"

My deepest fear, and I love him for saying it—even if it's not always true. "Let's hope it skips a generation." I joke, but we're not laughing.

He walks to where I stand with my back against the newly painted wall. It's cloud blue now and bears no resemblance to the beige patched-over mess I put my fist through not so many months ago when this was another kitchen. Another life.

I'm about to say as much when I realize he isn't wearing anything to cover his head. For the first time in months, I'm looking at all of him, and . . . shit.

I don't know when it happened but, quite suddenly he looks like himself again. The scar is there, obviously, but less visible now that hair is growing. He's gained some weight, too, and he's been working out. He looks good. Healthy, even, despite the setbacks and drama.

He looks like . . . David.

And this, the sight of him, this semblance of normalcy? This is what breaks me. The tentative hold I've kept on my emotions since last night crumbles, and tears begin to form. I turn away just as Kate interrupts with a shout.

"Josh! You're never going to believe this. Claire just sent me a text."

Of course, she did.

I wipe my eyes, careful to avoid David's gaze. "Better you than me," I manage, cringing as we hear Tessa pose the inevitable "Who's Claire?" question. Moments later, she appears, arms crossed.

"You were engaged, Josh? I thought you're against marriage."

Oh, for God's sake.

"Yeah, I am." I hold up my left hand. "Do you see a fucking ring?" This comes out far more cutting than intended, but I'm barely in control of myself. She stiffens just as Kate stalks in.

"Be nice," she chides, stopping short when she sees my face. Her expression immediately falters.

"Oh, no. Joshie, don't . . ."

I want to tell her I'm fine, but she throws herself at me. I'm wrapped up in a sea of curls and the kind of crushing hug only a sister can give. It's messy and much needed, and I'm not even ashamed when David and Tessa tiptoe out, leaving us alone.

It feels good to hold Kate. To cry with her. Sometimes I forget that it's she, and not David, who's been beside me all along. That it's Kate, and only Kate, who suffered the same childhood as me. Kate, who's always loved me, been there for me, never let me down . . .

"Do you feel any better?" she asks, once I've composed myself. She hands me a glass of water, and I catch a glimpse of my red-eyed reflection.

I hate crying.

But I do feel better. She follows me over to the rustic farm table she insisted on buying. It's a little large for the space, but I have to admit, it's cozy. And a great place to kick back and mope.

She sighs, fingering the yellow checked placemat someone left out. "You know, I thought I'd feel happier, seeing Nick humiliated. Like, I've fantasized about that. But I just feel sick. Those poor girls, Josh. He's such a pig." Her eyes fill with tears. "I mean, I'm not surprised given, you know, what he put you and David through, I just . . ." Her phone chimes, interrupting the thought.

"Same shit, different decade," I mutter, praying the subject drops.

Nick made a career out of sexual exploitation, is it any surprise his private life is infested with it? Especially considering he's never paid for his crimes. Why should this be any different? "He'll weasel his way out," I tell Kate. "If not, he'll go down swinging and drag us with him. You mark my words."

He might not even have to drag us. With all the recent publicity and our pictures splashed everywhere, it wouldn't take much for someone to recognize David or me. Embarrassment and fear have kept most of the men our fathers exploited from talking. But now, with Nick's fetishes on film for all to see, what's stopping them?

Kate looks skeptical. "Yes, but we have the upper hand for once. We may not have a body, but we have the recording from that night at David's house. And we have truth on our side. Who's going to believe him after all of this?"

I frown as she holds up her phone. "Enough about that, okay? Let's forget Nick for now. This will make you happy." She shows me the screen. "Anna just texted to say she and Rosa are bringing us dinner from the café."

At the mention of food, my stomach spontaneously rumbles, but for once, Kate's eyes don't roll. She leans across the table and hugs me instead. "We'll get through this," she says, pulling back with a resigned smile. "And if not, there's always Portland."

Friday, October 6th 5:14 pm

The media circus continues for days.

We keep a low profile and avoid life in general while Nick's sex-capades dominate the headlines. In a twist of irony, it's Angela who finally replaces him. Not my mother, Angela, you know, the woman he murdered? That would be too poetic.

No, it's hurricane Angela and her treacherous path along the east coast that ultimately shifts the focus. Apparently gossip reporters don't like flooded streets and gale force winds. By midweek, they've scurried off like ants at a picnic and we're water-logged, but blessedly alone.

Until Friday, when Nick shows up, unannounced, and on a rampage. It's just David and me. Kate's over at Anna's and Tess is working late. We're heading to the park during an interruption in the rain, when a blacked-out escalade rolls up. The back window comes down, and there he is—ball cap, sunglasses, and a sweatshirt tucked around his face.

"Get in," he commands.

My immediate reaction is a resounding, *hell no*, but the words don't form and seconds later we're crowded on the seat beside him, zipping off. A clear mistake, but I'm so accustomed to taking orders from this man, it barely registers we could have said no. Besides, it was only a matter of time before he showed up. We knew this. Nick wouldn't risk an open phone line, and there's too much damage to control.

As it is, we've been in constant contact with his personal attorney and the network's legal team. But we don't need advice—we want no part of this shit show. "No comment" has become our new favorite phrase. Even Tessa has gone radio silent on our behalf. Only the ass-throwing post remains.

But I'm guessing that's not what this little meeting is about. Nick glares at David and me. "Don't say anything until we park."

I almost say "No comment" just to fuck with him, but something tells me to keep quiet. In fact, I'm feeling downright magnanimous, looking at this pathetic shell of a man. A little apprehensive? Absolutely. But panicked and nervous as fuck? Nope.

Not yet, anyway.

We drive for several minutes, veering off O'Donnell Street just before the freeway. The car finally stops in an abandoned lot adjacent to a row of burned-out buildings. We're only a few miles from home, but it feels like another city all together. And suddenly I'm not feeling so composed.

The rain picks up and the driver exits. He huddles under the remains of an awning and lights a cigarette. The engine's still running, though, a sign this "meeting" won't last long. I brace for a list of dos and don'ts, followed by Nick's usual threats.

What I do not expect is a guilty admission. He already denied everything in a public statement through his attorney. A targeted attack, he called it. A misunderstanding, doctored photographs, consensual play . . . he's deeply sorry for disappointing his fans but promises to get to the bottom of this character assault, blah, blah, blah. Same old Nick— the man is a professional liar.

So, imagine our surprise when he immediately addresses David. "Tell me everything you know about Carol Brennan." I full body flinch, but David? The fucker doesn't move.

"Who?" he asks, innocent as all hell.

Is it any wonder I love him?

Nick's nostrils flare. "Don't fuck with me, David. I'm not in the mood. Carol Brennan. The man is your uncle, and you only have one. So, spill it."

David shrugs. "If you're talking about my mother's brother, Ian told me he died."

"Oh, he did, did he?" Nick pulls out an iPad with a video, already queued. And my altruism flies out the window. Panic sets in as I break into a cold sweat.

We are so fucked. He knows David met Carol! He thinks we're in on the Fully Exposed video. He's going to murder us right here in this parking lot!

I'm about to grab David and bust open the door when Nick presses play, and another story quickly evolves. We watch the distant figure of a maintenance man enter the 14th street D.C. venue that housed the premiere party. A few frames later he's on video, walking through the main event area where decorations for the night are still being strung.

Next, this same man is captured standing by the audio-visual equipment. He clearly messes with it, then looks directly at the security camera and winks. He fucking *winks*.

Nick zooms in on the man's face, and it's Carol, obviously. Even grainy and underlit, he's a mirror image of David. You know, if David were sixty-five and grossly haggard. But the resemblance is there.

"Carol fucking Brennan. Very much alive and well." Nick chucks the iPad on the floor, eyes dark as steel. "Now, I'm only going to ask once. Did either of you have anything to do with this?"

There's a breath of silence. An awful, guilty-as-hell moment that sends my heart into free fall, and I'm not sure I can swallow, let alone speak.

David, though? He holds it together. Instead of responding, he picks up the iPad, then looks at Nick. "If you knew I had an uncle all this time, why didn't you tell me? Why did Ian lie?" He presses play again, bringing Carol's face to the screen. "And how do you know this man is him?"

"How do I know?" Nick's fists clench and he purples with rage. "You little piece of . . ." Without warning, he explodes, lunging for David who still holds the iPad.

He uses it to shield his face as Nick's angry blows land on his chest and stomach. Backed against the door, David folds to protect himself, and I see nothing but red.

I don't know what comes out of my mouth, or how I get there, but not a millisecond passes before I have Nick pinned to the floorboard. He barely puts up a fight as I pummel his face, the fucking coward.

David pulls me off before any real damage is done. "Not worth it," he rasps, clutching his stomach. "Don't sink to his level, Josh."

Nick scrambles to his knees, wiping the blood trickling from his mouth and nose. One eye begins to swell, but it doesn't keep him from smirking.

Oh, it is so on.

I move at him again, but David stops me. And if looks could kill.

"Enough!" He maneuvers himself between us, making sure Nick and I back down before he begins speaking. "You know we had nothing to do with that video, or my uncle, if that's who he is. So, cut the bullshit and tell us why you're really here."

I'm literally vibrating. I want to smash my father's stupid face in for what he just did, and for being such a low life dumpster fire of a human. But David's right—he's not worth it. So, I relent, bracing for another onslaught of his wrath.

It doesn't come, though. He seems to accept David's reasoning before slinking back to his seat, mollified. David and I sit back too, and the three of us regard one another with a wariness born from years of mistrust.

And after an excruciating silence, Nick finally begins to talk.

5:54 pm

We listen to him rewrite history for five solid minutes.

Predictably, he casts himself as the victim and Carol as the vendetta seeking villain, which is not so far from the truth. Just not the whole truth.

He lays out an intricate web of scheming and deceit, years in the making. We hear of Carol's decades-long hatred, stemming from Nick's brief relationship with Elena when they were young. He goes on about mental illness, and how Carol had it in for him after he broke Elena's heart and married Vivian.

A lie. Elena is the one who ended things. Everyone knows she dumped his ass for Ian back in the day, but whatever. There's no point arguing. Nick claims he, too, was told Carol died years ago. Thus, it never crossed his mind Carol was the one stalking us and sending photographs back in the spring.

"It makes sense, though. Of course, Elena lied. She must have stayed in touch with Carol all along." He shakes his head, then turns to David. "Your mother was a fucking head case after you and Abigail were born. God only knows what crazy shit she told him."

Right.

Crazy shit.

Like how Nick was a cheating murderer. How she and Ian covered his crime, burdening themselves with a multitude of sins. Oh, wait. That's not crazy at all—that's what actually happened.

Every fiber of my being wants to call him out, but I'd be a fool to give away our hand. Especially when it seems Nick legitimately has no idea that we, one, are already acquainted with Carol, two, are privy to and unwilling participants in his vicious scheming, and three, know he has far more than degenerative sex videos as a means of taking Nick down.

Carol is the fucking man.

I love Carol.

I mean, I hate him, but like, I fucking love him. And I love how he's under Nick's skin, because I've rarely seen my father so fired up.

We endure several more minutes of his threats and ranting before our "meeting" ends and we're dropped back at home. The girls are still out, so David and I wander the kitchen, aimless. We pick at some leftover pizza and stare at each other, wordlessly chewing.

"So," he says, finally. "That was something."

"That was something all right." I swallow. "Nick's not going to take this shit lying down, you know. Carol better watch his back."

If my father made one thing clear, it's that he's out for blood. His team is going full ham. No matter, Carol has all but disappeared. The plan is to discredit him and his "highly edited," character assassination, i.e., the Fully Exposed video.

They already filed charges for burglary, vandalism, and crimimal tresspass, to name a few. And Nick expects our full cooperation. He threatened every evil in the book, should we even consider speaking against him. And in turn? He promised not to expose us. Expose us?

That's rich from someone no doubt facing a landslide of battery and assault charges. Not to mention he'll be implicating himself and lose any form of leverage if he does. No, I'm not too worried about Nick telling tales anymore, but I am worried about Carol.

David reaches for some water, swaying briefly on his feet, and I have to fight off an anxious shiver. He's fine. Just a bit shaken—we both are.

He retreats to the living room, and I follow, flopping onto the sofa beside him. The new sofa that's not nearly as comfortable as our old one. It's too deep, and the fabric is itchy, but I'm too tired to care at this point.

"I think Nick's the one who should watch his back," he says, yawning. "Something tells me Carol won't stop. Not if he showed his face. That was no accident—he knows what he's doing."

It's a good point. Carol hid for so long, why reveal himself now? Why risk inciting Nick's fury, unless he has something else planned. But what? And where is he? Still watching us, maybe? Watching Nick? He's like a loose cannon.

Fuck, my brain hurts. I switch on the television. "I'm too tired to think anymore. Let's put on a movie or something."

He nods, already drifting, curling comfortably into the fetal position right here on the couch. I stretch alongside him, grabbing a throw blanket to cover us, aware, suddenly, that even breathing seems a chore. I'm exhausted.

We shouldn't fall asleep here, not like this. But I'm done. I can't think or feel another thing. With the last of my energy, I lean into him, closing the distance until my face rests in the curve of his neck, finding solace in his warm, welcoming skin.

His breathing slows, and the noises around us fade. The house darkens, and I vaguely notice the

girls returning, their hushed whispers and flickering lights. But we don't speak, and we don't
move. And for a few blissful hours, I forget everything, and everyone, and everywhere but here.

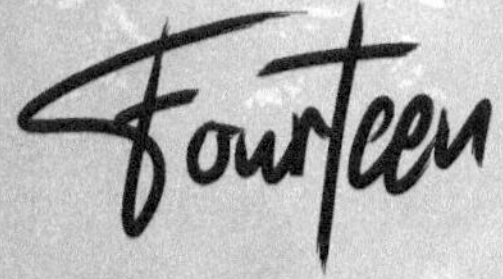

Aftershock Shindig

:: A friendly gathering in the
wake of personal upheaval

Kate
Thursday, October 19th 2: 12 pm
Harris Teeter Boston Street
Baltimore, Maryland

The premiere party is kind of like an earthquake.

The event itself is shocking, yet brief. Only, it doesn't end. Little tremors keep coming. Aftershocks, if you will. And just when things are back in order?

Another tremor.

Another scathing article. Another accusation against Nick. Another siege of photographs, old stories, new details, you name it. For weeks, I feel as if I'm walking around, exposed. Pun fully intended.

"I feel naked," I tell Tessa.

She looks up from her phone, frowning. "Did you forget to wear a bra?"

As if.

I don't even need a bra. A foreign concept for Miss Brazilian double D's. I tug at my shirt, nonetheless, laughing. "Yes, but that is definitely not it. I just . . . oh, never mind. Let's finish up and get out of here."

We're at the grocery store, and I'm feeling . . . itchy. No fewer than three people have stared me down. One took my picture, then scurried off, which Tessa must not have noticed. Not that she'd be bothered. She enjoys the spotlight.

David, Josh, and I? Not so much.

A fact that makes this shopping trip a bit . . . off brand. Why? Because we're shopping for a party. That's right. In the middle of Nick's scandal and with our lives on full display?

We are having a party. An aftershock shindig, if you will.

At our house.

Tonight.

"How many people are coming, again?" Tessa asks as we shuffle down the next isle.

I toss a brownie box mix into the cart, then another. "I've lost count."

This isn't an exaggeration—I have no idea how many people might show. Between Anna's roommates and their friends, our co-workers, and an eclectic group of random acquaintances—we could have a full house.

And the idea wasn't even ours.

Zach, Anna's so-called boyfriend and self-claimed contractor extraordinaire, suggested we hold this little soiree. I'm not a fan of the guy, but his crew did a nice job. Last week, after my room was finally put back together, he not-so-subtly planted the party seed.

I guess Josh agreed to host some type of event at the house once repairs were done—a goodwill promo kind of thing—so he couldn't say no. The timing sucks, though. What, with the freaking world breathing down our backs and all.

But, whatever. It's fine. I can make small talk over a charcuterie board if Josh can. My phone vibrates with a text and, surprise, surprise—it's him.

Josh: MORE CHIPS

I slow the cart. "Josh is adding to the list again," I tell Tessa. "Now he wants—"

Another vibration.

Josh: CHICKEN FINGERS

Chicken Fingers?

Josh: COOKIES

I roll my eyes at the ceiling.

Me: This is not a toddler party, Joshie.

Josh: 👆

Josh: BEEF JERKY

I pocket my phone as it vibrates yet again. And again. And then Tessa's chimes. "He says not to let you leave the store without cookies." Another series of messages roll in, and she laughs so hard she stops walking. Ugh. These two.

I'll be the first to admit Tessa's presence has been a welcome relief, especially for Josh. I know he invited her out of some misguided determination to push David and me together, but they really do get on well.

And is it any surprise? She's basically David, but like, chattier, and with extraordinary boobs. Not sure if that's a pro or con for Josh, to be honest. Despite Tessa's claim, I haven't observed anything overtly . . . physical between them.

Which isn't saying much. History has proven I'm oblivious to all things sexual happening right beneath my nose, but whatever. I've gone off track here . . . what was I thinking?

Oh right, Tessa!

In all seriousness, she's amazing. We love her. She is the therapy and comic relief we needed and has single-handedly kept us from breaking down. Also, thanks to me, she knows our darkest secrets. This fact alone should produce some level of anxiety, but it doesn't.

It's almost as if she's known all along, which is just . . . bizarre. But then, what isn't these days? And speaking of bizarre . . .

After Nick's Gestapo-like back-alley meeting with the boys—thank God I wasn't there—his PR machine shifted into full propaganda mode. Nick's innocence was all but declared, pics of our "wholesome" family started cropping up everywhere, and Carol, who is still missing by the way, was fully demonized. Little is known of Carol, which only helps Nick's cause. He's an enigma, according to the news.

Seems he changed his name a number of times, lived off the grid . . . I'm not sure how the man made money. Or where he would go now. Certainly not back to North Carolina. And he wouldn't stick around here, but I can't shake the feeling he's watching. Seems everyone is watching us.

But hey, a party should make that better, right?

"Come on." I tug Tessa toward the cured meat section. "The charcuterie board won't make itself."

6: 57 pm

Josh is still grumbling two hours after our return from the store.

"How do you forget chips?" he mutters, picking through the food Tessa and I put out. "Oatmeal raisin, Kate?" He shakes his head. "Why couldn't you buy normal cookies?"

David saunters in all freshly showered and looking like a snack. "Those are normal cookies," I say, winking at him. "They aren't as sweet as chocolate chips. I thought David might like them."

"Please. Your boy's never eaten a cookie in his life." Josh swats David's hand as he jokingly reaches for one. This is true, and possibly the only annoying thing about David—his distaste for sweets.

The doorbell rings then, and all eyes swivel from cookie platter to foyer.

Tessa's hand flies to her mouth. "It can't be time, yet! We're not ready."

But it is.

Moments later our living room is full of chatter. The Brewer's Hill crew, aka my summer roomies, are first to arrive. It's only been two months, but it seems like decades since we lived together.

Demetri's boisterous laughter echoes off the walls as he and Rosa exclaim over little intricacies like molding and trim. Josh literally beams. He's such a nerd for that stuff—he picked most of it out, even on this second go round.

"Zach's running late," Anna explains, hobbling over, her injured foot still in a walking boot from her fall at the café. She pulls me aside while Josh invites the others into the kitchen. "Jason and Brighton are stopping by, too. And Zach is super pissed." She lowers her voice. "It's a mess, Kate. I can't even begin to tell you."

So, I'm out of the loop, for obvious reasons. It's been weeks since I've caught up with Anna, but I did see her briefly last Friday at football. Yes, that's right. Josh and I got roped into playing flag football this season. It's not like we have anything else going on, right?

Friday nights in Patterson Park. It's fun, said literally no one. I mean, it's not awful. Whatever. There's beer, so that's something.

Anyway, Anna came to watch last Friday, and she brought her new coworkers, Jason and Brighton. Jason, she met while working at Joe Mama's, oddly enough. She's now working as an accountant for Zach's dad's company, and, in a bizarre twist of fate, so is Jason. They are totally into each other, by the way.

Not that they or anyone else acknowledges this because, you know, Zach.

Meanwhile, Jason and Brighton are not only coworkers, but roommates, too. They've been taking Anna back and forth to work, which is driving Zach crazy? I don't know. I can't keep up with my own drama, let alone hers.

"You need a glass of wine," is all I manage.

"More like a wine IV," she moans, and we limp our way towards the kitchen just as the doorbell chimes again.

David answers, and I hear his buddy Blake, followed by a few guys from Josh's station. Someone puts on music, and I float through our newly renovated rooms with sauvignon blanc and a forced smile. No mention is made of the Nick situation, but curiosity circles like a shark in blood infested waters.

It's only a matter of time.

We haven't offered much, and our friends are no doubt dying for details. But I, for one, am keeping quiet. I learned a lesson after the Chad West adventure—Kate plus intoxicants equals incoherent, babbling disaster.

So tonight? There's nothing but sugar in my brownies, and I'm limiting myself to two glasses of wine. I should be golden. Or, you know, at least bronze.

We're a half hour into the party when I find Tessa in the boy's room with Demetri. They're talking about her new job, and my heart sinks a little. Tessa's stay was always meant to be temporary and I'm happy for her, but I don't want to think about her leaving. It's all happening so fast.

I listen with mixed emotion as she explains how the offer finally came through a few weeks ago. A dream job—assistant events coordinator for one of the largest cruise ships in the world. Her contract starts the week of Thanksgiving.

"I am going to miss living here, though," she says softly. Her slender arms wrap around my shoulders, and she hugs me tight. "It's been a wild ride, hasn't it, Kate?"

You can say that again.

I nod, leaning into her warm embrace as Demitri looks on with interest. He wants to ask about the specifics of Nick and our wild ride in the worst way. But he doesn't. He congratulates her and makes some comment about the boy's built-in bookshelf thing instead.

"It's so spacious in here," he muses, running a hand along the bed. That would be bed, singular. There's only one, now.

With all the debris and destruction from the ceiling collapse, my furniture had to be pitched. Once the repairs were finished, the real debate began—buy me and Tessa new beds and return to my room as originally planned, or simply move one of the beds from the boy's room. There's really no need for four massive beds upstairs, so we went with the two-bed option.

It's raising some eyebrows, though. And not just among our guests.

We agonized over the decision. Like, literally, it's taken a week. We just moved the bed this morning. David's bed. So, now it's technically our room, mine and his. And the boy's room? That's now Josh and Tessa's. Will this arrangement work long term, as in, when Tessa leaves?

Not a chance.

Will it work tonight?

Doubtful.

But I, for one, am down with trying.

8: 11 pm

What I am not down with is a semi-drunk Zach, who arrives an hour late.

He then has the audacity to mock my charcuterie board.

"Sweet spread, Sunshine," he snarks, tossing back half the rolled prosciutto in one bite. "So, what do you think of your room?"

Ugh. I hate when he calls me Sunshine.

Let's ignore how he requested this little shindig and didn't have the decency to drive poor Anna, who's been stuck in a walking boot for over a month now. Not that she wanted to come with him, but it's the principal, you know? And then, to show up drunk?

No class.

He's cheerful, at least. I'll give him that. But it's the obnoxiously loud, snide kind of cheerful that sets everyone on edge. I don't respond about my room, and after downing a pound of salami, Zach moves on to David, greeting him with a thunderous voice and a leering stare that lasts far too long.

Josh intervenes, offering a hand. "Thanks for coming. Everyone loves what you and the guys did with our place. Come on in the kitchen, you want a beer?" He is all false smiles and forced diplomacy. Josh, like the rest of us, is fully done with Zach.

He's done with this party, too, poor guy.

"Go eat your cookies," I whisper as the two lumber off. Tessa dissolves into giggles and Josh offers us a very distinct finger before disappearing into the kitchen.

Not a second later the front door opens and in walks Jason and Brighton. Beside me Anna gulps as Rosa claps her hands. "You guys made it!"

Ignoring Anna's silent plea to tone it down, Rosa throws herself at Jason while a grinning Brighton approaches with flowers and wine in hand. "Congratulations on your place," he says, hugging me. "You're not armed with a bra, are you? I'm not prepared to defend myself."

So, here's a funny story about Jason and Brighton. Last month Anna, Rosa, and I were bra shopping at Target of all places—not for me—and we ran into them. They, too, were in the intimates' section, which is a whole other story. Anyway, someone (Anna) accidentally flung a bra at Jason's face, and from the way he's currently reddening, it's still a source of embarrassment.

It was funny at the time, though.

"No bra here," I joke, taking the wine and flowers just as Tessa appears.

"Ai, meu Deus, Kate. Again, about the bra?" She pats my shoulder. "It's okay if you don't need one. Nobody's judging."

Oh, for the love.

I'm about to explain when something on the television catches my eye. The Jaguars/Saints game is on, and there's a news ticker rolling across the bottom of the screen.

Nick Janney Fully Exposed Scandal: First Female Victim, Identified

David follows my eyes, sucking in a breath as he reads the tagline. We've been waiting for this, or any ball to drop, really. There hasn't been a new development in days.

Anna moves to put her arm around me as the room grows quiet. "I'm sorry, Kate. This has to be so hard."

I nod, noticing the confusion on our latest guest's faces. They might be the only ones here who don't know about Nick. Brighton cocks his head to the side, squinting at the screen. "You a big Saints fan, Kate?" The Saints are losing, and he, very understandably, must think I'm upset about the game.

If only it were that. "No, it's just—"

"It's just her dad's a fucking low-life," Zach offers, brushing past, nearly knocking the flowers from my hand. "Or have you two been living under a rock the last few weeks?" He claps his hands on Jason and Brighton's shoulders, turning them to face the living room crowd. "These lovebirds have been driving my Anna back and forth to work every day for almost a month, haven't you, boys? Real saints, these guys. They could teach your dad a lesson, am I right, Kate?"

Oh, how I loathe him, but I'm not about to defend Nick. And did he say lovebirds? Does anyone say that anymore? I glance at Anna, who looks mortified. Mor-ti-fied. But not surprised.

In fact, no one seems surprised except Josh, David, Tessa, and me. Even Jason and Brighton look . . . resigned, maybe? Irritated?

But Jason likes Anna, doesn't he? And last week Brighton mentioned crushing on some guy named Luke. He and Jason aren't together. Zach does not pause for these or any other considerations before plowing on. Oblivious to the room and its growing tension, he turns to David and Josh who stand feet from Jason and Brighton.

"Well, isn't this cozy. I'll bet the four of you have more in common than you think."

Reframing

:: Transforming the old into something new

David
Thursday, October 19th 8:55 pm
Foster Avenue Baltimore, Maryland

They say football has the power to bring people together.

It also has the power to entertain and distract, thankfully, because Zach's not so subtle implication is overshadowed by the Saints, who drive in a last second touchdown to tie up the game at the end of the first quarter.

"Zach is such a jerk," Kate whispers once we escape to the kitchen. "I wish he'd just leave already."

That's not happening.

As we speak, he's holding court in the living room, having moved on from Jason and Brighton's "relationship" to the actual reason for this party—the work he and his crew did on our house.

"Leave? He just got here," I say, listening as Josh's friends join the conversation. They've been upstairs and have nothing but praise, which Zach shamelessly eats up.

Josh, no doubt thoroughly annoyed, stalks into the kitchen moments later with Brighton at his heels. They join Kate and me by the charcuterie board where we aggressively attack what's left of the brie.

"I can't stand that guy," Brighton whispers, and Josh almost chokes on a cracker.

I don't know much about Brighton or Jason, aside from what Kate's told me. She and Josh hung out with them and Anna after flag football last week, but Tessa and I weren't there.

We were having dinner with Bennett who I haven't seen much of lately. He's been working crazy hours and is clearly run down. It's concerning, but I'm hardly in a position to lecture him. Even Tess has noticed, though.

Anyway, I do know Jason and Brighton are not a couple, as Zach implied. According to Kate, Anna and Jason like each other, but aren't acting on it because of Zach. Kate and Josh both took to Jason right away, and as for Brighton? They're smitten. Josh went so far as to claim he could be a taller, funnier version of me.

So, I was curious going into tonight.

I examine him now as he's laughing. He has very distinct features: wide, brown eyes, sharp nose and jawline, high cheekbones. His hair is dark and curly, but much shorter and tamer than mine. He only has a few inches on me, height wise. I wouldn't say we look alike, exactly, but there's something innately pleasing about his face and mannerisms.

And knowing Josh as I do? I can see the appeal.

Brighton goes on to explain how Zach is under the mistaken impression he and Jason are together. Sounds like Zach has jealousy issues where Anna's concerned—go figure—and they've agreed to play along to keep the peace. I guess he, Jason, and Anna all work for Zach's dad, so it's imperative they keep up the ruse.

I get the impression Brighton rather enjoys their deception. And the way he speaks of Jason makes me want to smile because he's very expressive and articulate. It's clear they have a close friendship. I wonder if I make people feel that way when I talk about Josh.

Or Kate, who's watching me watching Brighton, wondering what I'm thinking, no doubt.

What am I thinking?

I don't even know. I grab a beer for distraction, fully aware of her eyes still on me. I haven't had a drink since surgery, not that I drank much before, but she will find it monumental. As will Josh.

I'm tempted to down the entire thing, but I take a sip instead, returning my attention to the funnier, improved version of me who's explaining why he and Jason wanted to see Zach's work. Apparently, they're renting his sister's row home in Federal Hill. She offered a discount in exchange for labor.

"We're plowing through a mile long list of home improvement projects," he says, grimacing. "Sisters, am I right?" Brighton looks expectantly from Josh to Kate, to Josh again.

It takes him a moment to catch up. "Right, sisters. Yeah. Kate wouldn't know a tool if it bit her in the ass," he jokes. "But then, neither would David."

Really? "How did I get pulled into this?"

Brighton chuckles. "Come on, now. I don't believe that for a second. David looks like he could easily handle a power drill."

Josh snort-spits half his beer on the table as the room erupts in laughter.

"What?" Brighton smirks, shamelessly sporting a sorry-not-sorry, grin. "I just mean, you know . . . he looks like someone who knows his way around the equipment."

Kate almost drops her wine, and Josh laughs so hard that he has to hold a chair to keep from falling.

"Depends on the job," I manage, blushing so deep I can feel my cheeks glowing.

Brighton clinks his bottle against mine. "Hard work isn't for everyone, am I right?"

Zach calls for us, then, explaining how several girls from Kate's spa have arrived, and he wants to do a full-house tour. Kate scurries off to greet her friends, and the three of us grudgingly follow, still chuckling.

And though I don't mind the teasing, unease settles over me. It's beginning to feel overwhelming, all these people in our house. In our lives. Observing and commenting, making demands.

But we wanted this, right? At least, Josh did. Even without all the *Exposed* drama, having Tess here has forced us out of our comfort zones. And not in a bad way. She's great . . . and looking a bit frantic.

"I can't shake Kate's friend, Demetri," she whispers, joining Josh and me in the hall. She glances around, eyes wide, then takes his face in her hands. "Do something quick, Josh. Kiss me!"

And it's his turn to look frantic.

He lifts his gaze to mine, whether for help or approval, I'm not sure, but any momentary lightness from Brighton's teasing is forgotten. It's too much. This all feels so foreign. So surreal. So far from where we should be. But she's waiting, and he's growing more tense by the second.

It's just a kiss.

Tessa is supposed to be with Josh, after all. Isn't that what we're promoting? Our altered bedrooms testify to this fact. So, why does it feel . . . wrong?

Why am I sickened even as I nod, hating how I'm encouraging him? He hesitates, but what choice is there? I'm with Kate, and he's with Tess, and our house is full of people . . . watching. And sometimes, what you want isn't what you need, and so you do the hard thing. Even if the hard thing takes you farther and farther from where you want to be.

Which is exactly how I feel as their perfunctory kiss grows deeper. I turn before he takes her in his arms, and I pray my face betrays nothing of the pain I'm feeling. And as I follow the crowd into my new bedroom, my only thought is of how desperately I want this night to be over.

Friday, October 27th 3:52 pm

Much like the party, the week that follows is a rollercoaster of emotion.

One positive? We all agree—no more gatherings at the house. There's too much going on. Every other day, it seems, Nick's antics take center stage and we're back on edge. Just when we think the story has died down, another development propels him into the headlines.

More women from Carol's video are identified, and, unsurprisingly, some are barely legal. As for those who aren't—their stories remain untold. What's truly shocking is how several of the women support Nick's tales of consent, prompting his camp to proclaim his innocence and denounce Carol's criminal acts and manipulations through the Fully Exposed video.

Meanwhile, it's obvious to us, at least, someone's paying these women off. Or worse yet, threatening them. And it's definitely not my uncle, who remains MIA. Which leads us to think he might be planning something else, a disconcerting, yet oddly comforting thought.

One blessing is with the news focused on the women and their stories, we are largely forgotten. By the media, at least. We do hear from

Nick. And by Nick, I mean his team of attorneys. Nick, according to the news, is sequestered in his gated Florida community, surrounded by a support system of friends and family.

Which is a lie.

We know Vivian is staying with her sister in Southern Maryland, and Nick has no other friends or family to speak of. Aside from his agent and the legal team, he's likely alone. And no one's shedding tears over that.

What we aren't celebrating is Tessa's departure from Baltimore, which is fast approaching. She accepted an event planning position on a cruise ship and her contract begins in a few weeks. Despite my turmoil over her and Josh, I will miss her. But I can't deny part of me is looking forward to just the three of us again.

How that plays out, though? I'm not sure.

At any rate, Tess is excited. This is something she always wanted. Back in college, we used to daydream about sailing the world. And now, here we are, living under the same roof years later, and it's finally happening for her. Kind of crazy, how things come full circle.

She's actively recruiting, too. As a paramedic and masseuse, Josh and Kate would have no problem finding jobs onboard. Not that I think they'd consider joining her.

Nor would I. There's the nagging issue of my residual tumor that needs to be dealt with, and the equally pressing rod still in my arm. It's been in place since my fall in March, and due to come out anytime now. That'll be yet another surgery.

I stare out the car window and sigh. "I'm just one boring medical procedure after another," I mutter. Kate and I are heading to the hospital for X-rays and my orthopedic follow up—not exactly the fun-Friday date night she deserves.

"Well, at least you're in good company," she says and pats my leg.

Kate, too, has had an onslaught of recent health issues starting with last month's UTI. Her cycle has never been regular, but lately she's had pain and breakthrough bleeding, which she attributed to stress.

Not that she routinely talks to Josh or me about these things, but I guess she felt comfortable telling Tessa who encouraged her to see a specialist. She's planning to make an appointment when we get back from Nashville.

That's right—we're taking a little trip. A working vacation if you will.

Tessa's stepbrother, Gabriel, and his partner, Frances, have a condo in The Gulch, minutes from downtown Nashville. She lived there before coming here, so most of her belongings are still with them. They offered a free stay if we came and helped box her stuff. Sounds like they're planning some renovations.

Is anyone not remodeling these days?

Speaking of which, Brighton and Josh have developed quite a friendship since bonding over my um, handyman skills? It's actually kind of sweet. They have weirdly similar tastes in nerdy home

. . . everything. I even overheard him talking about meeting up at Home Depot.

As much as I detest Home Depot, I felt a little pang. I'm not going to say it's jealousy, but I'm not saying it isn't, either. Mostly, I'm glad Josh is connecting with someone.

Multiple someone's.

He and Tess are getting closer every day. But hey, that's what we wanted, right?

Kate parks and I check in, and we settle onto a couch together in the patient lounge for what will likely be a long wait. I could sleep, I'm so tired. And tired of feeling tired.

"D," she says, just as my eyes close. "Look at this."

I squint to read the article she pulls up on her phone. "Carol Brennan, Apprehended!" is the title, but the accompanying photo is not my uncle. It goes on to explain how yet another false Carol turned himself in. He's like the third one.

She shakes her head. "I don't understand people. Why pretend to be a criminal?"

Why, indeed.

I take her hand. "Nothing makes sense these days, but we're getting pretty good at pretending, aren't we, Sunshine?"

Nick and his reckless actions, the women and their denials, Carol and his cryptic warnings? I can't make it all compute and I'm so tired of trying. My eyes fall shut again, mind unwilfully playing his parting words.

You won't see me again, he said. *There's a package for the three of you. In a hollow rock. Go alone once the dust settles. Be careful.*

What could he have left for us and why tell me like that? How was he so certain we wouldn't see each other again? These questions have plagued me. I was honest with Josh, Kate, and Tessa about meeting Carol that night at the premiere party, but I didn't share everything he said.

Like the package? Josh would want to find that right away. And maybe we should. Maybe Carol's gone. Dead and buried somewhere, and inside the rock lies what could be the final nail in Nick's coffin. Or maybe it's something so upsetting, Carol couldn't bring himself to say the words.

Or maybe, and I'm beginning to believe this is the truth, we haven't scratched the surface of what Carol knows, what he's capable of, and what he's about to do.

Sunday, October 29th 3:45 pm

Josh glares at a blond boy zipping past in a red-and-blue cape.

"I'm about to lay a smackdown on Spiderman," he whispers. I shush him as a tiny brunette dressed like Dorothy from The Wizard of Oz takes a bag of skittles from my cauldron and skips off.

It's the Sunday before Halloween and we're volunteering at his station's annual fall festival. Well, I'm volunteering, Josh is required to work the event. His station does a lot of outreach activities for the community. It would be fun if we didn't have a million things going on. But I like seeing the kids all dressed up. I even have a Halloween costume.

Our English department usually picks a literary adjacent theme, and all the teachers dress accordingly. This year everyone voted for the Wizarding World of Harry Potter.

Coincidence? I think not.

But I can't let my scar go to waste, so Harry it is. I tried convincing Josh and Kate to dress as Ron and Hermione, but he found some Santa costume on clearance, and she and Tessa are dressing as Dolly Parton and June Carter Cash in honor of our upcoming Nashville trip.

Nothing can compare to Josh's Santa suit, though. It's awful. He looks more like Billy Bob Thorton in *Bad Santa* than Jolly Old Saint Nicholas. And am I the only one putting two and two together here because, Saint Nicholas? Nick? Does he realize the irony? You can't make this stuff up.

Spiderman sprints past again, cape flying as he snags more candy, chanting, "Santa stinks, Santa stinks!"

Josh grabs my shoulders, positioning me between him and the boy. "Cast a spell on this kid, Potter," he commands, laughing as Spiderman squeals then hurries off to his mom. The event's winding down, and this leaves us alone in our little tent.

He still holds my shoulders. I feel the scratch of his beard and the warm tickle of his breath.

"You're killing me with this costume," he says, leaning close. "It's unlocking all kinds of cosplay fantasies I never knew I had."

As he's saying this, the last group of children approach and I'm laughing so hard I can barely greet them. He fills their buckets then turns back with an intense look, eyes locked onto mine, shamelessly staring.

"It's the glasses," he says, head cocking to the side. "You should wear those all the time. But like, only for me."

Honestly, I could've predicted his reaction to this costume. But I didn't expect he'd say something here at his work with so many people around. He must reach this same conclusion because almost instantly, he sobers, moving away from me as we begin shutting down.

Pretense or not, we are committed to this Tessa-Kate couple thing. Or I should say, he's committed. I'm not sure I have a choice in the matter. But since the party and his public groping session with Tess on the stairs, it's public knowledge—they're together and I'm with Kate. In fact, his station's gossip-thirsty crew has done nothing but pester us for details all afternoon.

Which is great, right? I love Kate. We should be together. And Josh. I want him to have a chance at something meaningful with Tess, or maybe someone like Brighton if things with her don't work out.

We're moving forward. It's what we need to do.

Only, are we really?

I catch his eye as we fold up the table and chairs, and there's no question what he's thinking, because I'm thinking it too. How in the world are we supposed to do this? We've tried before, and it never works. Old habits are hard to break, and keeping up pretenses is exhausting. There's no roadmap for him and me. No, what not to say or do.

Just muddle our way through, I guess?

I don't know. I want us to move forward, but at the same time? I don't want anything to change . . .

We finish cleaning up in silence and are in the Jeep heading home ten minutes later. It's not uncomfortable between us—we're years past that. But it's . . . different. Off.

We make it to the highway before he speaks. "Did you know some people call Santa Claus, Saint Nick?"

I turn to face him certain he's joking because who doesn't know that? But no, his face is pure and preciously indignant. I'm not sure how he grew up Catholic and avoided this knowledge, but I play along. "Do they, really?"

He nods. "Saint fucking Nick. Can you believe that? One of the guys just made a smartass comment and it dawned on me." He flicks his hand toward his bad Santa suit crumpled in the back. "Now I gotta burn the damn thing."

"Well, I tried to get you to go as Ron, so . . ." I press my lips to keep from laughing.

"Wait a minute," he says, eyes narrowing. "You knew about the Saint Nick thing? And you just let me walk around all day like fucking irony in a fat suit?"

"What do you want me to say, Josh? It's Christmas 101."

His nostrils flare, and I can't tell if he's genuinely mad, or just playing. But before I can dodge out of the way, he leans across the seat and yanks my robe open, grabbing for the Gryffindor tie, a clip on. The cheap thing practically disintegrates in his hand, and I can't help it, I double over with laughter.

"Come on, J. Jolly Old Saint Nicholas? The Beach Boys' "Little Saint Nick"? You never made the connection? It's like common knowledge."

"Common knowledge," he scoffs, still clutching the tie. He chucks it at me, but his eyes dance even as I clumsily reattach the clips and pull on Harry's signature glasses. He shakes his head. "Well, now you're just playing dirty."

I brandish my wand to complete the look. "You know what they say, a wizard's work is never done."

"Is that so?" He yanks it from my hand then rolls the thin wood between his fingers. "Too bad this thing can't Incendio the shit out of the real Saint Nick. Now, that . . ." He lightly taps my nose with the tip. ". . .that would be the best Christmas gift of all."

The Watcher

Carol Brennan
Wednesday, November 1ˢᵗ 6:03 am
Hidden Spring Estates Naples, Florida

Nick Janney was going to pay.

On some level, Carol had known it would come to this. A showdown, decades in the making. He'd known when he let the security camera catch his face. He'd known when he dug up Angela's remains. Carol had known from the moment he sent those photographs to Nick last spring—he was setting a path in motion.

The beginning of the end.

And now, the end was upon him.

He had expected a backlash from the Fully Exposed video. Once Nick realized Carol had orchestrated the sabotage, he'd piece it all together. The photographs, his clandestine connection to Elena . . . everything. *Almost* everything.

Carol had taken painstaking efforts to ensure no ties could be made between him, David, and the

Janney kids. Yes, he used his real name with them, but his phone, his property, everything he touched was under an alias. Carol was virtually untraceable and cautious to a fault.

Approaching David at the premiere party had been his only risk. Emotion got the better of him. Carol had wanted to warn his nephew and, selfishly, he wanted to be near Elena's son one final time.

He'd taken the appropriate measures, though, disabling the cameras in that quadrant, disguising himself. He correctly assumed no one would suspect his presence as a member of the venue security staff. Not after it was discovered what he had done just prior to the party.

No, Carol had expected the backlash. He had expected Nick to go on the offensive. Lie, deny, plead with his fan base, whatever it took to keep from drowning. He had even expected the criminal charges they filed against him.

What Carol had not accounted for was the possibility that Nick's lies would be believed. That the girls he abused and violated, in many cases, would claim consent. Or worse yet, support Nick's assertion that photos and videos had been doctored.

In a few short weeks Carol watched with disbelief as the narrative shifted from Nick, perpetrator of disgusting acts, to Nick, victim of a madman's revenge. What little was known of Carol, had been dragged up, trampled on, and spit out in a vicious attempt to fully disgrace him.

But the final straw came when stories of Elena began cropping up. Nick had gone too far—it was time for Carol to put an end to the madness once and for all.

So, he headed south to Florida, yet again, and did what he did best.

Carol watched, and he waited.

As with the women, Nick made it almost too easy. Cowering inside his heavily secured mansion, behind the fortified gates of his exclusive community, he kept a predictable routine: up at five thirty, coffee, a check of the news, and then out for a jog. Alone.

He took the same route every day. A mile up his street, through the front gate out of his neighborhood, and down an obscure, vacant path, but for wildlife at that time of the morning.

After his jog, Janney spent the days alone—other than an occasional meeting with his attorneys or a food delivery. Vivian was gone. Despite what the media was reporting, Carol hadn't seen her once. It would be days before Nick was missed, the dumb fuck.

It was almost too easy.

And it was almost time for Carol to set the rest of his plan into motion.

Tangled

Part Three

Essential Pause

:: A necessary break from reality

Josh
Wednesday, November 1ˢᵗ 3:05 pm
BWI Airport Baltimore, Maryland

We leave for Nashville on November 1st.

"Do you think it's bad luck, flying on All Saints' Day?" Kate asks, not for the first time.

Beside me, Tessa groans. She leans closer to Kate and David, who are sitting in the row across from us. "Kate," she explains, just as the plane's engines roar to life. "All Saints' Day is about honoring Christian saints and martyrs who have passed in the faith. It's not about superstition. We are going to be fine."

"Are we? What about tomorrow, Tessa? Isn't it called All Souls' Day? The Day of the *Dead*! Don't you think it feels ominous? I'm not sure we should be flying."

As usual, Kate's timing is impeccable. We are literally pushing away from the gate as she considers this. I'm not a nervous flier, but I'd rather not be discussing sainthood and death while lifting off the ground. "Would you stop," I grumble, flinching as the plane jerks into motion. "It's fine. Just close your eyes and try to sleep like your boy over there."

Because of course David's sleeping.

For the last ten minutes, he's been peacefully snoozing with a plush neck pillow and headphones. He's resting on Kate's shoulder, all snuggled up in a fuzzy travel blanket without a care in the world.

Oh, to be him for a day.

Even on a packed flight to Nashville, he's as mellow as the morning sky. Though, I must admit, compared to our recent nightmare, this trip feels like a walk in the park. There are benefits to this pseudo couple thing. Like, Tessa planned every detail, down to my seat assignment. She even packed for me.

Plus, she has all these bonus rewards and club memberships. We were chilling in an all-you-can-eat lounge before boarding. And the flight crew loves her. She speaks like ten languages and communicates with perfect ease.

I feel like royalty with her. It's fun. And a far cry from the last time David, Kate, and I flew together. Though there is something to be said for narrowly missing a flight, scraping pennies for airport coffee, and praying you find seats near each other.

But those days are behind us, I guess.

Maybe for good.

Regardless, and despite Kate's fears, it's a short, uneventful flight to Nashville. You would think with Nick's job and the affluence he and Vivian enjoyed, Kate and I would've traveled more, but mostly they went without us.

And then Ian and David came into the picture and *Brought to Light* took off. There were lots of trips for David and me after that. Road trips, and not any place of our choosing. I thought those days were behind us, too, but Nick's degenerative antics have cast us all into the spotlight.

It wouldn't take much for one of the men Nick and Ian blackmailed to come forward. To point a finger at David or me. We were just boys back then, but still recognizable—especially him. No one forgets those eyes. And with our pictures splashed all over the news in connection with Nick? Someone could easily identify us.

Yet, despite this, we've been largely ignored. Sure, we've had to deal with random stories popping up here and there, and a few old friends and not-so-friends have crawled out of the woodwork, but nothing damning. And there's plenty of damning shit out there if someone really chose to dig. Which makes this trip all the more timely. A little escape from reality. Not that disaster can't find us in Nashville—I'm not naïve. But a few days away could be good.

We've never been to Nashville, and now, here we are, traveling in couples, no less, about to meet my faux girlfriend's stepbrother and his partner. Meanwhile, Ian's dead, Nick's basically under house arrest in his gilded Florida mansion, and Carol's off plotting God knows what. And we're just plodding along, waiting for the next ball to drop.

But that's life, right? So fucking bizarre.

As is being in a city other than Baltimore. The sun is setting when we arrive at Tessa's uncle's building, a modern high rise in the heart of the city. Shops and restaurants line the streets between colorful murals and lush, green spaces. People are out in droves, jogging, walking dogs, dressed up for the night. I pause, suitcase in hand, taking it all in as Kate wanders over.

"I already love it," she says, hugging me. "The city, its energy, the whole downtown vibe . . . it's perfect! And don't these buildings remind you of our old drawings, Josh? Remember?"

I scoff, but of course I remember. Growing up, we spent hours sketching out elaborate cities, neighborhoods, condominiums . . . anything. I was going to be an architect, and Kate was going to work in interior design. We had it all planned.

And now look at us—we can barely manage a row home.

"You could still do it," she says as we follow David and Tess inside. "You have an engineering degree, after all. You could go back and get your master's in architecture. The two go hand in hand."

"Or he could just work on the ship with me," Tessa quips, grinning over her shoulder. "Did you tell them?"

Kate and David full stop in the middle of the entrance way, both swinging around to gape at me.

Fuck.

"Tell us what?" he asks.

"Nothing." I glare at Tessa who shrugs. She's so like him sometimes, it's infuriating. Literally, nothing bothers her. He is looking legit concerned at the moment, though. And I feel terrible, yet oddly warmed by his alarm.

"We just read over the paperwork. Tess had me talk to some guy she knows in the hiring department. That's all." Based on their expressions, David and Kate obviously think this amounts to more than nothing, but I'm mercifully cut short by two men in the distance calling for Tessa.

As much as we've shared, she hasn't offered many details from her own past. For example, I know her stepbrother's name is Gabriel, and his partner is Frances, and that she came to live with them when she was a teenager. But they are the only family she speaks of.

She's never even shared a picture of herself from childhood, let alone any family members. So, when two athletic-looking guys in their late forties join us, I'm shocked. I was expecting Gabriel, at least, to resemble her, but he's as white as the day is long, and a good bit older than I imagined.

And Frances? He's a dead ringer for James Dean and, as we quickly discover, is almost completely blind. I hold David back once the introductions have been made. "Why didn't she tell us?"

"What do you mean . . ." he starts, but the girls are beckoning us to a crowded elevator. David waves them on. "Go ahead," he calls, "we'll take the next one." Once the doors close, he turns. "Who didn't tell us what?"

"Tessa. You think she might have mentioned Frances being blind. And Gabe is old enough to be her father, and very much not Brazilian. She could have mentioned that, too."

"Oh." He looks confused. "I thought she told you about Frances. And Gabe is American. He's the son of her mom's second husband, I think. He was in college when Tess was little. They hardly knew each other before she came to the States."

"How do you . . .?" I cut myself off because of course he would know all this. He dated Tess, for fucks sake. He's known her for years. And I just . . .

You're just pretending, asshole, jaded inner Josh grumbles. *And not very convincingly.*

Another elevator opens and we step inside. "Would you really leave?" he asks before the door even closes.

I'm focused on my internal monologue, so his question catches me off guard. I completely forgot about the cruise conversation. But David hasn't. Uncharacteristic lines crease his forehead as he awaits my answer, eyes wide and worried. Those beautiful blue eyes.

I want to tell him, no, of course not, I would never leave. No part of me wants to be on a ship without him. I don't want to go anywhere without him, or Kate. But that's selfish. Why bother with any of this if the end result isn't them, together?

Pretend or not, I need to show them I'm fine by myself or with Tessa, even. Because it's not all pretend; I do like her. I could be with Tess. I really could.

And so, I'm quiet until we reach the fifth floor. And as the doors slide open, I force a betraying shrug and say, "Yeah, I'm thinking about it."

6:38 pm

We spend the next hour getting to know Gabe and Frances.

I'm not even embarrassed to admit how much I like them. Aside from Nick and Ian, my experience with the male father-figure type is pretty much limited to Bennett, who, let's face it, only tolerates me because of David.

Gabe and Frances, though? They are a lot like him. Kind and genuine, down to earth. Pragmatic, but like, funny, too. And despite the age gap, they clearly have a bond with Tess, who must have done some explaining prior to our arrival.

Other than asking how we're holding up, no outright mention is made of our relationships, the *Exposed* scandal, or any specific . . . ahem . . . family members. Not that I'm complaining. Nick can take a hike in the everglades and get eaten by a fucking gator for all I care.

And since I'm on the subject, Tess clearly shared that food is my love language because while we chat, Frances puts out this giant spread of biscuits and croissants from a local bakery, and Gabe makes fresh espresso in a sleek machine that could literally devour our Keurig.

They give us a brief tour of the condo, and I do mean brief—it's a one bedroom with a den. The space is small, but meticulously decorated with floor to ceiling windows that provide natural light and stunning views.

I can't believe Tessa traded this for our dumpy little shit box, but I guess she didn't have much room here. Gabe explains how he's turning the den—essentially a doorless closet where she slept—into an actual office, hence the need to get her stuff out.

He's an accounting manager and plans to work from home part time to help Frances, whose vision is rapidly deteriorating. I don't want to ask, but they're forthcoming about his condition—a rare, genetic eye disease that eventually leads to complete blindness.

He gets around, though, and despite his limitations, he's an award-winning children's author and artist with no plans of slowing. Gabe proudly points out his work displayed throughout the condo.

It's warming watching them. The way they joke and tease back and forth, how they finish each other's sentences. They're like an old married couple, minus the marriage.

"He can't afford the ring," Frances jokes, but Gabe is quick to add how they both grew up in dysfunctional homes and for them, marriage was never on the table.

"Sounds familiar," Kate mutters as she and I exchange a glance over our espresso. I try to catch Tessa's eye, but she's looking past me.

David alluded to violence in her past, so I'm not shocked when Gabe explains how his father's marriage to Tessa's mom was volatile. Gabe had been a young man at the time, but Tessa was only a child. My heart aches at the thought of what she went through.

"I wish I could've brought her to the States sooner," he says, slinging an arm around Frances. "I don't know what I would've done without this guy." He reaches for Tess. "We got you out eventually, didn't we, Tessy? And we have each other now."

Tessy?

I grin at the nickname, filing it away for future use because she is clearly uncomfortable with this turn in conversation. Kate notices, too, quickly changing the subject to dinner plans. This sparks an immediate debate between the men—local and trendy versus crowded tourist trap.

Frances cleans up while they argue the merits of each, and I notice Gabe discreetly clearing a path, guiding him with the occasional, gentle touch. It's such a small, insignificant act, yet at the same time, deeply intimate.

I try not to watch David's reaction, but I can't help wondering what he thinks . . . of them, this place, us being here, everything. He always jokes about moving to a condo. Is this what he pictures?

Because I could see him and me living together like them, in a place like this.

What about him and Kate, you moron, jaded Josh demands. *What about Tessa? You wouldn't be here without her.*

I want to throttle the voice in my head, but it's true. We're only in Nashville because of Tess. And she's only involved because of me, and the lies she's perpetuating on my behalf.

Lies she must have told Gabe and Frances, who clearly think we're a couple. Which, I guess we kind of are, but not in a way that would make a father proud. They must know she dated David in college. I didn't even consider how awkward that would've been for her to explain.

It's bad enough I'm a liar; now I've turned her into one, too. The least I can do is quit the fucking fantasizing and focus on her. Without further thought, I walk to where she stands by the window. "Thanks for bringing us here," I say, taking her into my arms.

She smiles and leans in for a kiss, biting playfully at my lower lip. We're comfortable with each other now. Sharing a bed will do that, I guess. And your life story. Painful as it was, revealing our past, I'm glad she knows. It's made it easier, being with her.

Not that it's hard. Fuck. What is wrong with me?

I really do like Tessa. She's beautiful in every sense of the word. Sexy as hell, intelligent, funny . . . incredibly easy to talk to. She even finds my bullshit amusing. And she isn't looking for a long-term relationship.

On paper, we're perfect. I should be thrilled, right?

But as we embrace, I can't help looking past her to perfection himself, who's sitting on the couch beside Kate, pretending he doesn't see my every thought and plan unraveling.

And isn't that just fucked up on so many levels.

Thursday, November 2nd 7: 32 pm

Thankfully, our first full day is too busy for my intrusive thinking.

"Never mind working on a cruise ship," I tell Tessa as we dress to go out for the night. "I'm moving to Nashville."

She rolls her eyes.

Tess is over my fangirling, but I can't help it—I like it here. It's clean, the weather is amazing, the music is off the charts—ha ha—and food is the fucking bomb.

Last night, we ate at some elevated steakhouse—divine, Kate kept calling it. Then, we hit up Gabe's favorite dessert place for Boozy Milkshakes before heading to a local cocktail bar where Frances knew the guy playing acoustic guitar. It was after midnight when we made it back to their condo, exhausted.

I don't remember my head hitting the floor, which is where we slept. All four of us, in the den on a big bed of blankets and pillows. There's a guest unit in the building that Gabe reserved for our stay, but when we tried to drop our stuff off last night, it was occupied.

A scheduling mishap, the manager apologized. He offered to pay for a hotel, but we're only here three days. It seemed like a waste. Besides, the four of us are used to sharing a room.

We were up early, anyway; today being packing day and all. There was breakfast, of course. Homemade pop tarts from Milk and Honey, at Kate's request. They were pretty fucking good. As if I needed another reason to love it here?

Packing Tessa's stuff occupied the rest of our day, but we managed to squeeze in a few sights and attractions here and there. The strip, however, we saved for tonight . . .

"This is insane!" I tell David as the six of us jostle our way down Broadway. Last night was all about the local scene, but tonight we are in full tourist mode: hot chicken, honky-tonks, and boot shopping—another Kate request.

Only, it's impossible to move. The sidewalk is crowded to the point of claustrophobia, and the air literally pulsates with music and noise. Neon lights are everywhere, and the vibe is one hundred percent Vegas. Pictures and videos do not do this place justice—it is pure chaos.

People are hanging off balconies, dancing on barstools and railings, most of them drunk off their asses. In fact, half the people we pass look wasted. This whole downtown area seems ripe for disaster. I can't keep my brain from switching to work mode because all I see is a hotbed of medical emergencies waiting to happen.

"Forget what I said about moving," I tell Tess, side stepping a woman sprawled on the pavement. "You couldn't pay me enough to work down here."

She laughs. "Now that sounds more like the Josh I know."

Kate yanks my arm. "Would you stop talking about moving? You're upsetting me."

"Who's upset?" Gabe falls in behind us, Frances at his side. I don't even want to think about him navigating this crowd with limited vision, but he doesn't seem worried. Neither does Tess or Gabe.

"Everyone's fine," she assures him, linking arms with both men. "Where shall we take them first?"

The better question is where don't they take us.

We start with hot chicken at Hattie B's, followed by an agonizingly long stop in Boot Country where Kate falls in love with the ugliest pair of boots I've ever seen. They are a sickly lime- green color with hot-pink flames licking up the sides. Down the front of each is electric-blue stitching that zigzags erratically. But that's nothing compared to the heels. Clunky and mismatched leopard print, they are the worst part of the boots by far.

That is, until we discover the price.

"Four-hundred dollars?" Kate practically chokes. "They better walk by themselves!"

They don't, in fact. And they don't come off her sweaty feet, either. It takes the combined efforts of David, Tess, and Frances to get the damned things to budge. Meanwhile, Gabe and I laugh so hard we knock over a display rack and have to flee the store.

From there, we hit up a string of Honky Tonks where everyone sings, and the music's loud, and drinks flow like water. Gabe and Frances must party a lot, because wherever we go, they know someone. Bartenders, bouncers, busboys . . . we get free shots and VIP treatment all night long.

And then comes the dancing.

Normally, I hate to dance, but it's different here. The anonymity is intoxicating. There are so many people, you just blend in. We dance for hours in crowds of sweaty strangers, and no one cares who I am or who I'm with or where I'm from, and it is the best fucking feeling in the world.

I ride high all night until the buzz begins to fade, and the lights come on, and I, somehow the most sober of our group, am tasked with getting us home. We are minus Gabe, who hit a wall. Literally. Like, he actually walked into a wall. Busted up his nose and everything. We put him in an Uber about an hour ago.

And you have to love Frances because once he knew Gabe was okay, he laughed his ass off. He's still chuckling as our little entourage struggles up a much less crowded Broadway. He and David walk ahead together—cue the blind leading the blind joke I am dying to make.

But I exercise restraint, because at least they're still hanging.

Kate, on the other hand? She's not so much hanging, as hanging on me, complaining how her feet hurt. And Tess? She's riding on my back, alternately singing and whispering what sounds like dirty Portuguese in my ear. I have no clue what she's saying, but it's pretty fucking hot.

And David?

He keeps glancing back at us with a sweet, sleepy-drunk smile that makes me grateful for every second with him. What if things had turned out different this summer? We could've lost him. This trip? This moment? Might never have happened.

But it is happening, and we're here, together, very much alive and well and surrounded by people we love. And as we push into Gabe and Frances's lobby, a stumbling heap of drunk, giggling idiots, our troubles seem a million miles away, and for now, that's enough.

The Abduction

Carol Brennan
Friday, November 3rd 4:52 am
Hidden Spring Estates Naples, Florida

Carol was done waiting.

He was done watching. He'd had enough. He was sick and tired of Nick Janney and his pathetic attempts at deflection. It was time the man paid for his actions.

It was time to finish what he had started once and for all.

These were the thoughts cycling through Carol's mind as he sat, crouched behind a bush in the predawn hours of Friday morning. Every day for the last five days Nick had run by this exact spot, alone and unsuspecting.

And today, Carol was ready.

Parked just feet from the path and hidden by thick overgrowth was the car he had rented. Under an alias, of course. It was gassed up and ready to go, and so was Carol. He felt alive. Confident. Focused solely on the matter at hand.

Which is why he experienced no hesitation when Nick jogged past. Carol sprung like a coiled snake, precise and explosive, assailing the man with superhuman strength and speed. Not that it was necessary. The fast-acting drug Carol plunged into his neck took quick effect—Nick never stood a chance.

In fact, he didn't move or utter a sound as Carol dragged his limp body to the car. They were on the road minutes later. Carol driving as if he hadn't a care in the world. Nick bound and passed out in the trunk hidden beneath blankets.

It shouldn't have been that easy, but it was. Even the drive to Lake Lanier, though long, was uneventful. Carol kept Nick sedated, despite having restrained him. No need for complications.

His luck continued once they arrived under the cover of night. Carol was able to drag Nick's semi-conscious body from his trunk and get him loaded into a tiny fishing boat without incident.

Not that he was worried. The isolated cabin on the north shore was a perfect place to carry out his plan—private dock, deep cove, and no boat traffic. Besides, Carol would be long gone by morning.

Shivering, he pushed off into the water just as Nick began to move. Carol rowed for several minutes in silence, watching. The boat was in the middle of the cove when Nick finally lifted his eyes, still groggy.

"Where am I?" he slurred. "What's happening?"

Carol, still rowing, said nothing. But their eyes met, his wide and alert, Nick's foggy and blood-shot. It took a moment for recognition to set in.

Nick cursed, moving violently, but Carol had tied weights to his legs, and his balance was off. He fell to the side, grunting with the effort of steadying himself. Once he was upright, Carol handed him a water bottle which he raised to his lips with difficulty. Both hands were tied, but he gulped greedily, emptying the container in a matter of seconds.

"Carol Brennan," he said, voice steadier now, eyes clearing. "What the hell are you doing? I thought you were dead."

Carol had felt dead for years.

Losing Elena had gutted him. A pain that never dulled. But this last year, it seemed every time Nick spoke the wound opened wider and wider, until Carol could no longer contend with the man. And now, here he was. At the end.

"We're in Georgia," he replied evenly. "And you know why."

Nick's face twisted. "Elena? Oh, for fuck's sake. Newsflash, asshole. Your sister has been dead for years, and I had nothing to do with it. Now turn this piece of shit around and take me home before you do something really stupid."

Carol almost laughed out loud.

He was past stupid. He'd been drowning in crazy for years. There was no turning the boat around. No going back. He was finishing this.

Before Nick could move or say another word, Carol lunged at him, roughly covering his mouth with masking tape, silencing the man. He sat back satisfied as Nick's nostrils flared. Even in the moonlight, his steely eyes burned with hatred.

"Better," Carol said. "And yes, this is about Elena."

And for Carol, it was. But it was so much more. Nick was like a cancer. His destruction may have started with Elena, but who could count his victims? Certainly not Carol. He wanted to avenge his sister, and free his nephew, but if he rid the world of a monster in the process?

So be it.

He continued rowing as he spoke. "She and I never lost touch with each other, but you already figured that out, didn't you? And she confided in me. Here in Georgia, as a matter of fact. After she and Ian moved. You remember when they left Maryland, Nick? Right after your twins were born?"

The man's eyes widened.

"I'm sure you do," Carol continued. "It's not every day you strangle the mother of your child, then force your ex-girlfriend and her husband to help in the cover up. That's the kind of act a man doesn't forget."

Nick shook his head and made an inarticulate sound, but Carol recognized the fear in his eyes. The alarm.

"You didn't really think she'd keep that to herself all those years, did you? Not with Ian around—he was a fucking headcase." Carol made a *tsk tsk tsk* sound, enjoying Nick's discomfort more than he should. "She told me all about Angela, too, about what you did and how she died. Josh knows all about that, by the way. So does Kate. But we'll get to them."

At his children's names, Nick's head jerked back as if he'd been punched, and for a moment Carol regretted not sharing his plan with them. They too, deserved to see this sorry shell of a man humiliated and destroyed. The Fully Exposed video had accomplished that to a degree, but not completely.

Carol stopped rowing. He pulled the oars into the boat. "The thing is," he said, pausing to note how Nick watched his every move, "Ian didn't trust you back then and for good reason it would seem. In fact, he and Elena didn't destroy Angela's body at all. They buried her along with all the evidence, which I'm guessing maybe you suspected?" He met Nick's acrid stare and smiled. "You might be surprised where they buried her, though. In your old backyard, under your fucking nose, Nick. Can you believe it?" Carol shook his head. "Josh and Kate know about that, too. And David, of course."

Carol's voice cracked on his nephew's name. A reminder of his own shortcomings. What his apathy cost the boys and Kate; how they suffered. His sister would hate how he put her memory over the well-being of her child.

But it all ended here. He would finish this off and begin a new chapter, free from the guilt and anger that had weighed on him for so long. He was ready to let go.

"Look," he said, sighing. "We both know what a piece of shit you are. And I've wasted enough time on you. I never should've involved the kids—that was always your game, right? You and Ian? Those photos I took of them were a mistake but telling them the truth wasn't. David, Josh, Kate . . . they deserve better than us." He felt around in his pocket, pulling out a mini audio player. "Remember that night at Ian and David's? When you pushed Ian to his death, blamed Josh, then forced him, Kate, and David to burn the house down?"

Nick's skin went pale. He seemed to involuntarily shudder.

"What am I saying? Of course you remember. And would you believe this? I've got a recording of the entire thing. Let's have a listen." He didn't wait for a response, pressing play on the near-decade-old message Ian unknowingly left on his phone.

The shock on Nick's face was more than gratifying, and Carol let the full five minutes play out—every condemning word.

He pocketed the player. "The kids heard that, too. In fact, they have a copy," he said, sitting a bit straighter, sensing the man's building rage. It fueled him. "You should be thanking them. They knew all this before David's surgery. They could've fucking ended you. They should have, if you want my opinion. But they didn't. Why? Because they're better than you."

Better than me, Carol thought, but didn't say it. In truth, he was no better than Nick. While David, Josh, and Kate had known, Carol stole the evidence from beneath them. All they had was a copy of the message, and the contents of Elena's envelope. Damning, yes, but enough to take Nick down?

Probably not.

And now? It didn't matter. Nick was going down either way, and the kids would be free. There was only one thing left to share. A rumor, yes, but it bore mentioning. So much, Carol left it in a note for David and the Janney kids to find and investigate if they chose.

"Last thing," he said to Nick, who was now jerking side to side in his seat like a trapped animal. "I have it on good word your beloved Vivian wasn't having an affair all those years ago." The moving stopped. "That's right, Nick. She was so hurt by your infidelity, she lied about her own pregnancy." He paused for effect. "Which means, Katherine is your daughter after all."

In a shocking explosion of movement, Nick's hand whipped around his body, yanking the tape from his mouth. "You mother fucking piece of shit," he growled.

Carol sat unmoving, stunned to see the man had freed himself. His hesitation allowed Nick enough time to lunge, despite the tethers, knocking Carol to the floor of the boat. Even tied and coming off the drug, he was stronger than Carol anticipated.

The men struggled, wrestling one another as the tiny craft rocked perilously. Nick's one hand and both feet remained bound. Tied to him was enough weight to ensure his body would rest at the lake's bottom.

But as they moved, the rope securing that weight tangled around Carol, debilitating him. With frantic effort, he rolled side to side, attempting to free himself, but the boat rolled too, tipping enough to cast both men into the chilly water.

It happened so suddenly that Carol barely registered the cold. Bound to the weight, and each other, they sank fast, leaving nothing but a ripple on the quiet lake. Both men flailed wildly, to no avail. The movement only ensnared them farther.

As the surface and any hope of survival fled from Carol's grasp, he caught a final glimpse of the boat. Alone and adrift, as he had been for far too long. This wasn't his plan, but perhaps, he thought, this was meant to be.

Maybe it was all supposed to go down this way.

With blackness setting in, and pressure building in his lungs, he thought of Elena and of Abigail, almost sensing their presence. The peace that awaited him. And he thought of David and of Josh and Kate and the freedom they would have once Nick was gone.

And Carol stopped fighting.

Seventeen

Splintered

:: When connections crack
and foundations falter

Kate
Friday, November 3rd 5:02 am
Laurel Street Nashville, Tennessee

I wake suddenly, as if from a terrible dream.

It takes a disorienting moment to realize where I am, and another to determine I am, in fact, still drunk. My body feels like a wet bag of cement, and I am in desperate need of a bathroom. I think of the thousands crammed into the downtown area.

Do people really do that every night?

A stupid question, because of course they do. My own family is a prime example. Nick and Vivian rarely spent nights at home. And when they did, it was always with a drink in hand. They never went to bed sober.

And now? From what I can tell, my mother is perpetually high. And Nick? If I was as wretched a human as him, I'd drink myself into oblivion, too.

How do they function?

How did Josh and I turn out so different from them?

How—

There's a soft moan beside me, interrupting my thoughts. A female moan.

"Josh!" It sounds like Tessa.

She moans again, louder this time. And . . . did she say Josh's name? She did! Oh, no! Are they . . .? No! They wouldn't, would they?

The last few hours return in a foggy rush. The two of them, making out on the dance floor, our stumbly walk home from Broadway, Tess on Josh's back, the bright, echoing lobby, Frances and Gabe's den. We're packed in like sardines, Josh, Tessa, David and me. Side by side on the floor. And now she's moaning. And moving. I can feel her leg brushing mine.

Josh says something in a low voice, and she giggles. "Josh, stop! That tickles."

"Quit laughing and help me, then," he not-so-whispers. "I can't get in there."

Get in where?

Fully awake now, I press closer to David, who is on my other side and might as well be a body pillow at this point. He doesn't even flinch. How is he sleeping so hard already? We just got in bed.

I mean . . . I think we did.

I don't know. Logistics are irrelevant—I've got bigger problems. Two to be exact. And they seem to be getting it on inches from me. I shift so close to David; I'm practically covering him.

"It's just so big," Tessa murmurs.

My eyes squeeze tight. I want to shutter my ears.

"Stop pulling away," Josh grunts. "I'll be fast, okay? In and out before you know it."

In and out? Is he serious?

This has to be a nightmare. Maybe I'm still sleeping. They wouldn't do this with David and me right—

She gasps. "Ow . . . that hurts, Josh! Jeez. Be gentle!"

Okay, maybe they would.

"Well, it's harder than it looks. Why don't we use Vaseline or something. Lube will loosen the skin."

Lube? Sweet baby Moses!

There's shuffling, and cringing—that's me, by the way. I am cringing so hard I might crack a tooth. I can't believe this is happening. And now, lube? Here in the den, with no door, and Gabe and Frances in the other room, and David and me . . . in the splatter zone?

No. Just . . . no.

"Gabe and Frances probably have some," Tessa muses. "But it would be in their bathroom, and I don't think I can wait until morning."

No. Of course, she can't. And why should she when Josh is promising speedy service with his giant . . . um, tool?

I bury my face in David's chest while they debate, willing him to wake up. I even dig my fingers into his ribs, but nothing. Nada. Not even a snore, damn him.

"Oh, just do it, already," Tess decides. "I'll hold my breath."

Is that even a thing?

Have I fallen through a wormhole? This is mortifying. And like, what is she so afraid of? I mean, not to be like that, but I'm familiar with Josh's . . . member. He's not exactly hold-your-breath massive. And . . . yup . . . now I'm picturing it.

I squeeze my eyes tighter, but that's not helping. There's more shuffling, and then it sounds like a light clicks on. "There," he says. "I can see better now. Go ahead and spread open again. Yeah, like that. All right, I'm going for it."

No. No. No.

I can't just lie here and listen to this. I mean, I am all for them getting closer, but do I want to hear, feel, smell, and taste the . . . juices?

No. I cannot even.

My eyes fly open, and I bolt up so fast a tiny windstorm knocks several papers from Gabe's desk. "Stop!" I shout. "If you guys are going to have sex, you could at least wait until . . ."

I trail off because immediately something isn't fitting, and it's not Josh's fictitiously large pecker. Nope. In fact, instead of naked and fully aroused, I find them semi-clothed and sitting atop the blanket, facing each other, clearly confused by my outburst.

Josh holds Tessa's outstretched hand in front of a flashlight. In his other hand?

Tweezers.

Before they can say anything, the living room light comes on and Frances appears in the doorway. "You guys all right in here?" He glances around the room, pausing to linger on me. He blushes instantly. "Oh, I'm so sorry, Kate. I didn't realize you were um . . . that you guys were . . . I mean . . . . I'll just go."

He literally flees as I glance down at myself. Tessa hops up with a blanket which she gently wraps around my . . . nakedness. Yes, that's right. It would seem I am the one without clothing.

"How . . ." I sputter, looking from her to Josh, who is now laughing so hard he can't speak. Tessa collapses onto the floor beside him.

"You were hot," she practically croaks. "We tried to stop you, but you just ripped everything off and passed out next to David."

Oh, good Lord. That does sound like me. As soon as she says it, a vague memory returns. I glance at the bookcase instinctively cringing, yet again, because yup. There're my clothes. Right where I threw them.

I pull the blanket tighter. Wait a minute! "How could Frances tell I was naked?" He's not fully blind, but . . .

"I'm guessing he saw enough to draw his own conclusion," Tessa says pointedly. She and Josh exchange a look before simultaneously staring me down. "Guess he just assumed, huh? Sound familiar, Kate?"

Yeah. I did kind of do that, didn't I. I'd like to sink to the floor and join David in his hibernation, but I doubt they're letting me off that easy. I go on the defensive instead.

"Well, what am I supposed to think? You're moaning about 'it being so big' and Josh is talking about lube. You're spreading things, he's going for it. The logical conclusion is—"

"A splinter," Tess interrupts, holding up her hand. "Between my fingers. It hurt so bad that I couldn't sleep, so Josh offered to get it out."

Right. A splinter. That does make sense.

I drop down beside them, a mixture of shame and relief. I'm suddenly thrilled they aren't having sex, and maybe for reasons beyond the fear of lube splatter. There's a peculiar comfort in this realization which I am definitely not delving into. Nor am I focusing on my mortifying nudity. I will save that embarrassment for tomorrow.

A splinter, huh? The absurdity hits me all at once, and a giggle spontaneously erupts. Like, I'm legitimately cackling.

"I was worried you'd get lube on me," I howl, unable to stop. This sends them into a fresh fit of laughter, and we're all caught up. Awful, middle-of-the-night-drunk-belly laughter that has us clutching our stomachs and wiping away tears.

It is the perfect end to a perfect night, and we're so loud that sleepy the bear comes out of hibernation, props himself up with a beautiful blue-eyed squint and says, "What'd I miss?"

Thursday, November 9th 4:30 pm

The lube humor continues even after we return from Nashville.

We text jokes throughout the day. Tubes of lube appear in random places all over the house. Even at work, every time I pick up massage oil or a bottle of lotion, I hear the word lube in my head and laughingly relive the night at Frances and Gabe's.

So, when Thursday afternoon rolls around, I am only mildly surprised to learn my final client of the day is allergic to Jojoba oil and would prefer I use lube instead.

"I've never seen anyone request that," Megan whispers as she hands me the intake form. Only, I'm laughing too hard to comment because I have a good idea who this client might be. And sure enough, I catch a glimpse of dark, spiraling curls as soon as I enter the room.

Tessa. She's already on the massage table.

"So, we're using lube today," I say, grinning.

She pushes up on her elbows. "I brought my own."

"Of course, you did." I bend to give her a hug. "What are you doing here? Why didn't you tell me you were coming?"

She shrugs. "I thought a surprise would be more fun. Besides, I didn't want to leave Baltimore without at least one massage. I hear your hands are legendary."

I roll my eyes. "Well, you didn't have to come all the way down. I could've done it at home."

My brain trips over the word. *Home*. It won't be Tessa's home much longer. In a matter of days, she'll be gone, and it will be me and the boys again—a return to normal.

Only, not.

So much has happened. And Tessa's part of us now.

"It's going to be strange when you're gone," I say, applying oil—not lube—to her back in long, flowing strokes. I still can't believe this girl, this beautiful woman I once considered a rival, is now a best friend. A sister, even.

She knows more about me—the real me—than any friend I've ever had. And not only that, she is loved and cherished by the two men I love most. Stranger still? I don't feel threatened by her. And doesn't that just defy logic?

"Kate?"

I'm so lost in thought, my hands stop moving, and she turns, face falling as she regards me. "I'm going to miss you so much. I almost wish I hadn't taken the cruise job, but it's such a good opportunity, and . . ."

"No. Of course you should go." I wipe at a sudden tear threatening to fall. "We'll visit, and you'll come back. How long are you gone, like thirty weeks? You'll be done before you know it." Unless she extends or signs a new contract, or . . .

"Did Josh tell you he's thinking about flying down with me?"

Whoa. What?

I swallow. "You mean, like when you leave? To Miami?"

"Actually, we're going to stopover in Nashville first, for Thanksgiving with Gabe and Frances. Then to Miami for sign-on day. He'll fly back from there. I thought he told you guys."

Um, no. He did not.

"It's not definite," she says, noting the shock I do little to hide. "We were talking in bed last night and he said he got someone to cover his hours at work. He doesn't have tickets, though. So, he's probably still thinking . . ."

I doubt it. Josh is not exactly known for spontaneity. If he's messing with his work schedule, he's serious. And if they're talking in bed?

Heat creeps up my neck remembering how I accused them in Nashville. Despite the lube humor, the nature of their relationship remains in question. Probably because, other than a few playful kisses and a lot of cuddling—we are talking about Josh, after all—they seem more like friends than anything else.

Only talking in bed sounds . . . intimate. Like, Thanksgiving with your girlfriend's family, intimate. But would he really go? This is our first Thanksgiving since moving into the Canton house. I never imagined we would spend it apart, especially after nearly losing David this year. And with everything going on with Nick?

But then, I guess it's just a day. Does it really matter? It shouldn't. Only, it does. It really, really does.

"But he wouldn't leave David and me for our first Thanksgiving!" I don't mean to say this out loud. And I definitely don't mean to use a panicked, high-pitched whimper. But I do.

Tessa sits up straight. "Ah, não! I didn't even think about that. Of course, he should be with you guys. I'll just tell him there's been a change of plans at my end. He was probably just humoring me anyway."

Guilt and shame prickle my skin like tiny sweat beads. Why am I making a big deal out of this? They're basically together, after all. Josh has every right to spend time with her. To travel. To have a life outside of me and David.

What, he's supposed to sit around and watch us? Wait for David to make some kind of ultimate decision we both know he's incapable of making? Better yet, what if Josh really has feelings for Tess? I shouldn't get in the way. I love Josh. I want him to be happy.

But, do I really? Or do I just want him happy with us?

My body sags like a worn cushion. "No, don't do that. I'm the one who's sorry. You two should go, have fun together. Maybe some time away is what he needs." A fresh wave of shame rolls over me. What about Tessa and her needs? I haven't even considered what she wants out of all this.

"Ugh, I'm an awful friend, Tess. Here I am, so focused on the three of us, I'm not even thinking about what you want." I can't keep from grimacing. "I know I didn't handle the splinter situation very well, but if there really is more between you guys. If you're going to . . . what? Why are you laughing at me? I'm serious."

Her lips spread into a gentle smile. "No, I know. And I love you for it. It's just . . ." She pulls the sheet around herself and scoots closer. "I don't want to speak for Josh, but I don't want to mislead you about us, either." She lowers her voice. "All I'll say is, you weren't so far off base in Nashville."

She's searching my eyes and, Oh. My. God. No. "You had sex?" My voice is atrociously loud.

I clap a hand over my mouth as Tess dissolves into giggles, but she's shaking her head. "I didn't say that. Josh wanted a distraction so you and David could have more time together." She shrugs. "I'm just doing what he asked. And as for our relationship? Do I like him?" Her smile broadens. "Yeah, I do. I really do. And maybe one day, when we're both carrying less baggage, we'll figure it out. There aren't many guys like Josh, but I don't have to tell you that. He's all heart, you know? Problem is, it's already taken."

This is perhaps the best description of Josh I've ever heard. And so true. He's one of a kind. Salty and sweet, prickly, yet tender, loyal to an absolute fault. What little space David doesn't occupy in his heart is reserved for me. I guess the question is would he change that for Tessa?

Would I want him to?

She's watching. "Don't misunderstand, Kate. I'm not asking Josh for anything. I'm still getting my own life together. But here's what I know about relationships—there are people you move past and people you keep. And then there are the ones you only hold for a time. I'm not saying it's right but look at David's uncle and what he's done. That kind of commitment in the name of love is rare. Not that Josh is like Carol," she amends, quickly. "It's just, some people have an unbreakable bond."

"You mean like Josh and David," I say because we both know it's true.

"Yes." She hesitates. "Not just David, though. You, too. People spend a lifetime searching for what you three share. And if I'm lucky, maybe one day, that will include me. But right now, if I were you, I wouldn't be so quick to let go just because what you have doesn't fit some model of monogamy. Love is hard enough to find, Kate. You have to treat it like something precious."

Her eyes are piercing and iridescent blue, and I think, not for the first time, that she has the power to see straight through me. That given a different set of circumstances, she and I might have formed a relationship similar to Josh and David's. That we, too, share a bond.

But I say nothing, surrendering instead as she gently cups my cheek. I close my eyes, leaning instinctively into her embrace. The softness of her lips should catch me off guard, but it doesn't. In fact, kissing her feels like the most natural thing in the world.

Wait a minute. I'm *kissing* her.

It takes a beat for the full realization to sink in. Are we really doing this? Her tongue parts my lips, and . . . yup. We are definitely kissing. Her mouth is warm and vanilla sweet, and I can't even freak out because three intrusive thoughts immediately hijack my brain.

First, I should be taking notes because she is doing things with her tongue that shouldn't be possible. Second, I cannot believe David experienced this and still came back to me. And third? I am, sadly, not aroused in the slightest.

We pull away from each other, nervous giggling as we wipe at our mouths. Her face is flush and beautiful, and I have never wanted to be attracted to someone more. I consider faking it.

"So," I say, breathlessly, "that was nice."

Her eyes twinkle. "Just nice?"

"No. It was more than nice." I brush a wisp of hair from her forehead feeling recklessly charged, and regretfully certain of my sexuality. "Trust me, Tess. If that kiss did anything for me? I'd be the luckiest girl in the world."

She barks out a laugh. "Same! Life would be a lot simpler, right?" She squeezes my hand. "But, hey, it was worth a try."

I give her a fierce hug. "Come on," I say, blushing despite myself. "Lie back down. I'm going to finish your massage, and you're going to tell me exactly how you did that thing with your tongue."

7:45 pm

It's a busy evening, yet I think of nothing but the kiss.

Well, that and Josh and Tessa . . . having sex. Because while I refuse to pry any further, I am dying for details. Also, and simultaneously, I am wishing we could go back in time and not invite Tessa here. Not because of her—I love Tessa—but because of me.

As much as I thought I wanted David to myself and for Josh to fall in love? I'm not sure I want either of those things—at least not independent of one another. Which makes no sense. And the more I think about it?

Yeah. No.

Better to focus on the kiss, which also makes no sense, but was . . . educational, maybe?

I don't know.

By the time I'm alone with the boys, my poor mixed up brain is on overload, and I don't know what the hell I want. At least it's just us—Tess had a work thing. We're heading to a party at Jason and Brighton's house in Federal Hill.

It was only supposed to be Josh and Brighton swapping nerdy renovation tips, but Josh panicked at the prospect of one-on-one conversation and insisted on an entourage. Which is fine, because now Anna and Rosa are coming, too. But really? I can't focus on anything until I get this load off my chest.

I wait for a lull in conversation before rapidly spilling the tea. "So, I gave Tess a massage today . . . and we kissed."

Boom. Mic drop.

Josh, who is driving and zoned out at a stop light, grunts a little *uh huh*, while David's head immediately snaps up. It occurs to me, quite suddenly, they might not find this little nugget as amusing as Tess and I did. Especially if Josh has actual feelings.

I hadn't considered that.

"Wait." He's slow to catch up. "What did you say?"

"Um . . ."

David's just staring—looking amused, maybe? Hurt? I don't know, it's impossible to tell with him. Either way, he's surprised, and Josh is pissed, and I instantly switch into clean up mode.

"It was nothing," I say, feeling my cheeks crimson. "We laughed, after. Like, ha ha, now we've all kissed each other. And then we talked about how neither of us were like, turned on, you know?" Josh narrows his eyes, and God only knows what possesses me to carry on, but I do. "It was funny. Oh, and she did the craziest thing with her tongue that was just—"

Josh holds up a hand. "Immediately, no. That's my girl you're talking about."

His girl? That's awfully possessive.

"The tongue thing," David says. "I remember that."

I can't tell if he's joking, but the comment earns him a not-so-gentle shove from Josh. "You should be thanking me," David smirks, brushing him off. "Let's not forget who knew her first."

As if we could?

This conversation is not going as planned. What was I thinking, bragging about the kiss? How did I expect the boys to respond? Tessa's words play back through my mind, and I feel sick.

People spend a lifetime searching for what you three share. I wouldn't be so quick to let go.

That's exactly what I'm doing. I shouldn't be bragging; I should be begging Josh to stay home with us. I should be making David understand how serious this is. He needs to know everything I know.

"It doesn't matter who met her first," I blurt, with no forethought whatsoever. "And, just so you know, David, Josh's stupid little plan is working. They're having sex, now. And he's leaving us for her."

Sheesh, Kate. Dramatic much? That did not come out well.

It's a miracle Josh doesn't wreck because he's not paying one ounce of attention to the road. He shoots daggers at me in the rearview. "What the hell are you talking about?"

Don't say it. It's not the right time. Don't say it. Don't—

"Um . . . you and Tess hooking up in Nashville? Flying off to Thanksgiving with Gabe and Frances, then on to Miami? Ringing any bells, Joshua? She told me all about it, so don't act like it's not true."

Oh, Lord have mercy.

His grip on the steering wheel grows vice-like as David's carefully constructed mask begins to fall. I can almost taste the tension settling in between them.

"I'm not . . ." Josh stutters. "I mean, I'm just thinking about . . . fuck, I don't know. Damnit, Kate." He glares at me again before turning to David. "I offered to fly down and help her get situated in Miami, then she brought up Thanksgiving. What was I supposed to say?"

David's looking at his hands. "It's fine, Josh. You should go with her. It's the right thing to do." Our sweet pacifist. Only, his words don't match his tone. And I hate how I, yet again, am the catalyst of their conflict. I should just leave it alone.

Should being the operative word. But once I start . . .

"No, the right thing would be to stay home with David and me. Either that or fully commit to this Tessa thing. But for God's sake, Josh, don't go back to Nashville and lie to Frances and Gabe. Not at Thanksgiving. You should be honest."

Okay. I have definitely gone too far.

And didn't Tess say she's not looking for anything from him? If she's not offended, why am I? Besides, don't I want to be with David? Why am I so bent on what Josh is doing? I should want him to be happy.

But isn't he happiest when we're together? The three of us?

Ugh. It's all so confusing. Nothing fits anymore, and the Jeep suddenly feels stifling.

We pass the remaining time in a miserable silence. Josh kills the engine once we arrive and we sit, three splintered silhouettes. I ache to fix what's broken, but I don't know how.

"Josh . . ."

My hands rest on his shoulders, but he shrugs away, opening the door. One foot is out before he turns back to David and me. "Trust me," he says. "You two do not want my honesty."

The Escape

Carol Brennan
Wednesday, November 9th 8:03 pm
Roses Motel Gary, Indiana

Carol had been content to die with Nick.

There was something poetic, he thought, about the two men, drowning together. But fate had other plans . . .

Carol shifted in his motel bed, lamenting the sagging mattress, and the dank, airless room he'd been calling home since fleeing Lake Lanier. One week had passed and he still couldn't believe he'd made it out alive.

Even now, tucked beneath several blankets and a thousand miles from Georgia, he shivered. Carol had thought a lot this last week. He'd run every second of the scene with Nick over in his mind, yet still could not conceive how he'd escaped the lake's deathly grip . . .

After he and Nick tipped into the water, their descent had been rapid thanks to the weighted cords Carol had tied to the man. Unlike Nick, Carol had accepted the inevitable. He stopped fighting, and everything had gone black.

But then it seemed, only moments later, he was face down on the shore, sputtering and gasping for breath. Try as he might, even now, he couldn't remember how he'd gotten there.

But did it matter? He was alive.

And Nicholas Janney? There had been no sight of the man. No evidence of a struggle. Nothing. Even the little fishing vessel had disappeared, which was odd, certainly, but perhaps it sunk, Carol reasoned. Destined to rest on the bottom alongside Nick's lifeless body.

That night, Carol had remained face down for several minutes on the muddy shoreline as water lapped at his feet and legs. He had dug his fingers into the cold, damp ground unable to believe his luck. He should've been dead with Nick, but he'd been spared, despite his sin.

His many sins.

With effort, he had rolled to his back, squinting up at the nothingness. Few stars were visible in the night sky that stretched above him: a smooth black canvas. He'd never been a religious man, but he offered a prayer that night.

A thanksgiving and a vow to be better. What he did not ask for was forgiveness. Yes, he killed a man, but he wasn't sorry. It was a necessary crime. Nick had ruined countless lives, Carol's and Elena's among them.

Given enough time, he would ruin David's life, too. More than he already had . . .

Remorse crept in, as it always did, at the thought of his nephew. And of Josh and Kate. His actions this last year had put them through months of needless stress and worry. It was bad enough he'd used them to get back at Nick. Now they were caught in the *Exposed* scandal and would soon be faced with Carol's involvement in Nick's abduction and death.

Because it was bound to come out.

He had been careful, but it wouldn't take long for the police to tie Carol to Nick's disappearance. His death, however? Proving that would be a different story. Carol knew they could track him heading north, at least to Georgia, but there, the trail would run cold.

And so would the case.

He knew the investigation would be drawn out and painful for David, Josh, and Kate. Not that they would miss Nick. But each new development, each set back, would be a reminder of their shared, broken childhood, and of the man who brought so much turmoil into their young lives.

Eventually, though—and Carol clung to this— Nick's death would bring them peace. Freedom, even. The new beginning they deserved.

If Carol had been a different kind of man, he might have found a way to tell them what he'd done and ease their minds. But he couldn't. Wouldn't. He had made a promise with himself—regardless the outcome, there would be no more contact.

That's why he'd written down all he needed to say. Hidden it in a place only David, Josh, and Kate would know. And when the time was right? They, too, would have every piece of truth. Not restoration, but at least some form of redemption. He owed them that much.

When Carol spoke with David at the *Exposed* premiere party it had been to warn him, yes, but more importantly, to tell him where the letter was located. And he'd wanted to see his nephew one last time. His beloved sister's only living child. Fire and Ice, Elena had called them—David and his twin sister, Abigail.

Alone in his motel room, Carol conjured a vision of his sister and her young daughter, still awed he was alive. He vowed, for the hundredth time, to be even more vigilant. Nicholas Janney was gone and he had been spared.

His duty now? Protect David and the Janney kids.

Because threats still remained. There was Vivian Janney, for one. She was a trophy wife at best, and a sorry excuse for a mother. The woman posed no physical threat, but she knew things. Past things. Damaging things. And if she came forward?

Well, Carol would have to make sure she didn't. He hadn't come this far to let the bitch set his house on fire or run her mouth *about* the fire. Or the vast chasm of skeletons in both their family's closets.

No. Those secrets would die with Carol. And with David, Josh, and Kate, should they choose not to expose them. At least now, the decision was in their hands . . .

Carol lay back; the old bed creaking beneath his weight. He flicked on the ancient television, wondering if tonight he might finally get some sleep. He tucked the blankets around his body, lamenting the midwestern cold as he scrolled through the few available channels.

He landed, unexpectedly, on a national news program, abruptly straightening at the sight. He had watched nothing but reruns for a week and assumed there was no cable service at the motel. Only there on the screen was a reporter standing in front of the Janney's sprawling Florida estate. News of Nick's disappearance and apparent abduction crawled across the ticker. And at the bottom corner of the screen, a photo.

Carol's face.

It was an image of him captured on the security camera at the premiere party venue. Beneath his photo, the words: *Carol Brennen wanted in connection with the disappearance of media personality, Nicholas Janney.*

The station cut to another story as Carol sat, contemplating. It's happening, he thought. No turning back now. Instinctively, he rose and shut off the lights. He pulled out his travel bag and began packing in the dark, planning. He'd keep on the move until the trail went cold and the story died down. Because it would.

They would never find Nick's body. And even if they did, there would be no tie to Carol.

Of this, he was sure.

Eighteen

Submergence

:: The overwhelming sensation of drowning

David
Thursday, November 9th 8:32 pm
Birkhead Street Baltimore, Maryland

The tension follows us into Jason and Brighton's house.

Which is really nice, by the way. And smaller than ours, if that's possible. It's a one bedroom one bath. The original second bedroom was turned into a closet at some point, and that's where Jason sleeps. Brighton shows us around, but my mind is a mess of girl kisses, discreet hookups, and lonely holidays. I hardly pay attention.

It's not that I'm mad at Josh. Not really. I can always tell when he's hiding something. And lately? I've been getting that vibe. Plus, I know Tessa. That she'd make love to him or kiss Kate is not surprising. I'm not saying it doesn't sting, though.

And what did I expect? They've been sleeping in the same bed for weeks. I even encouraged it. And Josh is nothing if not dedicated to a plan.

But flying off with Tess for Thanksgiving? That, I did not see coming.

". . . and here's the bathroom," Brighton is saying. "This is the only space we completely gutted." He ushers us inside. "Everything in here is custom. Took forever, you know, but so worth it. And my favorite purchase so far?" He steps aside with flourish. "Meet John Flushington, our smart toilet. You have got to see this guy in action."

But before he can demonstrate, Jason calls him to the kitchen, and he begs off insisting we stay and take a test ride.

And we're alone.

Kate, being Kate, purposely ignores the tension and cracks a few smart potty jokes while drooling over the admittedly nice upgrades. Double chrome shower heads, ceramic floors, heated towel racks, and of course, Brighton's pride and joy.

Josh stalks around all surly, making mental lists, no doubt, because he can't help himself. And me? I can usually fake my way through anything, but I'm struggling. So, when the doorbell rings, and Kate makes a beeline to greet her friends, I follow. Josh holds me back, though.

He closes the door. "I'm sorry. I should've talked to you."

His apology stings more than it should, and I don't know which supposed offense to address first, so I go with the obvious. "You and Tess . . .?"

He sighs, the weight of his regret, palpable. "It happened in Nashville. I was . . ." he looks down, flushing, ". . . very drunk."

Oh.

That invites a multitude of questions I am not asking in Brighton and Jason's bathroom. I turn my back to him, feigning interest in the floating sink. "And Thanksgiving? You're going?"

He steps away from the door. "That's the plan. Tess said Gabe made reservations for the four of us. An Asian fusion place, so no turkey. Should be interesting, huh?" This all comes out in one breath.

"Sounds like you've made up your mind."

"I guess . . ." he takes another step, and I can feel the heat of him behind me.

"It's fine, Josh. Kate and I can go to Bennett and Julie's. She always hosts a big crowd." Except I don't want to go to Bennett's. I want to stay home. With him.

He swallows hard. "You're okay with all this?"

I nod, barely breathing, heart caught in my throat. I didn't think it possible to feel this angry, yet at the same time, unbearably sad. Confused. Frustrated. He's a foot away, but we're miles apart. And I'm just standing here.

He edges closer then, resting his forehead on my back. "I'm only doing this for you and Kate, you know that, right? Because I can't . . ." His hands close around my shoulders, trembling. "I can't let go if nothing changes."

His words ignite a war within my heart. Part of me wants to close my eyes and lean into his embrace while another part wants to whip around and shake him. I didn't ask for this, damn it. I don't want our lives to change. I just got mine back. What I want is him.

These words are on the tip of my tongue when the door bursts open. I jump about a mile, and his hands immediately drop. It's Kate, pale as a ghost, holding her phone outstretched as if it's on fire.

"Everything okay up there?" Brighton calls from downstairs.

Her eyes are wide and maniacal as she shouts, "Just showing Josh and David something. We'll be right down."

She hastily shuts the door then spins around. "I was outside," she pants. "My phone rang, and I didn't even look, I just answered. And it was Vivian, *crying*." She shoves the screen at us. "You guys. Nick might be dead."

We don't have time to react before she presses play. It's a short news clip. The female reporter is standing in front of Nick and Vivian's massive home in Florida. Behind her are police cruisers and miles of crime scene tape.

She explains how Nick hasn't been seen or heard from in days. Neighbors started noticing packages piling up, and lights that never went off. A welfare check was called, and the police discovered Nick, missing.

Vivian, still here in Maryland, was located and she confirmed she hadn't heard from him. Investigators determined Nick left for a jog early last Thursday morning and never returned.

Kate pauses the video. "That's when we were in Nashville," she says, incredulously. "He's been missing this whole time! Vivian said the initial thought was he disappeared on purpose to avoid the *Exposed* scandal. But she just got a call from the lead investigator." She sucks in a breath. "Guys, they found Nick's cell phone! It was a mile away from the house, smashed in some underbrush. And next to it? An empty syringe." She turns to me. "Vivian doesn't think they have any solid evidence connecting him yet, but David? They're already suspecting Carol!"

"Holy shit!" Josh is pacing, which equates to three steps in each direction. I shrink against the wall, mind swimming. Honestly, my immediate thought was of Carol as well. Nick wouldn't just disappear, that's not his style. But is my uncle capable of something like this?

Would he really abduct Nick? Would he kill him?

Either way, we need to get out of here. The media's going to be all over the story. I look at Josh and Kate, assuming we're on the same page, but they clearly . . . aren't.

"I'm going to be sick," Kate wails. "What if he's dead?"

"Good fucking riddance," Josh spits. He yanks the phone from her hand and begins replaying the video. Only his abrupt action upsets Kate's balance and she stumbles backward, landing with a thud on John Flushington's closed lid.

Josh and I watch in disbelief as the thin ceramic shatters like glass beneath her slight weight. And I'm not exaggerating—it explodes. A piercing sound ricochets off the tiled walls as Kate momentarily hangs before plunging butt first through the extra wide heated seat and into the water below. Stunned does not begin to describe her reaction.

Helpless, we turn to each other—the previous moment's tension lost. I have a ridiculous urge to laugh, which is terrible because he's clearly panicking and she's starting to ugly cry.

And Nick might be dead, and my uncle might be responsible, and everything's changing. It's all too much. I stand, fixated on the beautiful tile amidst shards of broken ceramic as Kate's wails grow louder. And then, there's a knock.

"Um . . . guys?"

It's Brighton.

"Oh shit!" Josh's eyes grow wide as Kate clamps both hands over her mouth.

"Everything all right in there?" He calls through the door. "Did something happen to John?"

Friday, November 17th 10:22 am

The next week passes with little progress in the investigation.

As expected, it's a media circus. We hear from the press who immediately pounce on the Carol connection, all but convicting him. The police are in touch as well, conducting phone interviews with each of us.

Fresh digging is done into my family, and I'm forced to relive details of my mother and Abigail's accident, my parent's tumultuous marriage, and the miserable *Brought to Light* years. Not to mention our pictures, which are quite suddenly everywhere.

Josh and I wake each day expecting one of the men our father's extorted to come forward and identify us. Even more so now with Nick potentially dead. The only thing holding them back I guess is fear of exposure—a powerful deterrent, and the only hope we cling to.

We also hold our breath every time Ian, or the fire is mentioned, certain new speculation will reveal our involvement. True crime junkies are all over the story with wild conspiracy theories, ridiculous allegations, and partial truths.

Yet, after a week, nothing of substance is found and, unbelievably, no tie is made between us and Carol. Nick's disappearance remains shrouded in mystery, and despite a handful of suspected assailants, my uncle's name remains at the top of the list.

He's good at covering his tracks, I'll say that. But who even knows? It's possible it wasn't Carol at all. Maybe Nick set the whole thing up and went into hiding—that's still a theory. Though my gut tells me otherwise. Carol would never have shown his face if he planned to end things with the Fully Exposed video. And how had he been so certain I wouldn't see him again?

The whole thing is baffling, not to mention his cryptic message about a package for us in a hollow rock. I have yet to share that unsettling information because what good can possibly come from it? I don't know. I'm going to have to tell Josh and Kate eventually.

On a positive note, we did learn from Anna that Brighton and Jason's new potty arrived, unscathed. Brighton, to his credit, handled John's demise surprisingly well the other night, laughing harder than all of us at Kate's . . . um . . . submergence? He did, to her complete mortification, promise to remind her of the incident as often as possible for the rest of their natural lives.

We offered to replace the entire toilet system but, lucky for us, John was under warranty. According to Anna, the company sent Brighton and Jason an upgraded model, which they christened Flush Gordon.

I just . . . can't.

If things don't work with Tessa, maybe Josh will go out with Brighton. We could use a little humor around here. Not that I think he would, or that I want him to. I don't want Josh with anyone if I'm being honest. Not even Tess.

But he's determined, as evidenced by his um . . . actions in Nashville, which I have yet to press him on. I'm not sure I need those details. Besides, there's been no time. Nick's disappearance is an all-consuming beast.

So much, that I hardly notice Tess packing to leave, or the plane tickets she discreetly buys on

Josh's behalf, or the way he avoids being alone with me. Note the sarcasm. I obviously notice all these things. And not just notice, but obsess over, which is odd for me. I can usually take everything in stride. But by the time Friday rolls around, I'm so out of sorts, I do something I've never done. I call Bennett from school during my planning period and unload . . .

After briefing him on the latest investigation drama, I blurt out what's bothering me. "Josh is flying to Nashville with Tess for Thanksgiving. And I don't want him to go."

It's quiet on Bennett's end as he absorbs this. "So, are they a couple, or is this like a friend trip?" Poor guy. We haven't exactly been forthcoming. God only knows what he thinks goes on over here.

"A little of both, I guess? He likes her, but I think he's going along with it for my sake." I pause, then decide to put it all out there. "The thing is, he wants us together."

"Who? You and Kate, or you and him?"

"Um . . ." I feel my cheeks growing warm. I've talked to Bennett about a lot of things over the years, and he knows how much I love Josh, but we've never specifically addressed the relationship. "Well, he would say he wants Kate and me together. But that's just Josh, he's . . ." I trail off. How can I possibly describe him and me in a way that doesn't diminish my feelings for Kate?

"He's in love with you," Bennett finishes, finally. "And so is she."

Well, that's certainly cutting to the heart of it. "No. I mean, yes, but—"

"And Josh thinks flying off with Tessa will what? Change the way he feels?"

He's more than flying off. I shake my head. "He's trying to force the issue," I tell Bennett. "He thinks if he leaves, if he's with someone else, then Kate and I will finally feel free to date, get married, move past him, I don't know. He's got a whole plan. But really, he just wants to make sure she and I stay together."

Bennett considers this. "Well, that's admirable, looking out for his sister. But what about you, David? I haven't heard you talk much about commitment, let alone marriage." He chuckles gently, likely remembering our conversation at dinner when Jessa first became a thing. "Grace would be thrilled with a wedding, by the way. Double, or not."

I have to smile, remembering her enthusiasm. "Yeah, I know she would. And a few years ago, I might have been all for it. But now? After this summer? It's like, I just want time with them. The other stuff? Doesn't matter."

I hear paper shuffling and picture him hunching over his desk at the college, cradling his phone, as he thinks. "That sounds like a pretty healthy perspective, given what you've been through. But have you told them how you feel? What do they want?"

What do they want?

Naming myself as the object of their affection seems arrogant, at best. And I'm not even sure it's true anymore. I mean, I know they love me, but is that enough? How long until my indecision drives them away?

"Listen, kid." Bennett stifles a yawn, reminding me of our last encounter. He seemed exhausted then, too, and the thought of something happening to him fills me with a deep unease. Bennett's like my anchor. What would I do without him?

What would I do without *them*?

"I know it's not easy," he says, his voice carrying a weight of understanding. "But it's not a bad thing, having two people to love. I can think of worse fates."

Me too. Like losing them both because I can't decide.

I slump in my seat feeling selfish. "I don't know. I'm practically committed to Kate. And what if Josh really likes Tess? She's good for him. And he's good for her. I don't want to get in the way of that. I just . . . I don't know. It makes me feel so . . . empty."

That's what it is. I feel empty when I think about Josh, gone. And not just physically, but like, moving-on-from-me gone. I don't want to be without him.

"Well," Bennett says, finally, "what if we take Tess out of the equation for a minute, because obviously her feelings matter, too. But if we're talking about you, Josh, and Kate . . ." He pauses. "Look, I'm not the best person to give advice about love, but I do know you can't commit to a relationship if any part of you is in love with someone else. It's not fair to either of you."

"Yeah, but—"

"Hear me out," he interrupts. "I think you guys have a different situation, though. I was in the waiting room with Kate and Josh during your surgery, and they suffered, David. Josh, especially. It was like he felt everything you were going through. And Kate barely spoke, let alone moved. I don't know what they would've done if . . ." He doesn't complete the thought but clears his throat instead. "Listen, I realize there's a lot I don't know, but I gather you three have been through hell and back . . . on more than one occasion."

He lets the comment hang, perhaps waiting for me to agree or at least provide some deeper insight into our past. Our relationships. And I should. He knows things aren't as they seem. We told Tess the truth, after all. Bennett's just as trustworthy.

And if Nick is dead, what's the point in hiding? But what if he's not, a little voice cautions. There's still so much we don't know.

"Here's the thing," Bennett continues, when it's clear I'm not going to respond. "I can't tell you what to do, or who to love. But I can tell you this— life doesn't come in a neat little package, and neither does love. It's messy, and painful, and . . . well, you know my story. If love isn't worth fighting for, then what is?"

I do know his story. He fought hard to keep his family together, and his love for Julie has always inspired me. "So, you think I should be honest with them, no matter what?"

"Why wouldn't you? And if you don't want Josh to go with Tessa, say it, and let him decide. Time is short, son. I don't have to tell you that. Why waste your life being anything less than real? And if you're lucky enough to find love? Don't let it walk away."

Sunday, November 19th 6:34 pm

Bennett's words stay with me.

Unfortunately, I do not put them to good use. In fact, in the days following our conversation, I hardly see Josh or Kate. He's working extra shifts, and when he is home, I'm sleeping. And she's booked solid at the spa. This happens before holidays, and it always baffles me. Like, wouldn't people need massage after all the forced family time rather than before?

Either way, between the spa and her job with Mia, Kate is fully occupied.

Tess is around, at least. She ropes me into planning for her upcoming months at sea, a good distraction but painful reminder of yet another change. Regardless of my inner confusion, I am going to miss her.

We spend Sunday shopping and evaluating each item she wants to take onboard. Space is limited, and she'll be sharing a small inside cabin with another crew member. This sounds like torture to me, but she's excited; so I do my best to keep things upbeat. Only the Josh dilemma hangs between us, and she clearly wants to talk.

By evening she's done with my evading. "You need to tell Josh how you feel."

We're standing in their room—my room—in the space where my bed used to be. It's now a maze of duffle bags and unzipped luggage. I pretend not to hear as I squat to unfold, then fold the same shirt three times.

She mutters something in Portuguese before dropping to the floor beside me. She puts a hand on my arm. "Why is it so hard for you to say what you're feeling?"

Um . . . good question.

I don't respond because no response is, in its own passivity, a form of response. Bennett's words come to mind, about being real and honest with people I love. Haven't I wasted enough time?

"I know you're right," I say, lying back. "I need to be more open." I rest my head on Josh's duffle, and she joins me, our shoulders bumping as we gaze, wordless at the ceiling. It could almost feel like we're back in college.

How odd, this life. The people that come and go. The things you remember. We used to lie like this for hours, not even talking. I was so grateful for her back then. But she wasn't Kate. I'll never love another girl like Kate. It's not even a question. And Josh?

Shouldn't he have a chance to experience the same feeling? And who better than Tess? If there's a woman he could love, it's her. Maybe some part of me knew, even back at Towson. Maybe that's why she and I connected.

I turn to face her. "I'm so grateful for you," I say, pressing my lips to her forehead. "You will never know how much I appreciate our friendship. Back then . . . now. You're part of us, here. I hope you feel that."

Tears form in her eyes. "I do," she says, pressing a hand to her heart, and then to mine. "I am deeply and forever changed by all three of you." She smiles even as a tear trickles down her cheek. Her eyes still hold a mischievous glint, though, and I know she's thinking about the kiss with Kate, and her and Josh. And her and I not that long ago. We're all bonded now. Physically, yes, but it runs deeper than that. And perhaps it should bother me, sharing them with her, sharing the past, and maybe the future. But there's an undeniable rightness in Tess being here. Being part of us.

She leans in and hugs me tight. "O amor é a única coisa que cresce à medida que se divide," she whispers, then pulls back to meet my gaze. "Love is the only thing that grows as it is divided, David. Sharing only makes it stronger."

Her words linger, much like Bennett's, even as the next few days pass in a blur. And before I've had time to process what's happening, I find myself on the couch with Kate, half asleep, waiting for Josh to return from work. He and Tess fly out early in the morning, and this is our last chance to see him.

It was hard enough saying goodbye to Tess, who's in bed, knowing we won't see her for months.

Josh, at least, will be back this weekend. A brief trip that somehow feels like a lifetime.

Despite both Bennett and Tessa's urging, I haven't said anything to him about how I'm feeling. I know with certainty, one word from me would keep him here. But if I love him, if I love Kate as much as I claim, wouldn't the right thing be letting him go? To share the love, as Tessa said.

As much as it hurts, he deserves a life outside our little trio. We bought this place with promises and hopes of starting over, after all. And while this is not how I imagined, maybe this is what starting over looks like.

I sigh, yawning as I reach to cover Kate's sleeping form. I'm about to down a whole diet coke so as not to give in to my own fatigue, when the front door creaks open. Josh drops his bag on the floor, then does a double take.

"You're up!" He shuffles over with bloodshot eyes and a wry, weary smile, all but falling onto the couch next to me. "Thirteen calls today." He kicks his feet up on the ottoman and leans back. "I'm fucking toast."

That's a lot for one shift. I glance at the clock. He and Tess are leaving for the airport in a matter of hours. The ticking seconds echo in our quiet room—a stark reminder of time, dwindling. "You should get to bed," I tell him, even as his head rolls to the side, finding a comfortable spot on my shoulder.

"I'll go up in a minute." He yawns, but neither of us move.

Lazy contentment settles over me at the weighty warmth of his body against mine. The subtle scent of cotton from his hair and skin, comforting and familiar. I inhale deeply, recalling how in the hospital before surgery, I was desperate to hold him. To memorize every detail.

So why am I letting go now?

He helps himself to my blanket, eyes already closing as his arms curl around me. The gentle rise and fall of his breathing lulls me into a peaceful haze. I, too, find myself yawning, surrendering to the warm comfort of his embrace. We end up lying together at Kate's feet, my back against his stomach, his face pressed into my neck.

There are a million things I should say, but I don't trust myself to speak as exhaustion wraps its way around us. All I want is to be with him. To lie here and feel the strong, steady thump of his heartbeat in a room that is quiet and familiar, and fading fast.

"Tell me not to go," he whispers so soft, I almost miss it.

I have to bite my cheek to keep from pleading. "It'll be fine," I say, though my voice lacks conviction. "You'll have fun."

He stiffens, and I feel my resolve crumbling, the weight of what I should say like a physical presence in the room. What if this is our last time together? What if, years from now, I look back and realize this moment, this decision right here, is where everything changed?

No regrets. Isn't that what I always tell him? What if my silence is what I will regret most?

As if sensing the conflict in my thoughts, Kate lifts her head. "Is that Josh?" she asks, all soft and groggy. "Are you staying home with us for Thanksgiving?" She rubs her eyes, focusing, registering his face, still buried in my neck, and his arm draped over the blanket we're sharing. I brace for the hurt I expect to see, but instead she looks . . . relieved.

Josh doesn't notice, though. He jerks away, stretching as he stands, the warmth of him abruptly gone. "Nah, I'm still going," he says, glancing at the clock. "Guess I better get some sleep, huh?"

She and I stand then, and I'm splitting inside. But I manage to hold it together as he pauses, then turns, pulling us both into a long, tight hug. "I love you guys," he murmurs, avoiding eye contact. "I'll call when we get there."

And before either of us can find the words to say, he pulls away and disappears upstairs.

Nineteen

Restoring Us

:: A reconstruction of that which was lost

Josh
Wednesday, November 22nd 5:59 am
Foster Avenue Baltimore, Maryland

Tess lets me sleep until the last minute.

She's showered, dressed and ready before I step foot out of bed. You have to admire her organization. She even has my bags downstairs all prepared to go. My only responsibility is showing up. A task that proves more difficult than it should.

I sit on the edge of my bed, breathing.

Kate and David aren't up, which is a good thing because after last night, one glimpse at either of them might derail me. Even still, I wish they'd come out and put a stop to this charade. Say something. Anything.

"Josh?" Tess calls quietly. "Are you almost ready?"

No. Fuck.

"Be right there."

With effort, I push myself off the bed, and head downstairs. Minutes blend, and lists are checked, and before I'm prepared, we're in the Jeep, on our way to BWI Airport. Tess is all smiles, but she's quiet, and me? I'm a mess.

You'd think I was leaving forever instead of a brief vacation. Nashville . . . Miami, those are fun places, for crying out loud. I should be excited. But no, I'm all sweaty palms and raspy breathing over here. It's a miracle we make it to long term parking, which is packed. And why wouldn't it be?

We do eventually find a spot, but neither of us seem bent on moving. We sit for a moment collecting thoughts. Or that's what I imagine she's doing. I take the time to give myself a man-the-fuck-up pep talk.

I can do this. It'll be fun, like an adventure, right? It's been years since I was in Miami, and I like Nashville. The food is awesome. Gabe and Frances are the best. And then there's Tessa . . .

I sneak a glance at her profile, which is masterfully put together, as always. She is stunning in every sense of the word, but the thing is I hardly notice anymore. Now that I know her, now that I've experienced her beauty on the inside? That is what I see. What I could love.

Maybe I do?

She's staring into the predawn. "You ready?" I ask, reaching for her. Resetting. This won't feel so daunting once we're on the plane. "The shuttle's going to take some time. We can grab coffee and breakfast once we're through security."

She hesitates. "Josh, I need to tell you something."

The gravity of her tone triggers a reflexive response, and I immediately run through a mental list of items she may have left behind. I glance at the clock to see if we have time to make it home and back, but she squeezes my thigh.

"Don't worry, I didn't forget anything, it's just—"

"What? What's wrong?"

She turns, locking eyes with mine. "I canceled your tickets yesterday. At no cost," she adds quickly. "They were refundable. I just thought—"

Whoa.

"Wait . . ." What the hell? "You canceled my tickets?" I glance around the parking lot, confused. "I'm here with you. At the airport. I don't understand."

Her eyes shine bright with tears. She has brilliant, unearthly eyes. Like David's, but brighter. A familiar pain cuts through my chest at the thought of him. Pain I've been pushing off for days now. Weeks. We keep drifting farther and farther . . .

She canceled my tickets?

"Josh, listen," she says, taking both my hands. "These last few months have been crazy, yes, but also some of the best of my life. And you." Her lips spread into a soft smile. "You, I could easily love. And maybe one day, we get our own story. But not now." Her eyes search mine. "You belong here, with Kate and David. I know it. They know it. I thought one of them would speak up and stop you. But when they didn't?" She shrugs. "Someone had to do the right thing."

"What? No!" Why is she doing this? "I . . . don't... understand . . ."

Only, I do. And I can't even argue because she's right. She's so right, my entire body aches with it. "But why?" I manage, gesturing at my bags. "Why go through all this? Why let me come here?"

"I know, I'm sorry. I should've said something, but . . ." She looks away. "I guess I thought maybe it would be better if you felt the loss, even for a moment. It's like, you don't know what you have until it's gone. Only, what you have isn't gone at all. You have a home with two people who love you more than anything in the world. And that's where you belong. Don't you see, Josh? You're trying to let go of what you should be holding onto. And I don't want to be the excuse you use to walk away."

"What are you, a fucking therapist?" This is more a question than a complaint.

Despite my anger, I can't hide how, with each passing second, I feel lighter. Her words are so freeing, so . . . right. As if she knows exactly what I need to hear. So much so that I can hardly keep the relief from my face.

She watches me wrestle with these thoughts— eyes a mixture of empathy and understanding. I'm going to miss the warmth in those eyes, her honesty, the laughter that effortlessly bubbles up. Even if she'd have me, I don't deserve a girl like her. "Tess . . ."

But she's shaking her head. "It's all right, really. This is what I want, too. Remember that day in Bennett's bathroom? I told you it wouldn't work, you and me." She cups my chin. "Jessa was a fun experiment, though. And I wouldn't change a thing. I have no regrets, meu amor, and neither should you. Whatever happens with your father . . . with our lives, and this next chapter? I will carry the three of you forever in my heart." She pulls me into a fierce hug, and I feel her tears hot on my cheek. "Let's not draw this out, okay? Or I'll end up canceling my tickets, too."

And before I can think about what's happening, she's opening doors, and grabbing bags, and on a shuttle bus waving goodbye. Gone from our lives as quickly as she came.

7:31 am

I drive home in a fog.

Hell, I don't even know how I make it to the highway. But with each passing mile, the haze lifts, and clarity settles in. I want to be mad, but for what? Tess was right about everything. And I'm probably a fool for letting her go, but she's right about that, too.

I should be here with Kate and David. What that looks like going forward, I don't know. But for now? I need to be at home, and I can't drive fucking fast enough.

When I arrive, however, the house is predictably empty. They do have jobs, after all. David's at school, and Kate mentioned a meeting with Mia in Virginia. I think she's gone most of the day, but he should be off at noon because of the holiday.

So, I busy myself unpacking and organizing, roundly ignoring a minefield of emotional pitfalls. That is, until I find a note from Tessa hidden in my sock drawer.

Stay on target, it reads.

A nod at our infamous axe throwing date. She signed her name and added a hand drawn winky face and a heart. The post is still gaining "likes" on Instagram, despite my pleading for her to take it down.

Don't take yourself so seriously, she admonished whenever I brought it up. A phrase likely scrawled on yet another note hidden somewhere else. If I know Tess, there will be others. And I do know her.

I clutch the tiny paper, falling back on my bed—our bed—missing her. It's not a sharp pang of loss, but more like a nagging ache. The pain of something cherished slipping away. I hate the thought of her on that flight to Nashville, alone . . . and Frances and Gabe, what they'll think.

I just left her at the airport. Should I have insisted on going? What if coming home is a mistake? A little seed of doubt worms its way in. It's not that I'm worried about Tess, she'll be fine. But what if Kate and David don't want me here? They didn't try to stop me, after all, and they are together. That part of my plan actually worked.

What if my unexpected return takes us back to where we started?

Stop being so negative, a Tessa-like voice chides. *Think about how much you three have changed. How far you've come.* I want to tell this voice to fuck off, but I at least owe her a moment of reflection.

She did talk me through some of the lowest moments this summer. Helped us navigate the Nick scandal, opened lines of communication, demystified the past, and showed me I can connect with someone new—even if I don't want to.

We may have stains from the past hanging over us, and we've yet to disentangle from Nick, but we are miles from where we were. If Tess were here, she'd tell me to be grateful. And I am.

I pick up my phone meaning to text her and find a screenful of missed calls and messages from Vivian, the investigator, Nick's attorneys, and a host of unfamiliar numbers. A reminder our nightmare is far from over.

Instead of responding, though, I silence my notifications, vowing to set the world aside, even if for a day. All I want is time with David and Kate— if they'll have me.

So what if we're messy and complicated, and completely unorthodox. Tessa's right, my pushing them together is tearing us apart. And for what? A fifty-fifty chance they find marital bliss? Those are terrible odds. Since when did marriage become the be-all-end-all of happiness? There must be a better way.

I suddenly have to see David. I need to tell him everything, look him in the eyes and hear him say we're going to be fine. Without thinking, I drive to his school, unsure what I'll do until I'm lurking outside his classroom like some lost, overgrown delinquent. There's laughter inside, and I hear his voice, a soothing tenor that instantly sets my mind at ease.

I sag against the door feeling numb with relief and mildly embarrassed for rushing over. Even more so when a group of kids scurry past, staring. I'm about to slink back to the Jeep when his door swings open and I stumble forward. Familiar hands catch my shoulders, righting me.

"Josh?" His shock is so complete, I almost burst out laughing. But then a bell rings, and curious students file past offering high fives and Thanksgiving wishes.

He shuts the door once the last child is gone, and we're in each other's arms. He smells like fresh coffee and well-loved books, and everything good and perfect about the world. I can't let go.

"I'm so sorry," I repeat, over and over until he threatens to call Tessa if I don't tell him what's going on. So, I do, following him around the classroom like a lost puppy yapping as he straightens.

I tell him about the drive to the airport and the canceled tickets, and Tessa's insistence I stay. But I don't stop there. He convinces another teacher to cover his last class, and I talk as we leave the building. I don't shut up the entire ride home, blubbering on about dumb shit like how Tessa snores, but I was too embarrassed to tell her, and how I lost my favorite pair of work boots, and the check I swear I sent Zach he never cashed.

I tell him every single thing that comes to mind because, suddenly? I can't stand him not knowing. I even tell him about Tess and me and what happened in Nashville. What we did (lube was not involved), and what I remember of it (not much, sadly).

What I do not tell him is to call Kate. There's no need. It's the first thing we do because, while time alone with him holds its own appeal, all I want is the three of us, together. Which I must repeat a thousand times.

And David, being David, listens with rapt attention because that is what he does. And I'm so stupid-happy to be with him, so drunk with gratitude at being home again, I almost forget that in my experience . . .?

Good things rarely last.

9:12 pm

It is a good night, though.

Really good.

Kate cuts her meeting short and makes it home before dark. And though less than a day has passed, we hug as if it's been decades. All I hear are Tessa's words.

You don't know what you have until it's gone.

How right she was. It took the act of leaving to fully wake me up. To help me realize how desperately I want to stay. I look past Kate's curls to David.

I *need* to stay.

And I need to thank Tess. Let her know how much I appreciate what she's done for me, for us. And I try to do just that when we Facetime her a little while later. But she's getting ready to go out with Frances and Gabe.

They have friends over, and the apartment is festive and loud. I could almost feel a pang of regret not being there—it would've been fun. But I don't doubt where I'm supposed to be.

During the call, both men lean over her shoulder to say hi and wish us happy Thanksgiving. I'm not sure how she explained my absence, but Gabe's kind smile makes me think she shared everything. Which is fine. I'm done with pretense.

And I'm not the only one . . .

"There is one more thing I need to tell you guys," David says.

It's late in the evening and he, Kate, and I are baking a pumpkin pie to take to Thanksgiving dinner tomorrow at Bennett and Julie's. A dinner that now includes me. And by baking, I mean, David and I are making the actual pie while Kate shuffles around ingredients because . . . well? We've experienced her cooking; it ain't pretty.

"I can at least roll the crust," she grumbles, interrupting David. I shrug her off and turn to him. "Go on. Finish what you were saying."

He hesitates. "So, it happened at the premiere party. And I promise, I told you everything but this." He stops mixing and looks at Kate and me in earnest. "Before Carol left the bathroom, he said one final thing. He said he hid a package for us in a hollow rock not far from the clearing behind your old house. That we should go alone once the dust settles, whatever that means." His eyes lock onto mine. "He told me I wouldn't see him again. And that we should be careful."

It takes a moment for me to realize I've completely mutilated the crust while he's talking, because what the actual fuck? How has he kept this from us? No wonder he's certain Carol had a role in Nick's disappearance. With that kind of warning, how could he not?

"Are you shitting me right now? Why didn't you tell us?"

"No, I know. I should have. And I'm sorry. I just thought—"

"It's fine, David." Kate gives me an admonishing nudge and takes the deformed dough from my hand. "He's telling us now, isn't he, *Josh*? Besides, it's not like we'd go wandering back there with Nick still missing. Can you imagine if someone saw us? How would we explain?"

I glare at David, but quickly realize this is only part of his reasoning. That, more likely, he fears the contents of what Carol left, if anything at all. The lying fuck could be toying with us again.

Whatever.

I'm not going to push. If I've learned anything this year, it's that David hides things to protect us, not cause harm. And while it's frustrating, how can

I not love this about him? Kate has a point, anyway. It's not like we'd go now, too much risk.

But we will.

"Whatever," I mutter, turning from them, realizing now is as good a time as any to share my own news. "As long as we're on the subject, you two are not going to believe this . . ."

Despite my vow to ignore all things Nick related, I did finally go through the messages on my phone. Most were the standard interview requests and repeated bullshit. But the investigator had some news.

Apparently, surveillance video picked up a car of interest, and police are working to identify the driver. They tracked the car, a rental, heading north, and it seems they now believe Nick was taken out of Florida.

And here all this time I've been thinking he staged it. That he's chilling on a secluded beach in Thailand or something, sipping Mai Tais, laughing his ass off. But given David's revelation about his uncle?

Fuck. Maybe it was Carol. And what the hell would he leave for us in the woods? What more could he know? What else does he have planned?

"They're broadening the search," I tell Kate and David. "And if it was Carol, they're having a hell of a time finding him. Sounds like whoever was driving ditched the rental and all but disappeared."

"It has to be Carol," Kate muses. "Do you think he has Nick hidden away somewhere?"

"More like buried." It would be fitting in a twisted, fucked up kind of way. Which reminds me. "Oh, and get this. Vivian left a message. She invited us to Thanksgiving dinner tomorrow at Aunt Lily's place in Southern Maryland."

Kate rolls her eyes. "She called me too. As if we'd go?" She shakes her head. "It's a little late to pull the mom card."

No kidding. Not to mention Vivian's family is completely intolerable. They hate Nick and always looked down on Kate and me. Vivian's not even close with them. Which makes her current living situation and this dinner invitation all the more bizarre. But what isn't these days?

We're all quiet for a time, thinking . . . baking. Kate reshapes the crust I mutilated, and David pours the filling. We get the pie in the oven and set a timer before retreating to the couch.

Kate sits on the ottoman in front of us, cross legged. "I talked to Anna today." She scrunches her nose. "Demetri told her Chad's been asking about me."

At the mention of his name, my blood immediately heats. Chad fucking West. I warned him to stay away. "That little piece of—"

"Relax," she says, patting my leg. "He still has my shoes and wants to return them. But I told Anna to say he should donate them." She rolls her eyes. "Trust me, I have no intention of seeing Chad West again."

"Good. Because, if he so much as calls you, I swear I'll—"

"Easy, killer," David interrupts, ducking the jab I throw at him. "How is Anna?" he asks, laughing as he pushes me away. "You haven't mentioned her or Rosa lately. What's the latest with Zach?"

Kate shrugs. "We only spoke for a few minutes. And I've been so distracted with Nick, and then Tessa leaving, I just . . ." Her voice trails off.

Tessa.

It's hard to believe she's gone.

"I miss her." This I say without thinking. But it's true. The house feels different. Like, everything's brighter when she's around. Not to take away from Kate and David, but Tess brought a sense of balance to us. I'm going to miss that.

"Yeah, I miss her, too," David says in a somber tone. I try to catch his expression, but he's leaning back, eyes closed.

"It is strange with her gone." Kate sounds almost wistful. "She could come back, though. Stay with us between contracts. She's family, now, you know? Like, part of us."

Us.

Such a small word to hold so much meaning. I look at the two of them, Kate with her bright, hopeful eyes and bouncing curls. David, all pretty and peaceful beside me, pretending he's not longing for sleep. And all at once, I'm struck by the simplicity of this moment. The beauty of us.

If this is all I ever have? It's enough. *They* are enough. I don't care what it means or what it looks like. I want to be with them, and I need to say it.

"Listen, guys. I'm sorry about the last few months." I take a breath, heart hammering. "I don't regret bringing Tess here, but I am sorry for how and why I did it. I just thought . . ." I look back and forth between them, swallowing. "I love you both so much. And I'd do anything to make things right . . . I just . . . I thought I could let go. That it would help if I . . . if you saw me with . . ."

I'm faltering and words aren't flowing as doubt creeps its way back in. What am I even saying? They don't want to hear this. They're finally happy together; I'm the one who can't move on. Fuck. Isn't this exactly what I vowed not to do?

Panicking, I stand abruptly, but they both grab hold of me.

"Josh," David says. "Stop."

Kate scoots closer. "Whatever you're going to say, it doesn't matter. We love you and we're never going to stop wanting you here, with us." She looks at David, then back to me. "We've talked about it, David and I. And we're not the same without you, Josh. We feel—"

"Empty," he finishes pulling me back down to the couch. "We feel empty when you're gone. Or even at the thought of you leaving. Like a piece of us is missing."

I'm shaking my head, trying not to get choked up. "Those feelings will pass, though. You just need time together." I gesture around our living room, a space that held so much promise when we moved in. But that's all it is—a space. "We could still sell.

It's not too late. You two could move, start over. Leave all this mess behind."

"And where would we go? Portland?" He wraps his arms around me. "You're not getting rid of us that easy. Because Kate and I?" She piles in, hugging us both. "We don't want a fresh start if it doesn't include you." He looks first at me and then at her. "I can't imagine my life without either of you. I don't know how we make it work, but nothing matters more than the three of us . . . together."

Kate nods, her eyes shining, and she's never looked more beautiful. We may not be related in the true sense of the word, but she is my sister. My best friend . . . a soulmate. I feel closer to her now than ever, and I sense she feels the same.

She gestures at our tightly woven trio. "I don't know how to explain what this is, but it's not complete without you, Josh. We don't need stupid titles or labels. Let's just be . . . us."

That word again.

The sound of it floods my heart with joy, only what is she really trying to say? "I don't understand, Kate. What does just "being us" mean?"

She smiles. "I don't know, but we'll figure it out. Maybe we take turns or something. Split our time. We'll make our own rules."

Even David looks surprised by this. We both sort of gape at her.

"What, like a timeshare?" *Has she lost her mind?* "We're not talking about claiming days in a vacation condo, Katherine. This is real life—people don't do shit like that."

But of course, they do, a little voice prompts. And would it be so bad? Isn't that what we've been doing all along? The only difference is transparency.

Kate gives me an exasperated look. "I don't mean booking time slots. Nothing that formal. I just mean . . . let's leave things open. Easy and fluid, like . . ."

I'm tempted to say lube because Kate's suggestion brings Tessa to mind. If anyone is down with fluid relationships, it's Tess. In fact, now that I think about it, she could be behind Kate's reformed thinking. And while I appreciate the sentiment, I'm not sure it fits . . .

"Like what?" I say, turning to Mr. Timeshare himself. "You're not buying into this, are you?"

Before he can respond, the oven timer goes off and all three of us pop up, grateful for the interruption. We pile into the kitchen, where we find an unexpected sight. The pie has nearly doubled in size, bubbling like a top hat over the crooked crust.

"Maybe it's the baking powder," Kate muses as we peer into the oven. David and I turn to each other. *Baking powder?*

"Kate," he says, in that patient, teacher voice I love. "The recipe didn't call for baking powder."

"Yeah, I know. That's why I added a few tablespoons. I wanted to make sure the pie would rise."

A few tablespoons? We turn back to the monstrosity in our oven. "Mission accomplished," I say, laughing. "We could feed the entire city with that thing."

She punches me. "It's not funny, Josh. Now we have to start over again."

Her words hit all three of us at the same time. Starting over—we're good at that.

A smile spreads across David's face. "I'm okay with starting over." He takes her hand and then mine. "But no recipe this time. We'll do it our way."

I take Kate's other hand completing the circle, and I'm thrown back five months. To chaos, and a hospital room, and the boy I love fighting for his life. How fitting, we should end up here where we started. The same, but different.

A chance to do it all again, only better. Maybe Nick's dead, and maybe he's not. Either way, he no longer holds the same power. And we have truth on our side. Once we find what Carol left, maybe it all goes away, and the past becomes the past, and we finally move forward, scarred but holding on, together.

Like clay jars.

There was a picture in the waiting room the day of David's surgery. A clay jar, all cracked and crumbling, yet still intact and holding dozens of wild daisies. We Have This Treasure in Jars of Clay, it said beneath.

I stared at it all day but haven't thought of it since. Of this fragile life and the precious gift we hold. How something as delicate as love can thrive, even when everything else is crumbling and torn apart.

And I was willing to walk away, for what? All I've ever wanted is right here. I pull them to me, and we hug each other tight in our cozy-quiet kitchen that smells of pumpkin spice and second chances and a life that suddenly feels too good to be mine.

No regrets. That's what David always says. Maybe it's time I start listening.

"I'm all for doing it our way," I say, holding tight to their hands. "But as for this timeshare nonsense?" Kate sticks out her tongue, laughing as David rolls his beautiful blue eyes. "I can't think of two people I'd rather get complicated with."

Epilogue

The Boat

Carol Brennan
Thursday, November 23rd 2:43 pm
Solomons Island, Maryland

He had spent Thanksgiving alone for nearly three decades.

Carol was no stranger to loneliness, but this year was different. He missed his quiet Carova Beach community, and his sweet dog, Gillie, who he'd left with a neighbor. He even missed watching David, Josh, and Kate. They were a connection, albeit distant, to a past which he could never return.

Since Nick's abduction was discovered, Carol hadn't stayed in the same place longer than a few days. He'd traversed the country, skirting cities, changing his appearance, and avoiding human contact whenever possible.

He'd slept in an abandoned barn, the backseat of his car, and even spent the night in an out-of-the-way bed and breakfast in Wisconsin. All the while watching and waiting as he'd always done. According to news reports, the investigators traced Carol's route north from Naples and into Georgia, but from there, as he'd planned, the trail ran cold. Carol had been shrewd, after all. He'd hidden a car in a rural town close to the border.

Once he and Nick were outside Florida, he ditched the rental and switched cars. With no cameras or witnesses around, police had little to go on. And, as Carol had expected, two weeks into the investigation, they hit a dead end, media attention waned, and he felt confident enough to step out of obscurity. At least, for a day.

Vivian was staying with her sister, Lily, in Solomons Island, Maryland, and though Carol had seen clips of her in the news, he wanted eyes on the woman. He'd seen clips of David, Josh, and Kate, too, though they wisely stayed far from the spotlight.

He longed, more than anything, to reach out to his nephew. To ask if they found his message, hidden in the woods. To learn if they, too, suspected Kate was Nick's biological daughter. Would they confront Vivian? Had they shared anything about Carol with the police?

He felt ignorant in his isolation, but still resolved to stay away. He would not risk bringing them down. Though with each passing day, it grew less and less likely Nick's body would be found. He had been careful, after all. But had he been careful enough?

Maybe not . . .

At the same time Carol hovered in the shrubs outside Vivian's sister's home on Thanksgiving Day, David, Josh, and Kate headed to Julie and Bennett's for dinner. And unbeknownst to all, another, unrelated group of friends headed out for a walk. A group of college students staying at an Airbnb on Lake Lanier.

While wine was poured in Southern Maryland, and turkey was carved in Baltimore, six-hundred miles south in Georgia, a small fishing vessel was being uncovered by the college students. It was near the shoreline in a thicket of trees, mostly hidden from view. Inside its narrow deck was a man's running shoe, several yards of heavy cord, and a tape recorder.

Now, the boat had been an object of concern for Carol. He clearly remembered watching it drift as he and Nick were pulled under, but when he woke on shore, the vessel was nowhere to be seen. He later convinced himself the drifting boat had been a figment of his imagination. That the same delirium which found him alive and on shore had conjured the false image.

The boat must've capsized and sank, he mused. It was old, after all, and they'd taken in substantial water during the scuffle. It was the obvious answer. Carol's only regret? He hadn't double checked the shoreline in his haste to leave that night.

And he should have. He really, really should have. Because, while the boat's discovery was damning, the presence of Carol's tape recorder was far worse.

Bringing it had been an unnecessary risk, but he wanted to see Nick's reaction, face to face. Only Carol was careless. He hadn't made a copy of the tape, other than the one he gave Josh and David. He brought the original with his name, the date of the fire, and the name *Ian Shaw* printed on the front.

The player had been in his pocket when the men went under. Carol assumed it had fallen out, and while he had been upset by the loss, he wasn't worried. The water and its corrosive powers would render both tape and player illegible and useless, should anyone find it.

But really, would they? It seemed an impossibility.

What Carol had not considered was the possibility of the player remaining in the boat. That the boat, hidden on shore and shielded from the elements, might remain relatively dry and intact. That hikers, upon discovering the vessel, might recognize Carol and Ian's names from the news, and call the FBI tip line.

No, those were the furthest thoughts from Carol's mind as he sat alone watching Vivian and her family on Thanksgiving Day. In fact, he thought little of Nick as he observed the slight woman sipping her way through a fifth of vodka and the forced festivities.

Muscles stiff, and mind reeling from hours of frivolity; Carol was ready to leave when he noticed Vivian, quite stealthily, retreating from where her family gathered. Several minutes passed before, out of the corner of his eye, Carol saw the figure of a woman in a long wool coat scurrying across the lengthy backyard.

He followed every movement as she made her way to the fence, hastily glancing from side to side. There was a small shed, and she entered it, still visible from where Carol crouched. Questions swirled in his mind until unexpectedly, a man appeared beside her.

Carol's blood ran cold as the two embraced, holding tight to one another. Not a stolen moment, but something deeper and far more intimate.

As if she had known the man for a very long time.

It was almost as if, Carol thought with mounting horror, Vivian were greeting her husband . . .

For the Author's Acknowledgements,
Book Club Questions, and more:

About the Author

Stephania Thompson is the award-winning author of *Woven*, Book One in the Charm City Threads Series. A poet and full-time novelist, she received her bachelor of arts in accounting from the University of Maryland, then went on to earn her CPA and work in both the public and private sectors before pursuing her passion to write.

A Maryland native, she and her husband are living the dream in their modern-day money pit with four children, a spoiled aussiedoodle, and one not-so-fire-breathing dragon. When not writing, working, or wrangling pets, she can be found hiking local trails or escaping in a book at her favorite café, iced latte in hand. She's a sucker for quirky romance, is addicted to audiobooks, and finds herself most drawn to flawed characters, raw honesty, and life's cringiest moments. You can visit her online at www.stephaniathompson.com *or find her on X @stephthmpsn and Instagram @ stephtwrites*

Bound by a devastating secret, childhood friends David, Josh, and Kate take on home renovation as a means of healing from a dark, shared past.

Their only promise? Friendship first—no hookups.

Only several months after moving into their Baltimore fixer, the aptly nicknamed Canton Catastrophe, walls are crumbling, sparks are flying, and promises are getting ignored.

Josh, a paramedic, is plagued with panic attacks, haunted by the past, and sharing a room with David, who he is definitely not attracted to. And then there›s Kate. She›s having a job crisis, popping pills, and pretending she doesn't notice how distant the boys have grown. And David? The eternally calm, blue-eyed beauty's health is deteriorating and he's mysteriously blacking out.

But when they learn someone may have discovered their darkest secret and is now stalking them--and blackmailing Josh›s father, a conservative media personality with secrets of his own, renovation and relationship woes take a back seat. Suddenly, their past is unraveling, and the shocking truths unearthed will have them questioning everything from family ties and friendships to love, loss, and the lengths they're willing to go for each other.

Want to know how it all began? Check out Woven,
Book One in the Charm City Threads Series